✂ - - ✂ - - ✂ - - ✂ - - ✂ - - ✂ - - ✂

LE 26 MAY 2016

28. JUN 16.   12. AUG 16.

12. MAY 17.   23. SEP 16,

26 JUN 2019

20. AUG

_____ LE

Rhif/No. _____ Dosb./Class ____F____

Dylid dychwelyd neu adnewyddu'r eitem erbyn neu cyn y dyddiad a nodir uchod. Oni wneir hyn gellir codi tal.

This book is to be returned or renewed on or before the last date stamped above. Otherwise a charge may be made

LLT1

D1610668

✂ - - ✂ - - ✂ - - ✂ - - ✂ - - ✂ - - ✂

GW 3435568 5

"I wish I could think of something we could do for Sarah that didn't involve kidnapping or breaking-and-entering, but with her family so firmly in place, it's going to be hard."

"I got nothing, if we can't bend the law a little."

"Are you making any progress on your Pratt family background checks?"

"Howard seems to have had several ex-wives who are curiously dead before their time. I'm still digging on Seth, but I think he's running an internet discount prescription drug business. Based on Connie's suspicions, he may be getting his drugs from illicit sources, but I can't make a direct connection on that yet. I'll keep digging until I can prove it one way or the other."

Fred came into the kitchen and meowed loudly.

"Don't even try it. Aunt Beth told me she fed you at five o'clock. And she gave you some bites of sliced chicken as a treat, since you had to spend the day alone."

Fred poked his nose in the air, swished his tail forcefully and left the room.

"He's got an attitude prob—" Lauren was cut off by the kitchen phone ringing.

"Hello?" Harriet said. "Hello?" She flicked the speaker phone button so Lauren could hear the conversation and looked at the caller ID. "Sarah? What's wrong?"

"Help me," said a rasping voice. "Help me."

The phone went dead.

"Come on."

ALSO BY ARLENE SACHITANO

The Harriet Truman/Loose Threads Mysteries

Quilt As Desired
Quilter's Knot
Quilt As You Go
Quilt by Association
The Quilt Before the Storm
Make Quilts Not War

The Harley Spring Mysteries

Chip and Die
The Widowmaker

A QUILT IN TIME

A Harriet Truman/Loose Threads Mystery

ARLENE SACHITANO

ZUMAYA ENIGMA   AUSTIN TX

2014

A QUILT IN TIME

© 2014 by Arlene Sachitano

ISBN 978-1-61271-243-7

Cover art and design © April Martinez

"Zumaya Enigma" and the raven logo are trademarks of Zumaya Publications LLC, Austin TX. Look for us online at http://www.zumayapublications.com/enigma.php

Library of Congress Cataloging-in-Publication Data

Sachitano, Arlene, 1951-
   A quilt in time : a Harriet Truman/Loose Threads mystery / Arlene Sachitano.
      pages ; cm
   ISBN 978-1-61271-243-7 (pbk. : alk. paper) — ISBN 978-1-61271-244-4 — ISBN 978-1-61271-245-1 (epub : alk. paper)
   1. Quiltmakers—Fiction. 2. Abused women—Fiction. I. Title.
PS3619.A277Q8545 2014
813'.6—dc23
                                   2014007522

To Malakai, Amelia And Claire

Acknowledgments

Thank you to everyone who supports my writing process, from the idea phase through the work of writing and the never ending promotional activities. My friends, family and business associates. I'd like to especially like to thank Jack and Linne Lindquist for hosting me in their booth, The Craftsman's Touch, at many large quilt events. Thanks also to Deon and Rich Stone-house at Sunriver Books and Music for our annual event.

Domestic violence is a serious subject and I've made every attempt to base my story in fact and to that end researched the subject before starting my story. Any errors are my own. The memory retrieval in my story is based on research I found on the Internet. The research is in its early phase and may or may not work as easily as I portrayed it or at all.

As always, many thanks to Liz and the team at Zumaya Publications for all the work they do on my behalf. Thank you, too, to my brilliant cover artist April Martinez.

Last but not least, thank you to my spouse Jack, our children and our children's children.

Chapter 1

Lauren Sawyer set her messenger bag next to the wing-back chair as she sank into the seat.

"I can't believe I'm sitting in your quilt studio at o-dark-thirty on a Wednesday morning and I don't even know why."

Harriet Truman kept a tea and coffee setup on a library table opposite the entrance and reception area of her long-arm quilting studio. However, she'd moved the cream and assorted sweeteners to the smaller pie-crust table that sat between the two upholstered chairs when she saw Lauren coming up the driveway.

Lauren scooped a heaping spoonful of sugar into her coffee cup.

"I'm not sure even coffee with sugar is going to get me through this…" She waved her hand. "…whatever kind of meeting it is."

"Aiden said it was important," Harriet poured hot water over the teabag she'd put into her mug and sat down in the other chair. "That's good enough for me."

"That's big of you, all things considered." Lauren looked at Harriet over the edge of her cup as she sipped.

"I'm giving him the benefit of the doubt. He's going to counseling, which is a big step for him. He and the counselor decided he needs to take one thing at a time. First, he'll deal with his sister and all her baggage; his brother's going with him for support on that one. After they've sorted that out, we'll work on *our* relationship. In the meantime, the counselor says it's okay if we see each other, as long as we keep things superficial for now. No decisions or big talks."

"Aren't we just the grownup in the relationship...oh, wait, you *are* the grown-up. How much older than him are you? Nearly old enough to be his mother?"

"Oh, stop," Harriet swatted at her across the table. "You know very well it's ten years. And it's too early for you to be poking at my insecurities."

Lauren blew across the surface of her coffee and took another sip.

"You're safe for now." She pointed to the window. "Someone else just pulled in."

Mavis Willis, who at seventy-one was the oldest member of the Loose Threads, came through the door a moment later.

"I hope you have coffee on."

"Right here," Harriet said and indicated the carafe on the table between her and Lauren.

"You *are* going to tell us what this is all about, aren't you?" Mavis asked.

She poured a cup of coffee as Harriet got up and let her have the more comfortable chair, sliding over one of her rolling worktable chairs for herself.

"I was just telling Lauren I've told you everything I know, which is nothing. Aiden just said to ask everyone to get here early because he wanted to ask something of us, and he had surgery starting at eight."

"You know, honey, your aunt Beth wouldn't be offended if you reupholstered these two old chairs now that you own the studio. She didn't like this floral when she bought them secondhand twenty years ago."

"She's welcome to do any upholstery projects on my behalf she wants to, but I've got bigger fish to fry right now."

Lauren and Mavis didn't get to hear what those fish were because Robin McLeod and DeAnn Gault came in followed by Connie Escorcia and Harriet's Aunt Beth.

Harriet was glad to see Robin—she was a stay-at-home mom and part-time yoga teacher, but she kept her license to practice law current just in case a need arose among her friends and family. It was to be hoped her skills wouldn't be needed this morning, but since Aiden hadn't told Harriet anything, it was nice to be prepared.

Connie took off her coat and draped it over the back of another rolling chair, moving it into the circle. She shivered and rubbed her hands together.

"I'm having flashbacks of the early-morning staff meetings at the grade school," she said. "I never understood why the fourth-, fifth- and sixth-grade teachers got the afternoon meeting time just because their kids were older than ours. By the way, Jenny isn't going to be here. She's meeting with family in Lynwood."

"I don't envy her those discussions," Mavis said and shook her head.

"They've been estranged for so long, you wonder if everyone might be better off letting it be," Connie suggested.

"If I were them, I'd want to reconnect, no matter how painful it might be at first," Beth said.

"Are we going to be doing any stitching while we're here?" DeAnn asked. "I took the boys to early drop-off at school, and my mom took Kissa for the whole morning, since we weren't sure what was going on."

"I don't have anything pressing for the morning, so everyone's welcome to stay and stitch if they want," Harriet offered. She knew everyone in her quilt group would have at least one hand-stitching project in her purse or in a bag in her car.

Robin looked like she was about to speak when Aiden arrived. He took his fleece jacket off and tossed it toward an empty chair as he strode over to the coffee carafe.

"I hope you ladies didn't drink all the coffee," he said as he tilted the container. "Carla's right behind me. She was doing a drive-by at the coffee shop to get Wendy a hot chocolate. I offered to do it for her, but she told me she was the housekeeper and I was the boss and left before I could argue."

"That was bold of her," Lauren said.

"She's getting real cheeky," He looked around the circle of women. "I'm guessing that's thanks to the influence of you all." He stirred sugar into his cup then stepped into the middle of the circle of chairs to address the group, who were now all sitting with coats off, leaning forward with coffee mugs clutched in their hands.

"You're probably wondering why we're here," he started. "And by the way, thanks for coming so early. I'm sure Harriet told you I'm scheduled for several surgeries this morning.

"When my mom died, I inherited a bunch of stuff, including her charitable foundation. There's a board of directors that oversees the choosing of charities, follows up to see how the money we donated is used, etc., and there are also a couple of paid employees who handle the day-to-day responsibilities. But at the end of the day, I have to say yea or nay on where the money goes."

Carla came in, interrupting Aiden's speech.

"Sorry," she said and slid her daughter Wendy off her hip and onto the floor, shrugging off her own jacket in one smooth move. She handed the little girl the foam cup of hot chocolate she'd been holding and sat in the chair Aunt Beth slid toward her.

"Abuela," Wendy cried in delight when she spotted Connie. Connie held out her arms and Wendy went to her, smiling as her substitute grandmother pulled her into her lap, shushing her as she did so.

"As I was saying," Aiden said and pretended to give Carla a stern look, failing when he couldn't chase the laughter from his eyes, "I do have a say in what charities get money from the foundation. I usually just approve whatever the very competent board chooses. What I'm here to talk to you all about is that I've personally identified a need in our community and am planning to fund the solution."

"Since we're not your very competent board, could you just cut to the chase and tell us what you want?" Lauren interrupted.

"Okay." Aiden rubbed his hands together as he paced across the space within the circle of chairs. His brow furrowed as he thought. "It's come to my attention that some battered women in our community are reluctant to come to the shelter because they can't bring their pets with them."

"That seems a little harsh," DeAnn said.

"The shelter often takes women with children," he continued. "Some of those kids potentially could have asthma or allergies that would preclude living with pets." He looked at DeAnn. "Like you, I thought that was a little harsh. I happen to think that pets are an important part of most people's support system. Pets are also on the front lines in a home when abuse is taking place. The sooner the pet can get out of the home, the better off it is, too."

"So, you want to build a shelter for the animals?" Lauren asked.

"Yes, but not like you're thinking. I want to add a kennel behind the existing house. Complete with a 'family room' for socializing with the animals and letting them have some normal time with their owners.

"For the safety of the residents, it needs to have a secure connection to the house, so we'll build it with an air-shower and positive-pressure entrance so the animal dander won't be transferred to the main residence. It will all be enclosed in heavy chain-link fencing, carefully made to not look like a prison."

"That sounds pretty cool," Harriet said.

"Where do we come in?" Aunt Beth asked.

"Like most shelters, they have a pretty tight budget. As a result and, again, like many shelters, they let civic groups 'adopt' or sponsor various public rooms at the home. The volunteers have to be carefully vetted so as to not compromise the residents' safety also.

4

"Enter the Loose Threads." He spread his arms wide. "I was hoping you might want to make quilts for both the pets as well as some larger ones for the residents to use in the social room, and any other homey touches you can think of. I'll pay any expenses, of course."

"After it's all set up, would we have an ongoing obligation?" Lauren asked.

"Lauren," Mavis scolded, tilting her chin down and looking over the top of her half-lens reading glasses. Being the oldest member of the quilting group made her the unofficial sergeant-at-arms.

"It's a good question," Aiden replied. "And no, you're under no obligation at any point. Most groups do take on the maintenance of their room, but what that entails varies depending on what room they ad-opt."

"I think it's a wonderful idea," Aunt Beth said. "We can make quilts for the people beds, too."

"Whoa, let's not get ahead of ourselves," Lauren cautioned. "Some of us work for a living. And even if my computer business is from home, I still have to put in the hours."

"You don't have to do anything you don't want to," Mavis gave Lauren "the look" again.

"I think it's a great idea, too" Carla said. "It really meant a lot to me when I got my baby quilt from the young mothers' quilting group when I was pregnant with Wendy."

"Sure," Robin added. "And I can make people quilts, too."

"When will the room be done?" DeAnn asked.

"They're breaking ground this week on the addition."

"We better get busy, then," Beth said and stood up. "Shall I make another pot of coffee or shall we switch to tea?"

"How many pets will you be accommodating?" Harriet asked Aiden while the others told Beth their drink preferences.

"The shelter is intended for six women, but they have a loft space that's approved for several more beds, so I'm planning on six indoor-outdoor dog runs, the same number of small animal enclosures, and an eight-foot counter with heat lamps and plug-ins for really small customers."

"That sounds pretty deluxe."

"The foundation can afford it, so why not? I want it to feel like home, not an upscale hotel and not an institution. I'm hoping you and the rest of the Threads can help me keep it personal."

"You know who you need to talk to?"

"I know you don't think a lot of me right now, but I do know who the best architect in this area is, and I wouldn't let my project suffer because of any feelings I might have about Tom and his relationship to you."

Harriet held her hand up in a peace gesture. The other Threads looked everywhere except at her and Aiden.

"I'm sorry, my bad," Aiden said. "We're supposed to be keeping it light. Let me rephrase. Tom is the architect we're using to build our very green, very environmentally pleasing animal facility."

"Good choice," Harriet said and walked away.

"Thanks, everyone." Aiden raised his hand in a half-wave as he headed for the door. "Gotta go."

"We're happy to help," Connie told him.

✂ - - - ✂ - - - ✂

Harriet and Connie rearranged the chairs, placing them around the large work table while everyone refreshed her drink and Mavis pulled out a bag of oatmeal raisin cookies she'd kept hidden until Aiden was gone.

"I was afraid the young doctor would see these as a distraction, since we weren't sure how serious this meeting was going to be," she confessed and bit into a cookie.

"I don't know what anyone else is thinking," Aunt Beth said as she took her place at the table while Mavis passed the cookie bag to Connie. "But for the pet blankets, I still have a lot of dog-print fabric left over from when we were trying to figure out our quilts for the dog adoption benefit last fall."

"Maybe we should divide into two groups," Harriet suggested. "Some people could make as many pet blankets as they can and the other half could work on a couple of lap quilts."

"That would be a start," Robin said as she reached into the cookie bag. "We should probably see if they'll allow us to tour the place and assess. Aiden told us what they need for the pet room, but maybe there are other, greater needs we should be aware of."

"I guess it *would* be bad if we made fabulous pet quilts and the children were using tattered rags to sleep with," Lauren said.

"I'm sure that's not the case," Robin shot back, "but we need to be certain."

"So, what's appropriate for a women's shelter?" DeAnn asked. "Do we go with soft and soothing or bright and hopeful?"

"I don't think there's a single scheme that applies to all people in this situation," Aunt Beth suggested. She rubbed her chin as she spoke. "I'd imagine women with young children might want something practical and perhaps more colorful. Older women or those who don't have children might want something more soothing."

"I like Robin's idea of at least one or two of us going to meet with who-ever runs the place," Harriet said.

"In the meantime," Carla said, "maybe we could make some sets with a large quilt for the parent and smaller quilts in the same color-way that could be for the kids."

"I like that," Connie said. "Then the rest of us can get started while our representatives go gather information."

"Good idea," Mavis agreed.

They spent the rest of the morning planning quilts and dividing up the tasks. Robin, Harriet and Lauren would set up a meeting as soon as possi-ble with the shelter director. Afterwards, they would all meet at Pins and Needles, Foggy Point's best and only quilt store.

Chapter 2

ave you ever been to a woman's shelter?" Lauren asked Harriet and Robin as they sat around a table at the Steaming Cup coffee shop. The shop was divided into function areas—tables and chairs in the center of the room, several groupings of upholstered chairs and small sofas around the perimeter, and a long computer table sporting electrical sockets every two feet down the center near the third wall.

Harriet had her hands wrapped around her mug of hot cocoa.

"I haven't," she admitted.

"Unfortunately, I have. Before the kids were born, when I was working fulltime, I represented more than one victim of domestic violence, so, yes, I've been to shelters before," Robin said. "Not here, though. It was back in my Seattle days."

"What should we expect?" Harriet asked.

Robin leaned back in her chair and pressed her lips firmly together in thought.

"They're all different, depending on what sort of building they're in. Some were made to be a group facility from the get-go, others were adapted. But they also had some things in common. To function, the house has to be very organized, and they're security-conscious to a degree that will probably feel paranoid to you. Believe me, it's necessary."

Harriet sipped her chocolate.

"Our tour guide will tell us how many people are staying there, right?"

"She'll give us some general information and will let us see a representative room or two. The resident who occupies it will have removed any iden-

8

tifying pictures or other information that would let you know who they are.

"I don't know if they do that here in Foggy Point, but in Seattle they took no chances. Anyone who came past a semipublic visiting room had to have a criminal background check and references. And, Lauren, no wise cracks. They'll throw us out at the slightest hint that we're there for other than our stated purpose."

"Okay, Mom, I'll behave." Lauren rolled her eyes upward then looked to Harriet for support. Harriet gave a small shrug but didn't say anything.

"Everyone done?" she asked a few minutes later. She took the three mugs and returned them to the collection tub near the counter.

"Where to now?" Lauren asked Robin.

"We meet the assistant director downtown, and she'll take us to the shelter. As we suspected, they don't let people drive up and park by the front door."

"Okay, in all our scenarios, I never imagined we'd be going to a large apartment building," Lauren whispered to Harriet as their host, Georgia Hecht, drove into the below-ground parking lot under the blocky beige sixties-era apartment building. She used a passkey to open an iron gate across the entrance. "Where will they keep the pets?"

"Don't worry," Georgia answered. "This isn't the shelter. This is the smoke and mirrors. We rent parking spots from the landlord, who also allows us to use a rather obscured entrance to our property."

They followed Georgia into the building's laundry room through a door at the back of the garage and on the same level. When they were all inside, Georgia looked carefully around before pulling a keychain from her pocket and selecting a key, which she then slipped into the lock on a door that appeared to lead into a utility closet.

"Close the door behind you," she ordered when they were all inside the small space. "It's a tight fit for four people, but we don't open the exit door before closing the entrance—ever."

Harriet did as directed, and Georgia pulled a shelf full of cleaning supplies toward her. It was hinged on one side and swung open to revealed a short passageway with another door at its end. Georgia peered through a peephole in the second door before using a different key on the same keyring to open it. She stepped aside and made a sweeping gesture with her arm, indicated they should precede her.

The quilters found themselves in a room dominated by a garden work-bench. The air smelled of earth and plants and the sort of oil used to lubricate yard tools.

"You can go on out into the yard," Georgia directed. "Once the door out of the laundry room is locked, we're safe."

Robin led the way out into a forested back yard.

"Follow the path into the back yard and wait for me on the deck," Georgia called after them as she turned to lock the door.

"I like it," Lauren said with a smile.

Harriet looked around the property, trying to imagine how it would look in satellite view on a map as they made their way toward the house. The house was well obscured by large, old-growth trees; someone had put a good deal of thought into this location. Sticks and flags marked the perimeter of what must be the new animal addition, and there was freshly turned earth at one corner.

"The house is on what was once a flag lot," Georgia explained when she rejoined them. "We planted an arborvitae hedge behind the front house, which we also own. The hedge goes across the old driveway, so from the front you'd never know a second house was back here."

"Like that guy in California who kidnapped the girl and held her in his back yard for eighteen years?" Lauren asked.

"That was unfortunate, but, yes, even parole officers couldn't find her, and they visited on a regular basis that whole time. Our situation is one hundred and eighty degrees from that one, but with luck, our house will never be discovered by anyone who isn't welcome."

"Thank you for letting us come tour. Hopefully, the new animal facility will help ease the journey for your residents with pets," Robin said.

"We appreciate the generous donation from Dr. Jalbert and the foundation. It will mean the world to the woman who live here."

"Our group is hoping to make a few bed quilts for you, also, if that's appropriate," Harriet added.

"Let's go inside," Georgia said and headed for the back door. "Dr. Jalbert has vouched for you, so you're free to tour the entire house. I'll show you around, and you can get an idea of what our needs are."

"That will help," Robin told her.

They waited while she unlocked the door and led them across a screened porch. She stopped to unlock the door into the house, and Harriet noticed the porch's screening was more heavy-duty than normal—another security measure, she assumed.

Georgia split them up for the tour, sending Harriet and Robin with residents and showing Lauren around herself. When they'd finished looking at the facility, she escorted them back out through the apartment building and drove them back to the downtown office.

Robin had suggested they not talk about what they'd seen until they got to Pins and Needles. Even Lauren was sufficiently sobered by what she'd seen to not argue.

"Did somebody die?" Marjory Swain asked from her post behind the cash register when Harriet, Robin and Lauren entered the quilt store.

Lauren only stared at her, her pale face whiter than usual.

"We just got back from a tour of the women's shelter," Harriet said as she slid out of her coat. "Come back and listen if you have a minute. I don't know about the others, but I'm not sure I can give my report twice."

The Loose Threads were sitting around the table in the larger of the two classrooms at the back of the store; hot drinks, bits of fabric, threads and pincushions littered the surface in front of them.

"The coffee and water pots are hot in the kitchen," Beth told them.

"Carla brought apple and cherry turnovers," Connie added proudly. "She made them herself."

"Connie showed me how." Carla's cheeks pinked at the compliment.

Robin, Lauren and Harriet fixed cups of tea and settled in vacant chairs at one end of the table. They looked at each other and then at the expectant faces of their friends.

Finally, Harriet began.

"I'm not sure what Robin and Lauren expected, but I was unprepared for what we saw."

She picked up a scrap of fabric from the table and twisted it in her fingers. Mavis took her plastic rain hat from the top of her quilting bag and began absently folding it into increasingly smaller triangles. Connie rhythmically stirred her tea, although Harriet knew she was drinking an orange-spice blend and had added neither cream nor sugar.

"Before you ask, the facility is well hidden and probably meets all the city codes for form, fit and function. That said—by necessity, according to our host—most of their funds went into providing security for the residents. The interior is colorless, industrial and bare-bones. The individual rooms have wood-frame beds and dressers like they have in college dorms, army surplus blankets, and white towels and bedding from a hotel seconds store."

"Diós mio," Connie said as she dropped her spoon with a clatter and put her hands to either side of her face. "Those poor babies."

"It's hard to imagine how they build much hope in the women and their children," Robin agreed in a grim tone.

"Even their computer is an antique," Lauren lamented. "How are they supposed to find jobs and start new lives with that sort of equipment?" She shook her head. "I expected the facility to be grim, but the part I wasn't ready for was the condition of the women themselves. Two of them had just arrived and were covered in bruises. One woman had a split lip that was so swollen she couldn't talk clearly, and another had a cast on her left arm up to the elbow." She shivered.

Harriet picked up the story.

"All of them had visible scars. My tour guide said the emotional scars are even worse. A lot of them are conflicted about being there. They're so used to being controlled by their abuser, and they've been isolated from their friends for so long, it's hard for them to help themselves, much less each other."

"Someone is doing art therapy with the children, so the kids have decorated their rooms with their drawings, but that's just about the only color in the place," Robin added. "And it ends up being more sad than uplifting."

"Sounds like we've got lots of opportunities, ladies." Mavis dropped her crumpled rain hat into her bag. "What do you think?"

"We can make the dog blankets Aiden asked for, but I'm thinking those bland rooms do need some quilts," DeAnn said.

"The children definitely need quilts," Connie said. "And probably matching pillows."

"Do the bedrooms have windows?" DeAnn asked.

"Yes, each room has a window," Robin answered. "But the house was made to be a shelter home, so the windows are clerestory style—above eye level. Their main purpose is to let light in, so curtains wouldn't work. The kitchen and bathrooms could use them, though, if that's what you were thinking."

"I can give you gals a good discount on fabric and batting," Marjory said, leaning against the doorjamb where she had a view of the cash register. "If you can use anything from the sale shelf, I'll give it to you at my cost."

"Thank you," Aunt Beth said. "That's very generous of you."

"I'd like to make a quilt, too. When you decide on a plan, let me know what I can do."

She straightened as the front door bell jangled, summoning her to the shop floor.

12

"I'll check with Pastor Hafer and see if he'd be willing to ask the congregation if anyone has any spare bedroom furniture in good condition they'd be willing to donate," Beth said.

"So, what is the actual breakdown?" DeAnn asked. "Do we know how many rooms they have and how many are occupied?"

"They gave us a summary sheet," Harriet answered. She scanned the paper she'd been given. "Looks like they have six resident rooms plus an attic loft they'd like to put two more beds in. There are five women and four children in residence right now. Two woman have one school-age child each and another has two younger children."

"I'd like to make children's quilts," Carla volunteered.

"Mavis and I can handle the pet quilts," Beth looked at her friend. "Like we said the other day, between us, we have a piece of every dog-print fabric ever made."

"I've got a couple of cat prints, too," Mavis added. "So, we're good to go ᴜn that. Beth and I could make some simple curtains for the bathrooms, too. We could do muslin with colored trim that would coordinate with the bed quilts."

"We can make lap quilts for the...what did Aiden call it? The socialization room?" Beth asked. "Animal prints should be fine for that."

"That sounds good," Connie said. "I can start a bed quilt when I finish making the adult bibs for the senior home. They're having an open house in two weeks, and I wanted to have one for each of the residents who uses one. I found a cute pattern that looks like a shirt or blouse front and completely covers the person's real shirt. Unless you look close, you can't tell they're wearing anything other than their regular clothes."

"Aren't there a lot of people who need them?" Lauren asked. "That's going to be a big job."

"I was going to talk about this when we were finished discussing the quilts for the shelter." Connie reached into the canvas bag sitting by her feet. "I brought copies of the pattern in case anyone wants to help." She set a stack of printed pages on the table in front of her. "I just found out about it at church yesterday. Diana was talking to Sarah's mother about how ratty the bibs they have look. I guess her mom lives there. Sarah's mom, Elaine, said they spent a lot of money building the new wing and that the stained bibs are functional. One thing led to another and..."

"...and you volunteered to replace all the bibs?" Lauren asked. "Seriously?"

Connie looked around at her friends.

"What could I do? Would you want your loved one to be sitting there with a stained rag around their neck when the whole community troops past their room during the open house?"

"Still." DeAnn joined the discussion. "That's a lot of work to take on at such short notice."

"Isn't the senior center where Rod's aunt lived before she died?" Robin asked. "I thought Rod said you weren't happy with them."

"Is that why you volunteered?" Lauren asked, her eyes bright with excitement. "Are you going undercover?"

"That's not a good idea," Robin cautioned. "If you have some reason to believe there was anything suspicious about the way Rod's aunt was treated, you need to hire an attorney or go to the authorities, depending on what you're thinking happened."

"I like it," Lauren said. "Count me in. Harriet?" She looked at her friend.

"I'm not playing private eye, but I'd be happy to make some bibs."

"Me, too," DeAnn offered.

"If they're not too hard to make, I can try," Carla said.

"You can work with me," Connie told her. "I'm sure you'd be fine on your own. They're pretty simple. But it will go faster if we work together, and Rod can keep Wendy busy."

In the end, everyone took a bib pattern and committed to making a few.

"Now that the bibs are taken care of, let's get back to the shelter quilts," Harriet said. "Carla is going to make baby quilts, Aunt Beth and Mavis are going to make the pet covers and lap quilts for the new room. Connie will make a bed-sized quilt. I can make another bed quilt. Anyone else?"

"I'll do a bed quilt, too," Robin volunteered.

Lauren raised her hand without saying anything.

"I'll make one, too," Marjory said from the doorway, where she was sweeping threads from the floor. "If that's okay with you all."

"Of course," Harriet said.

"Put me down for one," said DeAnn.

"Maybe we can get Jane Morse and some of our other friends who sew to make pillow cases to coordinate with the quilts," Beth suggested.

"We better get busy," Harriet stood up. "Did you get any information about what sort of fabric we should use for the bibs?" she asked Connie.

"Let me show you."

Connie pulled Harriet's copy of the pattern out of its plastic sleeve. The rest of the quilters gathered around.

Chapter 3

Harriet stopped the long-arm quilting machine when she heard a knock on her studio door. Aiden came in as she grabbed the knob to open it. He brushed past her and stormed into her work space.

"Come on in."

"Something's wrong," he blurted. He spun around to face her.

"You want to tell me about it? Sit down." She pointed to one of the wingback chairs and then went to sit in the other one.

"It's Rachel," he said, crossing his legs and bouncing his foot then uncrossing them again.

"Rachel?"

"Sarah's cat."

Harriet let her breath out, having briefly feared he was about to confess some previously unknown transgression that had come out in his weekly therapy session.

"What about her cat?" She got up and poured a cup of coffee from the thermal carafe on the library table then pressed it into his hands.

"Drink this," she said.

He sipped it and began again.

"I think Rachel is being abused."

"Oh, Aiden, I can't believe that. Sarah may be many things, but she loves that cat."

"I know that. I don't think it's her. That's why I'm here. I think Sarah herself is a victim of violence."

Harriet leaned toward him.

"What makes you think that?"

"She brought Rachel in this morning with a broken leg and a story about the cat trying to jump on the counter and slipping. She said she fell wrong when she hit the floor."

"Cats don't fall wrong, do they?"

"It's possible, I suppose, but a young healthy cat like Rachel? Not likely. And falling from the height of a kitchen counter it's *really* not likely. Fortunately, it was a clean break and should heal without complication. When I told Sarah that, she asked if Rachel could stay at the clinic until her leg healed. I told her it wasn't necessary and that I couldn't just keep her there. Then she started crying and asked if I knew of anyone who could take her into foster care."

"Wow."

"Her tears washed some of her makeup off, and she was covering up a black eye. I took a good look at her then and realized she didn't look like herself. Her clothes were baggy—she's lost a lot of weight. I asked about it, but she denied it."

"What did she say?"

"That everything was fine. I asked if I could help her, suggested she call the domestic violence hotline. I asked if I could call anyone for her. I told her I could get your aunt or Mavis to come pick her up."

"She wouldn't go for any of it?"

"Nope. She said she was fine, that she just needed a place for Rachel. I agreed to keep the cat for a couple of days to see if we can find someone, but Rachel is clearly the least of her problems."

"She has been pretty withdrawn from the group lately. And now that you mention it, Lauren thought she saw bruises on Sarah's neck a few months back. We've all tried to reach out to her, but she's not having it."

"Do you know her boyfriend?" Aiden set his cup down on the pie-crust table.

"She's been very secretive about him. She lives at his cabin most of the time, but several of the Threads have dropped in unannounced and no one has ever caught him there. She's always alone."

"Are you sure he exists?"

"Jorge has seen him. He says he's a good-looking smooth talker. Sarah hasn't talked much about him with any of us, as far as I know. She says general stuff—how smart he is, and how successful—but nothing specific. And it's been a while since she's even done that."

"I don't want to be overly dramatic, but I think your friend is in trouble. As part of our continuing education program at the clinic, we've had two training sessions put on by the Humane Society on the topic of domestic violence toward pets, and that's just since I've been here.

"They told us that people who abuse and/or kill people often hone their craft on neighborhood pets. It was kind of creepy. The speaker said the police figure if they vigorously pursue these people while they're in the animal phase, they may be able to prevent them from escalating. We vets are supposed to be the front-line offense."

"I tried to tell Sarah once things wouldn't get better without her getting help, but I could tell I wasn't getting through. She would only talk about the cat. Listen, let me talk to my aunt and Mavis and maybe Robin. They'll have ideas about what we can do."

"Thanks." Aiden set his barely touched cup on the table and stood up. "That's all I can ask."

"How are *you* doing?" Harriet asked. Before she thought about what she was doing, she stood, too, and slipped her arms around his waist. He put his around her shoulders.

"No one said therapy would be easy, and it isn't." He sighed. "My therapist tells me things will get better. And he keeps telling me to eat, rest and exercise a little."

"Sounds like good advice. I'm glad you're doing it."

"If this is what it takes for us to be us, it will be worth it. I never said I was going to enjoy the process. Especially the part where we can't really be together."

Harriet was silent.

"I know, we can't talk about it. I better go. I've got appointments. I just wanted to get you and the Threads on the job with Sarah."

She laughed. "Thanks, I think."

"Let me know what you find out and what you decide to do."

✂ - - - ✂ - - - ✂

Robin shook the rain from her jacket and put it on the back of her chair before she sat down at the big table in the back room at Tico's Tacos.

"DeAnn said to tell you she got your message and she'll be late because she's got playground duty this week at lunch time."

"I know it was short notice for everyone," Harriet said from the doorway, "but Aiden stopped by my place on his way to work this morning, and I didn't think this could wait."

Aunt Beth and Mavis arrived a few minutes later, followed by Connie and then Carla. Jorge brought baskets of warm tortilla chips and bowls of red and green salsa.

"Are you going to let us in on the mystery?" Aunt Beth asked.

Harriet pulled the door shut and joined them at the table.

"Sorry, but this isn't the sort of problem that can be discussed over the phone. Lauren said she's coming. I was hoping to wait until everyone got here before I go into it."

"Lauren's present. Are we taking roll call?" She came in and shut the door behind her before sitting down across from Harriet. "I take it from the locked door that we're telling secrets on someone."

Harriet stood up.

"Aiden stopped by this morning with some disturbing information," she began. "Sarah brought her cat into the clinic with a broken leg she said was from a fall. Aiden doesn't believe it—he thinks the cat is a victim of domestic violence."

Connie sat straighter in her chair.

"Sarah would never hurt that cat," she said.

"Hold on," Harriet told her. "He didn't say he thought Sarah hurt the cat. He thinks Sarah is also a victim. She was trying to get someone to foster Rachel, and when Aiden said he couldn't take her, she started crying and when her makeup ran, he could see she had a black eye."

"Diós mio."

"She *has* been acting weirder than usual for months," Lauren said and popped a chip into her mouth.

"And you said you saw bruises on her neck that one time, too," Harriet reminded her.

"I did. It looked like someone had choked her. She tried to cover it but her scarf slipped."

"How could we have missed this?" Aunt Beth leaned back and massaged her temple with her fingertips.

"She hasn't been around for us to miss anything," Robin reminded everyone. "Pulling away from friends is typical of women who are experiencing domestic violence."

"Is it the woman pulling away or the abuser keeping her away?" Carla asked.

"Good question." Robin turned to her. "I'm no expert, but in the cases I've dealt with, the abuser usually isolates his victim from all support systems so the only information she's getting is from him. He can tell her she's worthless, and there's no one to contradict him."

"That's what my mom's boyfriend did." Carla twirled a strand of her long dark hair around her finger. "He used to hit her, too, but it was because she'd argue with him and make him mad."

"Carla," Robin said firmly, "let's be very clear, here. It is never okay for a man to hit a woman. Or any adult to hit another adult, for that matter. It doesn't matter what your mom did or said. It was *not* okay."

"Okay," Carla whispered, her cheeks hot and pink.

"This is important," Mavis added. "I know you've had a rougher life than most of us can imagine, but it's important you understand this. Violence is never okay as a response to anything in a relationship."

The group was silent until Jorge came in with a handful of menus.

"Anyone need one of these? Or do you all know what you want?"

"Do you have a special today?" Harriet asked.

"Indeed I do. I have two pork tamales with a chicken enchilada, and I have chicken avocado soup."

The group ordered one or the other of the specials, except Robin, who stuck with her customary salad. Jorge spoke to his waitress before taking the menus and leaving. A moment later, she returned with three heaping bowls of guacamole.

"Back to Sarah," Harriet said when the door was closed again and the group was alone. "First, can anyone take Rachel? Second, how can we help Sarah? Anyone?" She looked around the table.

"Curly and I can take her," Mavis volunteered. "My dog hasn't met another animal she doesn't like."

"Okay, so what are we going to do about Sarah?" Harriet pressed.

"Do we have to do anything?" Lauren leaned forward and scooped dip onto her chip.

"Of course we have to do something," Mavis said. "How would you like it if you were in trouble, and we just sat around eating chips and ignoring your distress?"

"I think we both know I wouldn't be in that kind of trouble," Lauren shot back.

Robin stood up, pacing behind the chairs as if they were a jury.

"You might be surprised to hear that many victims of domestic violence are otherwise independent, intelligent women. It can happen to anyone." She turned and paced back to the end of the table and faced her seated friends. "I think our first step is to establish that she is, in fact, a battered woman. We're just assuming she is." She held up one hand and ticked off her fingers with the other. "Number one, her cat is injured. Number two, we've seen bruises. Number three, she's withdrawn from her social support network. Anything else?"

"I think that covers what we know," Harriet said. "So, what do we do?"

Mavis looked at Beth.

19

"Beth and I could talk to her when we talk to her about me taking Rachel."

"How soon do you think you can do that?" Harriet asked, looking from her aunt to Mavis.

"She should be working," Mavis said. "We can go after lunch."

"What if she admits her boyfriend is beating her?" Lauren asked. "What then? She's not coming to live with me, I can tell you that. Two days with that woman, and I'd probably hit her myself."

"It's really sad, but that used to be the standard prosecutors used to determine if they were going to go after abusive men. If fifteen minutes with the defendant made them want to hit her, they wouldn't take the case to court," Robin told them. "And that wasn't that long ago."

"We can guess she's not going to agree to leave her boyfriend just because a couple of us tell her she needs to," Lauren said.

Robin sat down again.

"I could go by and offer her legal advice," she said.

"She probably doesn't have anywhere else to go," Harriet said. "One of my quilt customers is living in her old apartment. Unless she got a new one, she's probably staying full time at that cabin."

"I wonder if they have room at the shelter," Mavis said.

"They were talking about putting some beds in their attic space," Harriet said. "Plus, I think they have one empty private room. I could call Georgia and ask. I need to take measurements for the bathroom curtains we need to make, so I have to call her in any case."

Jorge backed into the room, followed by his waitress, both of them laden with plates of steaming food, ending the conversation for the moment.

Harriet took a deep breath.

"This smells so good," she told him.

"All for the pleasure of the lovely mujeres."

Jorge smiled, set down his armload of plates, and left the room, returning quickly with a large tray of plates and bowls. The waitress set a pitcher of iced tea and a stack of glasses in the middle of the table.

"Do you need anything else right now?" he asked, looking from one end of the table to the other.

"Thank you, I think we're good," Harriet said.

Conversation ground to a halt as the women focused on their meals. Eventually, Connie put her fork down and leaned back from the table.

"I can't eat another bite," she said.

"Me, either," Harriet concurred. "Let's talk about where we are with Sarah. Mavis and Aunt Beth are going to go see her about taking her cat and will try to get her talking about her own situation, maybe suggesting she needs to make a change. Is that correct?"

Mavis and Beth nodded.

"I will check and see if the empty room at the shelter is, indeed, available, and whether, at first glance, they think Sarah qualifies. I'll tell Robin, and she'll go see Sarah and ask if she would like her to provide any legal services to help her get away from her abuser. She'll also talk to Sarah about going into the shelter."

"I'm taking the bibs we're making to the seniors at the end of this week," Connie said. "When I called Sarah's mother to arrange a time, she invited all of us to the open house. If we haven't gotten through to her individually by then, maybe we can talk to her as a group."

"Sounds like a plan," Lauren said.

Carla cleared her throat then coughed.

"If Jorge *has* seen Sarah's boyfriend, maybe he can tell us something about him." She swiped at a lock of hair that had fallen over her eyes.

"Oh, honey, that's a great idea," Mavis said.

"I'll be right in," Jorge's disembodied voice said over the intercom.

"It creeps me out when he does that," Lauren said. "He knows we forget he has that thing." She pointed at the speaker mounted near the ceiling.

"I heard that," Jorge said as he came in. "Just remember where your favorite guacamole comes from, missy." He tried to sound mean but burst out laughing at the end. He pulled out a chair and sat down near the middle of the table, then leaned forward before speaking in a quiet voice.

"I have learned some information about the señorita's boyfriend, and it is very troubling."

The women waited to hear what came next.

"She is dating her brother."

"What?" said Lauren loudly.

"Shhh," warned Jorge, pointing at the intercom speaker again. "Not her *brother* brother. They share no blood, but his father is married to her mother, and they lived under the same roof for a time."

"That complicates things," Harriet whispered.

"No joke," Lauren whispered back.

"We still need to try to reach her," Connie said. "Even if there's every probability that she'll refuse our help and tell us to mind our own business. I couldn't live with myself if something happened to that girl and we could have prevented it."

Mavis put her coat on and picked up her purse.

"We'll just have to make sure it doesn't come to that."

"We'll let you know how it went when we have the cat settled at Mavis's," Aunt Beth said as she hurried to gather her own coat and purse and follow her friend out the door.

Chapter 4

Oh, thank you, honey." Aunt Beth took the cup of tea Harriet offered to her as she sat on the sofa in Harriet's upstairs TV room.

"So, how did it go?" Lauren asked from her perch in the overstuffed chair.

Harriet reclaimed her seat at the opposite end of the sofa, setting her appliqué project back in her lap and picking up her own teacup. She picked up the TV remote and muted the sound.

"Okay," she said. "I'm settled. So, how *did* it go?"

Aunt Beth frowned. "It was a total bust."

"Did you at least get the cat?" Lauren asked.

"We did get the cat, but that was about all. Sarah wouldn't talk about her boyfriend, her bruises, what really happened to Rachel, or anything else."

"I guess that's no real surprise," Harriet said. "If she'd really wanted our help, she would still be coming to quilting. Or she could have called one of us."

"I don't think it works that way," Aunt Beth said. "If he's got her brainwashed, she probably doesn't feel like she can reach out. Having it be her stepbrother makes it even more complicated."

"It probably doesn't help that she works for her family, either," Harriet mused.

"So, we're on to plan B?" Lauren asked.

Aunt Beth stirred her tea, lost in thought.

"You know, our plan sounded so simple at lunch, but after talking to, or really, talking *at* Sarah, I'm not sure there's any point in Robin trying."

"How did she look?" Harriet asked.

"Terrible. She had a scarf wrapped high around her neck, and she was wearing knitted half-gloves so only her fingertips showed. And they keep that place warm for the old people, even in the reception area."

"Back to plan B," Lauren prompted.

"I'm not sure there *is* a plan B," Aunt Beth said. "My sense is we might have better luck if we could get her away from work, so she won't feel like the family is so close. We'll have to put our heads together and think about how we can do that."

"Since we can't solve the problem tonight," Harriet said. "Lauren and I were going to watch a British murder mystery DVD. Would you like to join us?"

"Well, I did feed and walk Brownie before I came over to report. I guess I could stay a while."

Harriet turned the TV's volume back on and hit play before setting the remote on the table.

✂ - - - ✂ - - - ✂

"Hit pause," Harriet told Lauren an hour-and-a-half later when her phone rang. "Hello? Connie, is that you? I can't hear you very well...Yes, Aunt Beth is here with me. Lauren, too." She listened a few moments before assuring Connie they would be right there.

"Where are we going?" Lauren asked.

"To the hospital," Harriet said as she turned off the television and gathered the empty tea mugs. "Plan B just presented itself. Connie went to drop off a hot dinner for her daughter-in-law, who is working night shift in the ER, and guess who she ran into in the triage area?"

She led the way downstairs and grabbed her purse and coat.

"Let me guess," Lauren said as she put on her own coat and slung her messenger bag over her head and settled it onto her shoulder.

"Sarah," Aunt Beth said and followed them to the garage. "How bad is it?"

"She was sitting in the triage area as opposed to coming in on a stretcher, so it didn't sound life-threatening. Connie said there were a few other people there, but said we should hurry anyway."

"Have you ever gone to the emergency room and gotten out in less that four hours?" Lauren asked.

"No, but there's a first time for everything, and it will take us a good thirty minutes to get there," Harriet said as she turned on the ignition.

"Stop talking and get driving, then."

24

"Mavis and I just saw her…" Aunt Beth glanced at her watch. "…not four hours ago."

"It probably doesn't take much time for someone to fly into a rage and inflict a lot of damage," Harriet suggested, turning onto the street.

"I think this is a case of 'be careful what you wish for,'" Lauren said.

Harriet turned to stare at her.

"What do you mean?"

"Eyes on the road, missy," Lauren ordered. "What I mean is, we couldn't think of a plan B; now we don't need to. If this doesn't convince Sarah to make a change, nothing will."

"Unfortunately, this isn't her first trip to the ER," Aunt Beth said. "If it didn't convince her the first time she went, she may not be willing to listen to us now."

"That will depend on how badly she's hurt," Harriet said.

"We aren't going to know that till we get there," Aunt Beth said and stared into the dark outside the car window.

They were silent until Harriet guided her car into the hospital parking lot.

"Let's go find out what's going on," she said.

Aunt Beth pointed to a car two rows over.

"Isn't that Connie's car?"

"Looks like," Lauren said. "If she's still here, Sarah must be, too."

✂- - - ✂- - - ✂

"We're here to see Sarah Ness," Harriet told the woman at the reception counter.

"We're out in the waiting area," Lauren said into her cell phone at the same time. She touched the face of her phone, ending the call, and turned to Harriet and Aunt Beth. "Connie will be out to get us in a minute."

Harriet mouthed a thank-you to the receptionist, who was fielding another call, then followed Lauren to a row of plastic chairs in the middle of the room.

"Over here," Connie called to them from one of the two doors that led to the interior of the hospital. She held it open as they filed into the hall beyond.

"She's having another x-ray, but we can wait in her cubicle."

"How bad is it?" Harriet asked once they were all crowded into Sarah's space.

"Her eye socket may be cracked or broken, and her right arm has a bad enough break that she's going to need surgery. If nothing's broken on her face, her eye will certainly have to be stitched up. They're trying to get a plastic surgeon here tonight to look at it."

"That sounds awful," Beth said, her face pale.

"I don't suppose we can just kidnap her," Lauren suggested.

"That would make us like her abuser," Harriet said. "Sure, we'd be kinder and gentler, but we'd be making decisions for her she should be making herself."

Lauren stood up and rocked from her toes to heels and back again.

"But she's not taking care of her own safety," she argued.

"We might need Robin," Harriet said and pulled her cell phone from her purse. "I think I'll give her a heads-up, and she can decide if she needs to join this little party. I'm going to step outside to make the call."

She returned a few minutes later. Sarah wasn't back yet.

"Robin says to let her know what Sarah says. The only way anyone can intervene is if Sarah's declared incompetent, which is a long court process, or if we observe her in imminent danger, in which case we can call nine-one-one."

"That's not very helpful," Lauren said.

"Unfortunately, it's the law," Harriet told her.

The curtain at the end of the cubicle was swept aside, and Sarah entered, riding in a wheelchair pushed by a young woman dressed in pink scrubs. A clip-on badge said the woman's name was "Taylor Morgan, RN."

"You all can't be in here," she said. "Two of you can stay, if Ms. Ness wants you to."

Connie took Lauren by the arm.

"Come on, let's go find some coffee."

"If you go back to the reception desk and take the left-hand door, you'll be in a hallway that leads to a family waiting room. There are vending machines, and the coffee one isn't half bad," Taylor told them with a practiced smile. She ducked out of the room, returning a moment later with a second wheeled stool, which she slid to Harriet. "I'll let you three talk while I go check with the doctor."

She gave Harriet a silent but telling look before turning and leaving them alone.

"Can you tell us what happened to you?" Aunt Beth asked.

"I told that nurse. I was out on the porch at the cabin. It was raining, and I slipped and fell down the steps." A tear slid from Sarah's swollen eye.

"Sarah," Harriet said in a soft voice, "things won't get better if you just ignore them. And next time you might not be as lucky as you were today. You're hurt, but you're still alive. I'm afraid for you."

"You don't care. None of you do. My family's mad at me. He's all I have." Tears were now flowing freely.

"Honey," Aunt Beth said and got up, crossing the small space to crouch in front of Sarah's chair. She took Sarah's good hand in hers. "We *all* care about you. That's why everyone has tried to get you to come to quilting, or come to coffee with us. That's why we're here. We want to help you. You need to let us in."

"We're going to be married," Sarah said with a sob. She took her hand from Aunt Beth's and raised her ring finger, displaying a small solitaire diamond.

"You can't be serious," Harriet said before she could stop herself.

"See, you don't understand." She let her hand drop to her lap.

Harriet wheeled her stool next to her aunt. Beth slid onto it, smiling at her niece as she did. Harriet crouched down in her aunt's place.

"I'm not judging you," she said. "I just hate seeing you like this. You have to be in tremendous pain."

Sarah looked down at her hands.

"Aiden is working on a project at the women's shelter—making a pet enclosure so people can bring their animals with them. He asked the Threads to make quilts for the pets," Harriet continued. "Robin and Lauren and I went to tour the shelter. We decided to make quilts for the women, too. It's a safe place you could go. I know they have room." She hoped she was telling the truth. "You could take Rachel with you when Aiden's building is finished."

"The location is kept secret from the outside world." Aunt Beth took up the story. "No one could come there unless they'd been cleared, and no one who's related to the residents is allowed in except for their minor children."

"But we're engaged," Sarah blubbered.

"Honey, if he loved you, he wouldn't do this to you." Aunt Beth reached out and retook Sarah's uninjured hand in both of hers. "Can you at least think about it? Maybe talk to the women who run the place?"

"Where are you going to go when you're released from here?" Harriet asked.

"Home." Sarah sniffed. "To the cabin."

"With your fiancé?" Aunt Beth asked.

"He stays in an apartment at the senior center during the week. He gets paid extra to sleep there and take care of any problems that the night staff can't handle."

"So, he won't be back until Saturday?" Harriet asked.

Sarah nodded, her black hair falling into her face.

"Connie mentioned you'd be having surgery. I assume that will be to-night or tomorrow," Harriet continued. "That means you wouldn't be re-leased until at least tomorrow night or even the day after. I can bring you an application for the shelter before you leave here. Then, if everything goes well, you could move there before the weekend."

Sarah sighed. "How can I leave him?" she moaned. "Who will do his laundry? He's helpless when it comes to taking care of himself."

"He's a big boy," Aunt Beth said. "And he can't go on hurting you like this."

"He doesn't mean to hurt me," Sarah whined. "It's my fault. I knew he didn't like spaghetti. I didn't know he was coming for dinner, but I should have known he might. Some nights he does come home, and I know he hates spaghetti."

"Sarah," Harriet said as gently as she could, "this isn't about spaghetti. You don't break someone's arm because they made spaghetti for dinner."

"But I should have known," she protested.

"Honey," Beth shook her hand gently to get her attention. "Look at me. This is not about what you did or didn't cook for dinner. It's about power. Right now, he has all the power. It's time for you to take some back.

"A man who loves a woman would never break her arm—not for any reason. I know this is hard, but there are plenty of nice men out there, men who will love you just like you are. You don't need to settle for this guy."

Sarah sighed, and it sounded to Harriet like she had the weight of the world on her shoulders.

"It's so much more complicated than that," she said finally.

"Will you at least consider what we've said?" Harriet asked.

Sarah was quiet for so long, she was afraid she wasn't going to answer.

"Okay," she finally said.

"Can we bring you anything?" Aunt Beth asked. "Pajamas or toiletries?"

"Could you go by the cabin? I could use a change of clothes and my overnight kit. Maybe a nightgown."

"Sure," Aunt Beth replied. "We'll wait until they tell you what the plan is. Do you have the key with you?"

"The nurse put my purse in the cupboard back there," Sarah nodded toward a cabinet at the back of the room then winced in pain at the movement.

Harriet located the purse and pulled a key ring from it.

"It's the one with the purple rubber thing on it," Sarah said.

"How did you get here?" Harriet asked as she put the blood-splattered purse back in the cupboard. "Tell me you didn't drive yourself."

Sarah's silence was all the answer they needed.

✂— - - ✂— - - ✂—

Harriet and her aunt found Connie and Lauren in the family waiting room a half-hour later.

"They took Sarah to check into a room for the night," Harriet told them. "She'll have her surgery first thing in the morning. We told her we'd get her some stuff from the cabin."

"Oh, good, you're still here." Nurse Morgan came through the door from the emergency room area and joined them near the coffee machine. "Did Sarah listen to you?"

"The jury's still out," Harriet said. "We're bringing her an application for the women's shelter, and I'll see if they have anyone who can talk to her, but she's not convinced yet."

"If he'd shot her or stabbed her, I'd already have the police here, but failing that, our hands are tied. She has to be willing before the hospital can call anyone."

"One of our quilting friends is a detective," Aunt Beth said. "We can let her know what's going on."

"I hope someone can get through to Ms. Ness," Morgan said. "If not, there will be a next time, and it will be worse."

"Thanks for letting us stay with her," Connie said.

"No problem. She wouldn't let us call anyone, and no one should be in her condition with no support." She turned toward the door. "I've got to get back to work."

Harriet waited until the door closed behind Nurse Morgan then turned to the others.

"Anyone up for a road trip?"

"To the cabin?" Lauren asked. "I wouldn't miss it."

"Connie and I better come along and make sure you two don't get into trouble," Beth slipped her coat on and picked up her purse. "Let's not dawdle. Brownie's waiting for me to come home and tuck her in for the night."

"Yeah, yeah, yeah," Lauren said. "You're not the only one with responsibilities."

Chapter 5

Boy, it's dark up here," Aunt Beth murmured as the road wound up Miller Hill. "Jorge said there's been a cabin here since before they had building codes. It's built on a rocky shelf of land that's the only buildable spot on that whole section of the hill."

Harriet slowed her car.

"So, apparently, the county isn't going to spend the money to pave the road."

Her car jolted as they left asphalt and drove onto hard-packed dirt sprinkled with a thin coating of loose gravel. The road narrowed as it wound its way up the steep hill.

"This can't be a very fun commute when it's icy," Lauren observed.

"Can you imagine how this was during last winter's storm?" Harriet said. "And she was here all by herself!"

"Whose house is this, actually?" Lauren wondered.

"I thought Sarah said it was her boyfriend's place," Aunt Beth said. "But I'm not sure. She said she had to take care of his cat at the cabin. I assumed it was his place."

"Didn't she live in that apartment in town when I first moved back to Foggy Point?" Harriet asked.

"That's what I thought," Connie said. "It's been so long since Sarah has been her old chatty self, I'm not sure what's true and what she let us assume was true."

Harriet guided her car through an opening in an overgrown bramble hedge.

"Here we are," she announced. "Let's go in and see what the cabin can tell us."

✂ - - - ✂ - - - ✂

Harriet had envisioned a log cabin, since everyone kept calling Sarah's place "the cabin," but in reality, it was a small, square cedar-sided house with a wide porch across the front and the dormant stems of some sort of climbing plant dangling from the front gutter for most of that length. It was probably lovely in the summer, when the stems would be green and laden with fragrant flowers.

A wrought iron bench sat under a picture window to the right side of the door; an old-fashioned wooden milk box was to the left. A one-foot-square ceramic tile with the log cabin quilt pattern glazed onto its surface and "The Cabin" painted in black cursive letters hung beside the door, below the house number.

Aunt Beth joined Harriet at the screen door.

"Are you going to open the door or just stand here and stare at the place?"

"Sorry. It just isn't what I was expecting."

"Me, either," Lauren said as she and Connie joined them on the porch. "I thought there'd be logs and an outhouse."

"I have to admit, I didn't expect to find such a pleasant little cottage," Connie agreed.

Harriet opened the screen door and slipped Sarah's key into the lock, turning the knob as she did so. The door let them into a tidy living room that was simply furnished with an inexpensive sofa and two chairs upholstered in a nondescript gray fabric. A black wood stove sat at one end of the room, judging by the cool temperature, the only source of heat for the house.

"Be honest, group, raise your hand if you thought Sarah's quilts would be all over the place," Lauren said. "Anyone?" She looked at the other three. "Who expected the drab gray decorating scheme?"

"Shush, you," Aunt Beth scolded. "If Sarah is a victim of domestic violence, this would be one more way for him to control her—not letting her have her quilts or any other personal items."

Harriet walked toward the back of the house, where a central hallway opened into a kitchen on the left. Sarah's bedroom was behind the living room.

"Hey, guys, come look at this."

A beautiful red-on-white Baltimore Album quilt covered the bed. The traditional flowered squares had been hand-appliquéd and then embel-

31

lished with embroidery. Touches of blue, green and yellow accented the red baskets, birds and flower vases that made up the pattern.

"I hope you're not going to try and tell me Sarah made this," Lauren said as she joined Harriet. "There is no way our friend did this. No amount of battering could have turned her into this kind of quilter."

"Of course she didn't make it. The question is, who did? And why does Sarah have it?"

"What have you got in there?" Aunt Beth asked as she, too, came into the room. "Wow," she said. "Connie," she called to her friend. "Come here, you need to see this."

"Sarah didn't make this, right?" Lauren said. She looked at Connie and then at Aunt Beth.

"Anything's possible," Beth said. "But you're right. It's not likely."

"I guess the question is, who did?" Harriet mused. "But let's worry about that later. We need to get Sarah's things together. She needs pajamas and slippers, her toothbrush, hairbrush. She has some vitamins in the bathroom," she said."

She crossed to a closet that went the length of the outside wall and opened the folding doors. The blazers and slacks she was used to seeing Sarah wear were nowhere in evidence. Instead, five long black skirts hung in a neat row next to several dark tunic-style sweaters.

"What on earth is going on here?"

"What?" Connie asked her.

"There is no trace of the Sarah we knew in this place. It's like she joined a cult or became a Stepford wife or something." Harriet found a nylon duffel bag on the floor of the closet then crossed to the unfinished wood dresser that sat opposite the end of the bed and started pulling nightclothes and underwear from the drawers. "See if you can find anything that isn't long and black for her to wear home. If not, maybe we can buy her something."

Connie opened a large cardboard box that was deep in the back corner of the closet.

"There's something here," she said and pulled out a pair of pants followed by a jacket and blouse. "I think there's a quilt underneath the clothes."

"Let me help," Harriet said, and together they hauled the box out then dug out one of Sarah's quilts.

"That's more like it," Lauren said. "Machine appliqué with stiff fusible web between it and the background fabric."

"Don't you make fun of that poor girl while she's lying there in the hospital with a broken arm," Aunt Beth said.

"I was just saying," Lauren mumbled.

"Why don't you go see what you can find in the kitchen?" Harriet suggested.

"What am I looking for?"

"I don't know. Anything that might explain any of this. I'd certainly like to find some evidence of the boyfriend."

"Let me see what I can do," Lauren said. "You know I can probably find out more on my computer and do it in half the time."

Harriet stopped packing and glared at her.

"Okay, okay. I'm going."

Aunt Beth went through the bedroom door and crossed the hallway to the bathroom.

"I'll get the vitamins." She slid open the pocket door and disappeared.

A stacking washer and dryer filled the end of the hall between the bedroom and bath. Connie opened the dryer unit.

"There are clothes here," she called out. "And the pants look like they belong to a man."

"Whoever he is, he keeps his toiletries on a shelf in the linen closet," Aunt Beth reported from the bathroom. "And there's an empty shelf below it where he probably puts a duffel bag when he's here."

"At least we know he exists," Harriet said. "Not that there was any real doubt, given the beating she's taken."

Lauren returned from the kitchen.

"Nothing special in there, unless you consider that somebody eats a lot healthier than Sarah. There's soy milk in the fridge along with tofu and a lot of kale."

"Judging from his toiletries, our mystery man has short, straight black hair and covers his acne with flesh-colored concealer. Other than that, nothing out of the ordinary," Aunt Beth said as she came back out of the bathroom. She had a small zippered mesh bag containing several bottles of vitamins and other over-the-counter remedies in one hand and a hairbrush, toothbrush and toothpaste in the other. "Has anyone found any sort of makeup bag I can put this stuff into?"

"Can anyone think of anything else we should look at before we take this stuff back to the hospital?" Harriet asked. She stretched her hand out to her aunt. "Let me put those into the bag with her clothes."

"I can't think of anything," Connie said.

No one else could think of anything, either, so they locked the cottage back up and returned to the hospital.

Chapter 6

I 'm going to take this as a sign you're feeling better," Harriet said to her little rescue dog Scooter as she rewound the roll of toilet paper he had spread all over the floor of the half-bath off her kitchen. "You, however…" She turned to her gray cat Fred. "…are in trouble. Don't think I don't know who jumped up and jiggled the latch free so he could get in. I double-checked that door, and it was shut before we went to bed last night. Don't even *try* to suggest it was a ghost."

"Have you finally gone around the bend?" Lauren asked as she came in from the studio. "I knocked on the door, but no one answered. Now I can see why—you were busy talking to yourself."

"I wasn't talking to myself, I was talking to these two clowns." Harriet turned around. Her dog and cat were nowhere to be seen." She sighed. "I suppose you never talk to Carter?"

"Of course I talk to my dog. Only he's in the room with me when I do it."

"They were right here."

"Sure they were. You know, if you put a basket or box with a lid on the back of the toilet you can put the toilet paper in it and avoid this problem."

"Scooter hasn't been well enough to get into trouble until the last few days. The wound on his back is finally healed."

"Not to change the subject, but did you connect with Georgia and did she have time to see us this morning?"

"She's meeting us at the Steaming Cup in an hour."

Lauren looked at her watch then stared into space, thinking.

"That should work," she said after a moment. "I've got a client call this afternoon, but if we don't spend hours at the shelter, it should be good."

"Aunt Beth is going to the hospital to check on Sarah and then meet Connie at the senior home. Connie has some of the adult bibs to drop off, but that's just an excuse to see what they can find out from Sarah's family."

"Let's get this show on the road, then. I'd like to have my coffee before Georgia gets there. She didn't strike me as the 'relax and have a cup' type."

"You two behave," Harriet told her pets and grabbed her coat and purse from the closet by the back door. "I'll drive."

✂ - - - ✂ - - - ✂

"Everyone here appreciates what your group is doing for the shelter," Georgia said when she'd locked the door of the shelter behind them.

Harriet pulled a measuring tape, a small notebook, and a pencil from her purse.

"It's our pleasure. I wish we could do more."

"Brightening this place up is huge. Anything and everything we can do to restore their sense of self-worth is one more step on the path to a normal life. Most of the women have been systematically torn down, mentally as well as physically. Feeling they deserve a nice place to live is one more piece of the puzzle."

"We're happy to help," Harriet told her. "I'm sure having their pets with them will be a big help, too."

"We can't even begin to thank Dr. Jalbert for supporting the pet annex. We've been talking to him about us taking in a few rescue dogs to keep here permanently as therapy for some of the women and children who don't have pets of their own."

"Are all the bathroom windows the same size?" Lauren asked before Harriet could respond to Georgia's last comment.

"Unfortunately, no. Our house design is a delicate balance between our security issues and the building code requirements for the number and size of windows. Let's start down here and work our way up to the attic."

✂ - - - ✂ - - - ✂

"Can I ask you something?" Harriet said to Georgia when she and Lauren had measured their way up to the top of the house.

"About time," Lauren mumbled so only Harriet could hear her and covering the words with a cough.

"Let me guess—you know someone you suspect is being battered."

"You get that a lot?"

"It's a sad fact that virtually everyone knows someone who is if not battered then at least bullied."

"You're right," Harriet conceded as she measured a long narrow window. "She's one of our quilt group members. She's been withdrawn from the group for months, and last night she resurfaced in the hospital, badly beaten. So far, she's unwilling to bring charges against the man."

"That's fairly common," Georgia said. "Are you hoping she'll agree to come here?"

"Am I that transparent?"

"No. Well, okay, yes, but it's not a bad thing. Your friend is lucky to have people who care about her. Plenty of women let good friends and even relatives be cut away from them by an abusive boyfriend or spouse, and those friends and relatives don't ask a single question. So, don't apologize to me for caring."

"We've approached her about moving to a shelter, and she said she'd think about it."

"She's going to have to do more than think about it," Georgia said. "We can provide all the support she needs, but she has to be the one to make the break from her abuser."

"Say she agrees," Lauren said. "What are the steps in getting her from the hospital or her home to here?"

"It's reasonably simple. Once she decides it's a go, she can meet us at a safe location we maintain away from here, and we begin the intake process. She'll need to fill out some paperwork. We'll run a criminal background check, do an internet search on her name and call her references."

Harriet made a quick sketch on her notepad then closed it and put it in her purse. She turned to Georgia.

"Is all that necessary?"

"Unfortunately, it is. Abusers will go to great lengths to find the women they batter, including trying to send other women they can control to the shelter so they can discover our location."

"That's sick," Lauren said.

Georgia laughed. "That's not the half of it. We've caught two journalists trying to get in to do undercover stories on us. We've also had half a dozen women running from arrest warrants."

"I suppose you get homeless women looking for a free bed, too" Lauren commented.

"You're getting the idea. We get at least one or two of those a month."

"Back to our friend," Harriet said. "She'll pass all those checks, so then what?"

"After the checks, one of our staff will do an in-person interview, again at that same safe location. If both we and your friend still think it's a good idea for her to live with us, we arrange to move her in. Depending on the circumstances, that can all happen relatively quickly.

"We usually have the woman stay at a safe house—that location changes monthly—for a few days to make sure she's going to stick. That way, if her abuser is really tenacious, he'll find her there, where fewer people are in jeopardy, instead of here."

"Hopefully, we can talk her into taking the first step," Harriet said.

"It's important that you understand she has to make this decision on her own. What she needs from you is support, not judgment. She's already getting plenty of that at home."

"Thank you for answering our questions," Harriet said. "I think we've got what we need for the windows."

"I'll take you back to your car. And I hope for your friend's sake she makes the decision sooner rather than later."

Harriet and Lauren spent the remainder of their time with Georgia identifying needs the shelter had and discussing how they might be met.

"I can't promise anything," Lauren said as they stood beside Georgia's gray sedan. "But this is the sort of project one of my clients likes. I'm pretty sure they'd be willing to donate computers and software your women could use to take online classes and job training."

Georgia handed them several business cards.

"The first one is for business contact. If people want to make donations, have them call this number. The second one is for your friend. It's our emergency number. Someone answers this phone twenty-four-seven. Someone is on call to pick up victims, if that's what's required, in less than an hour."

Harriet took the cards.

"Thank you. With a bit of luck, you'll hear from our friend. And for sure, you will hear from us regarding donations."

"What she said," Lauren echoed.

"Thank *you*," Georgia said. "Talk to you soon." She got into her car and drove out of the Steaming Cup parking lot.

Lauren's phone trilled, immediately followed by a similar sound from Harriet's. Lauren tapped in a security code.

"Looks like we have a summit meeting at Tico's."

Harriet glanced at her own unsecured phone screen. Aunt Beth had texted her, requesting she come to Jorge's restaurant as soon as they were finished.

"Let's go see what they want," she said.

Aunt Beth was in the kitchen at Tico's Tacos deep in conversation with Jorge when Harriet and Lauren entered the restaurant and headed for the back room. She looked up as they passed but kept talking.

Robin and DeAnn were seated at the big table, and Carla was at the server station pouring glasses of water. There was none of the laughter that usually accompanied Loose Threads gatherings. Robin was dressed in her usual yoga pants and pastel stretch top, but her face was all lawyer. DeAnn had on an oversized tie-dyed T-shirt she'd gotten at the previous month's 1960s festival; her demeanor was no match for its bright colors.

Sarah had irritated everyone in the group at one time or another, but none of them wished the kind of beating she'd taken on her or anyone else.

"So, why exactly are we here?" Harriet asked.

"Lunch, I hope," Lauren said

"We're not sure," Robin offered. "Your aunt said she'd explain when we got here."

"Which I will," Aunt Beth told them as she came into the room carrying menus. "Anyone need one of these?"

"Do we know the specials?" DeAnn asked.

Jorge's disembodied voice came over the intercom.

"Today, we have chiles rellenos with a chicken tamale, albondigas mexicanas—that's meatball soup for you gringas—and *tacos al pastor*, a slow-cooked street-style pork taco." He paused. "And of course, whatever salad Blondie wants."

Jorge prided himself on knowing his regular customers' dietary preferences, and Robin was definitely a salad person.

"I'm torn," Harriet said. "I love the chiles rellenos, but the tacos sound good, too."

"Say no more," Jorge said from the intercom.

The rest of the group told him their requests, and Aunt Beth set the menus on the server station and joined them.

"I'd like to wait for Connie to get here," Beth said. "Mavis can't come. She's getting her hair cut in Angel Harbor and was just getting in the chair when she got my message. Here's Connie now," she added as her friend came into the room.

"Do you want to begin or should I?" she asked Beth.

"Go ahead."

Connie stood behind her chair.

"Today I took a few of the completed adult bibs to the senior center, using the excuse that we needed them to try them out and see if they were the right size. Normally, I would have talked to Sarah at the front desk, and she would have taken care of whatever I needed.

"A new young woman was there. I've never seen her before, so I took a chance and pretended I didn't know what had happened to Sarah."

"Did she buy it?" Lauren interrupted.

Connie straightened her shoulders, drawing herself to her full height of just shy of five feet.

"I think so. She said she usually works in the back office and was filling in for Sarah while she recovered from a recent 'illness.' I told her I knew it was a family business and wondered if she was part of the family. She doesn't look like Sarah, I might add. She's fine-boned and blond—the opposite of Sarah. She said her dad owns the place. I didn't let on that I knew Sarah's stepdad and her mom are the real owners."

"Wait, does that mean she's Sarah's sister? Or half or step? Why have we never heard about her?" Harriet asked.

Lauren looked at her.

"Really? Think about it. When did Sarah ever talk about anything other than herself? She talked about her boyfriend when they were first seeing each other, but even then, it was always in the context of what she was going to wear or where they were going to go. She mentions her parents only when it has to do with their work demands interfering with her social life."

Aunt Beth cleared her throat.

"Let's remember who the victim is here."

"Sorry." Lauren sat back in her chair.

"Did you see anything else?" Harriet asked Connie.

Connie walked the length of the table then returned to her place before speaking.

"I saw the elusive boyfriend."

"Whoa," Carla said. "What was he like?"

"I only spoke to him briefly. He was delivering medication for a patient we were going in to see. He was charming, handsome and very smooth. He's the resident pharmacist."

"That seems odd," Harriet noted. "How can they afford to pay their own pharmacist?"

"Of course, that didn't come up. Nothing was said about why a licensed pharmacist would be sleeping over at a small-town nursing home, either."

"That will bear some investigation," Harriet said.

"On it," Lauren said and pulled her laptop from her bag.

Connie sat down.

"That's all from me. They again invited us all to the open house and, of course, thanked us for the bibs."

Jorge came in carrying three baskets of chips balanced on his arm, a bowl of guacamole in each hand.

"That family has always been a little strange, if you ask me."

"Strange how?" Harriet asked.

"The stepfather is very active and prominent in the business community—Chamber of Commerce, Small Business Association, the local business association. The señorita's mother is as invisible as he is visible. I've heard it's the mother who owns the business, but he controls it, along with his son.

"There are other kids attached to the family, too. The man has a daughter with his second wife, and there is a blond boy in there somewhere. I don't know who is the mother of the dark-haired son that is the señorita's boyfriend."

Lauren snapped her laptop shut as the waitress started bringing everyone's lunch in.

"So far, I found the pharmacist in the family is Seth Pratt. He is, indeed, licensed and in good standing. There have been no complaints against him—at least at first glance. Beyond that, I need to do more digging."

Jorge's waitress set a plate with a small chile relleño and two tacos al pastor on it in front of Harriet.

"This looks good," she said. She glanced at her aunt.

"I'll wait until we eat to tell you about my morning," Beth said.

✂ - - - ✂ - - - ✂

Lauren crumpled her napkin and dropped it onto her plate. Twenty minutes had passed since the food had been put before them.

"I'm glad you ladies have all day to lunch, but I need to get back to work." She looked at Beth.

"Okay." Beth pushed her chair back from the table and stood. "As some of you know, I spent this morning at the hospital. Sarah came through her surgery with no problem and was released, but not before I was able to make one last plea for her to leave her fiancé and move to the shelter."

"Did you make any headway?" Robin asked.

"I think I did. Possibly because she was taking pain medication and her resistance was lowered. I think I got through."

"But?" Harriet prompted when her aunt didn't continue.

"Her mother showed up. Sarah knows she can't go back to the cabin by herself right now. I didn't know if the shelter could take her immediately, so when her mother came in and told her she was going to take her to the senior center and have her stay in the skilled nursing wing for a few days, what could I say?"

"So, she's going to stay with her abuser?" Lauren said. "I mean, didn't Sarah say he was the night manager there?"

Beth's shoulders drooped.

"When her mother showed up, there was nothing I could do."

"Surely, she'll be safe while she's in their nursing wing," Harriet said. "And that'll give us time to make arrangements with the shelter, if she'll let us."

"I wouldn't make any assumptions about her safety there," Robin said. "Abusers can be incredibly persistent."

"Short of staging a raid on the place, can anyone think of anything else we could do immediately?" Harriet asked.

Carla raised her hand as if she were a child in school.

"Oh, honey, you don't need to raise your hand," Beth told her.

"What if we visited her a lot?"

"We can't be there twenty-four-seven," Lauren pointed out.

Harriet leaned forward, her elbows on the table.

"That doesn't mean it's a bad idea. If we set up an irregular schedule, so people are coming and going several times a day and evening, he'll never know when we're going to show up."

"It would be better if someone could be with her all the time, but I suppose visits would be at least a partial deterrent," Robin said thoughtfully.

She pulled a yellow lined tablet and a pen from her purse and drew a grid with Loose Threads names in a vertical column and the hours of the day across the top.

"I'm putting myself down from one to three." She looked at her watch. "I'll be late today, but starting tomorrow I can go there after yoga class and stay until the kids get out of school."

"I can go from nine to noon Monday, Wednesday and Friday," Carla said. "Wendy can go to playgroup at the church."

"I'll go at dinnertime, whatever days you need me to," Connie said.

"Put me down for whatever dinnertimes Connie doesn't do," Aunt Beth said.

"Kissa goes to a late-morning playgroup, so fill me in then," DeAnn said referring to her toddler.

"Put me wherever you need fill-in," Harriet said. "I'm working on a big quilt I'll be stitching on for days; I can pretty much take a break anytime."

Robin noted the times and put the pad and pen back into her bag.

"I'll e-mail the schedule to everyone when I get home from my visit with her. Connie, if you could go during dinner tonight that will give me time to get the schedule made and emailed to everyone."

"Sounds good to me," Harriet said. "Everyone?"

She looked around the table. One by one, the Threads nodded agreement.

Robin stood up.

"I'm going to head over to the senior center. I'll be in touch."

"I better go get stitching so I'll be ready when I get my assignment," Harriet said. "By the time you get back, Mavis should be done with her hair appointment, so you can give her a buzz. I'm sure she'll want to do a shift, too."

With that settled, everyone left for their various assignments and activities.

✂ - - - ✂ - - - ✂

"Come on in." Harriet called as she pressed the red stop button on the hand grip of her long-arm quilting machine. "It's open."

She hadn't heard the car pull into her driveway over the noise of her machine, but she recognized Mavis's silhouette through the curtained bow window beside her studio door. If Mavis hadn't seen Harriet at the machine through the same window, she would have let herself in instead of knocking; but she wouldn't have wanted to risk startling Harriet and causing a misplaced stitch.

Scooter jumped from his bed under Harriet's desk and began barking at her as she came in.

"Your timing needs a little work," Mavis said with a smile. She bent and picked the little dog up. Scooter licked frantically at her face, causing her to laugh.

"Some watchdog, huh?"

"He'll get there," Mavis said. She pulled a small plastic bag from her purse and took a strip of dog jerky from it. "Here you go, little one." She handed Scooter the treat and set him gently on the floor.

"You want some tea?" Harriet asked. She stood and bent forward, reaching for her toes. "I've been stitching on this quilt for hours. I could use a break." She straightened back up. "Hey, your hair looks great."

A redhead in her youth, Mavis's hair had been a faded rusty gray before today's makeover. It was now a more distinct auburn with golden highlights.

42

"Thanks, and yes, I'd love some. My daughters-in-law got me a gift certificate for a new hairdo for my last birthday."

"That was a few months ago, if I'm not mistaken."

"Well, it's never good to rush these things. Anyway, I went to Mr. Max in Angel Harbor, and I have to confess, I like his handiwork."

"How are you going to break the news to Miss Shirley?"

"That's why the girls got the gift certificate. They knew I wouldn't waste the money they'd spent buying it for me, and they also knew it would take something like that to get me to break away from Shirley."

"It looks good. You look younger."

"He cut the sides shorter and added a little color. I swore I'd never color my hair, but he said highlights don't really count."

Harriet circled her. There were lighter areas, but it was obvious Max had darkened the background color as well.

"Mr. Max sounds like a smooth talker. Come on, let's go to the kitchen, and I'll see if I can scrounge up a snack to go with our tea."

Mavis filled the kettle while Harriet dug in her cabinets, coming out with a box of gingersnaps.

"Will these do?"

"I love gingersnaps, and they don't have to be homemade to be good."

"Has anyone filled you in on what our lunch was about?"

"Not yet. I called your aunt when I got done, but she must have the sound turned off on her phone."

Harriet poured hot water into their mugs and put the cookies on a plate, then brought it all to the kitchen table.

"So, we seem to be in the bodyguard business," she said when she'd finished explaining to Mavis what had been decided at lunch.

"I'll call Robin when I get home and get on the schedule." Mavis picked up her tea and took a long sip. "I wasn't completely slacking today on that front."

"Do tell." Harriet leaned forward in her chair.

"Mr. Max and I were making small talk, and I mentioned making the adult bibs for the senior center. As it turns out, he's familiar with the center. He went to school with Howard Pratt."

"That's interesting."

"It gets more so." Mavis took a bite of her cookie. "Howard's been quite the marrying man. Sarah's mother is his third wife, that Max knows of— that was how he put it. And the first one died under mysterious circumstances."

"Mysterious how?"

43

"Mysterious as in everyone thinks she was murdered, and no one was ever arrested."

"That *is* interesting."

"Max says Howard played the hero, adopting the second wife's son after she killed herself. He says there wasn't any other family to take the boy, and Max didn't doubt Howard would have made sure the boy never forgot that. That last part was him speculating—he didn't have any direct knowledge."

"We need to get Lauren to dig deeper into Sarah's family. According to Georgia at the women's shelter, domestic violence tends to be generational. I realize that doesn't excuse Sarah's abuser, though."

"It *would* be good to know. And Connie and Rod have been suspicious about Rod's aunt's death at that center. Maybe Howard is one of those angels of death you hear about."

"If that's true, it's even more important that we keep an eye on Sarah while she's there and get her out of there as quickly as we can. If we convince her she's being battered, that might make her a liability in Howard's eyes."

"I hadn't thought about that," Mavis said. "Maybe we should talk to Detective Morse."

"I don't think we're to that point yet. So far, this is all speculation—except for Sarah being battered, of course. You know, I suppose there'a chance it's really Howard who's beating her. Except she did say Seth hit her because she cooked the wrong thing for dinner,.."

They finished their tea in silence, and Mavis stood up.

"Have you worked on your pet quilts for Aiden's shelter room yet?"

"I signed up to do a bed quilt, but I've spent all my time the last week on the customer quilt you just saw on the machine. The woman wants to enter it in the Tacoma show, and if it does well, she's thinking about Houston or Paducah.

"To be in either of those shows, though, the quilting has to be really dense. I'm hoping she realizes that the top winners at the big shows have what must be hundreds of hours of stitching in them. So far, she's not asking me to do that much."

"Want to get together tomorrow and work on them? I've cut out some pieces, but that's all."

"Sure, I'll dig out my dog prints and see if I have something that coordinates with any of the ones you're using."

"Let's meet for lunch at the Sandwich Board. Then we can cruise the sale shelf at the quilt store. Marjory might have something we can use for backing."

"Sounds like a plan. I think most of the Sarah-schedule openings are before noon, so that should work fine."

Chapter 7

"What are you two up to?" Lauren asked. She pulled a chair up to the table Mavis and Harriet were sharing at the Sandwich Board Deli in downtown Foggy Point the following day. "Mind if I join you?"

"Of course not," Mavis said. "Since when do you need to ask?"

"Just checking." Lauren pulled her laptop from her messenger bag and opened it on the table then spun it around to face her two friends.

"What's this?" Mavis asked.

"My attempt at Sarah's family tree. As you can see by the dotted lines, I'm not sure of all the connections, but this is what I've got so far."

Harriet tried to follow the branches of the tree.

"So there *are* two girls, Sarah and Hannah, and two boys, Seth and Joshua. Am I reading this right?" She looked over the top of the computer. "Sarah's not related by blood to any of them?"

"That's right. Hannah is a half-sibling to each of the boys, but the boys aren't blood relatives."

Mavis sat back and rubbed her hand across her chin.

"And Sarah says she's engaged to Seth?"

"That's what she told us," Harriet said. "At least, it was true when she was in the hospital. I talked to Carla this morning, and she thinks we've gotten through to her about going to the shelter, so hopefully that means the engagement is off."

"I swear I will kidnap her and take her far, far away if she tries to marry that jerk," Lauren said. "If you guys won't help me, I'll call the geek squad."

Lauren had a group of computer programming students she worked with who saw themselves as superheroes of the cyber world.

"We need to try to talk to her sister and mother when we go to the open house," Mavis said.

"Are you going to tell them about the shelter?" Harriet asked.

"No, I'm not suggesting that," Mavis said. "It would be useful to get a sense of whether they're going to help or hinder, though."

"I want to talk to Seth and see what he's all about," Lauren said.

"Just be careful," Harriet cautioned. "We can't tip our hand."

"We can pray she'll move to the shelter *before* the open house," Mavis said. "We've only got three days for that to happen, but I think they move quickly once the victim agrees to go."

"Did you find out anything about her biological father?" Harriet asked Lauren.

"His name is Peter Ness. Other than that, nothing. I'll keep looking, though."

"It would help if he were available to Sarah," Mavis said. "Maybe she could live with him until she gets her feet under her again."

"I think we need to find out if he's alive and make sure he's not worse than Sarah's current family," Harriet cautioned. "I mean, there must be some reason she's so close with her mom and stepdad, and we've never heard of her father."

"Numbers twenty-three, twenty-four and twenty-five," called a small woman with short dark hair and a tattoo sleeve covering her right arm.

"I'll get them."

Harriet stood and went to the service counter. The woman put three wicker plates loaded with deli-sandwiches and kettle chips onto a tray and slid it toward her.

Mavis took her turkey sandwich from Harriet.

"You have to wonder how that blue frog on her arm is going to look when she's my age." She tipped her head toward the woman behind the counter.

"I'd think twice before I put any image on the part of my arm that's destined to become a flap," Harriet said.

Lauren's Rueben sandwich was halfway to her mouth, but she stopped to laugh before taking a bite.

"Young folks never think it's going to happen to them," Mavis said. "But I can guarantee—no matter how fat or thin you are, when you hit menopause, your arms are going to flap."

Lauren set her sandwich down on her plate, still laughing.

"Thanks for sharing that little pearl of wisdom."

"Hey, what sort of friend would I be if I didn't help you prepare for your future? Who knows, you might have gotten an ill-placed tattoo if I hadn't warned you." Mavis smiled at her.

"Yeah, like that was going to happen."

"On a totally other subject," Harriet interrupted, "do you want to go look at fabric with us when we're done here?"

Lauren swallowed her bite.

"I need to. I'm still struggling with my idea for a bed quilt for the shelter. I know I could just do something pretty, but I'd really like to do something inspiring."

"I've been grappling with the same thing," Harriet said. "I assumed there were symbols associated with hope or healing that are universal, but I guess not."

"You were worried about that for the pet quilts?" Lauren asked.

"Hey," Mavis said. "We get that the pets don't care, but there's an owner associated with each of those pets, and she might be inspired by our quilts."

"Whatever."

"I signed up for a bed quilt," Harriet said. "If I ever finish the customer quilt I'm working on, I'm going to try to do one or two pet beds, too."

"Aren't you just the overachiever," Lauren said. "Now I'm going to look like a slacker if I just do my bed quilt."

"Stop it, you two," Mavis scolded.

Harriet stood when they were finished eating.

"Everyone done?"

Mavis and Lauren nodded, and she picked up the baskets and took them to the bussing station, dumping the papers into the garbage and stacking the plates on the table. When everyone was ready, they headed down the block for Pins and Needles.

"Honey? You ready to go?" Aunt Beth called from the base of the stairs.

"Just a minute," Harriet called back.

Scooter ran down the stairs at the sound of Beth's voice. Like the other Loose Threads, she carried a small bag of dog treats in her purse to use as part of the ongoing socialization process of the formerly hoarded dogs several of them had adopted. Scooter was learning fast. Any time he heard a Loose Thread voice, he came running in hope of a treat.

Harriet descended the stairs a moment later, buttoning the three lowest buttons on her cardigan.

"Since we're all going to be there today for the open house, Robin went to sit with Sarah this morning," Aunt Beth reported.

"I was hoping she'd be in the shelter by now."

"I don't know if you saw her yesterday, but she had to go and have some of that hardware that's sticking out of her arm adjusted. She was in rough shape. I'd have thought her pain meds would have knocked her out, but they didn't seem to."

"They must have some provision for injured residents at the shelter. I'm guessing it's not unusual."

"Probably, but still, it's not all bad that she's in a skilled nursing facility."

"Lauren's meeting us here. We figured parking might be at a premium." She led the way through her studio to intercept her friend, who had just pulled into the driveway.

"Okay," Harriet said when everyone was in the car and had their seatbelts on. "Let's check in with Sarah and then each take a different family member, see if we can learn anything."

"Do we know they're all going to be there?" Aunt Beth asked.

"I'm assuming they are," Harriet answered. "I thought Sarah said they all work there."

"We know some of them do, but I'm not sure they all do," Lauren said. "I'm with Harriet, though. I figure they'll all be present. Opening a memory care wing is a big deal, at least according to all their advertising.

"I did some work on their software the other day, and I saw their VIP RSVP list. They've got some heavy hitters coming—hospital executives, politicians, and even a couple of B-list actors."

"Wow, maybe we should have dressed up," Harriet said.

"We're fine. It's a senior care center, not a four-star restaurant," Aunt Beth assured her.

"Yeah, besides, this is Foggy Point," Lauren added.

Carla, DeAnn and Robin were standing beside Robin's minivan when Harriet pulled into the senior center parking lot.

"Any sign of Mavis or Connie?" she asked them.

Robin rose onto her toes to look past her to the street.

"They're pulling in now. We were talking in the car on our way over about what our strategy should be."

"We were, too," Harriet told them. "We were thinking we should each try to find and observe different members of Sarah's family."

"Sounds like great minds think alike," Robin said. "We were thinking the same thing. We figured we could take turns staying with Sarah, too. She seemed sort of restless when I was with her this morning."

Carla twirled a strand of hair in her fingers.

"Has anyone else noticed how uncomfortable Sarah seems to be?" Her face turned red as she spoke.

"I did think she was in a lot more pain than she should have been when she got back from the hospital the other day," Aunt Beth reported. "I mean, if her boyfriend is a pharmacist, you'd think he'd be all over it."

"I think she's afraid to take her medicine," Carla told them. "I'm usually there when they bring her lunch tray, and there's a cup of pills on it. She takes them and immediately goes to the bathroom—every time. And then she doesn't get sleepy or anything. Her arm seems to hurt all the time, too."

"Very good observation, Grasshopper," Lauren said. "I also thought she seemed to be in more pain than someone in an institution should be."

"Why does she call me Grasshopper?" Carla whispered to Harriet.

"It's an obscure TV reference. Don't worry, it's nothing bad. I'll tell you about it later," Harriet whispered back.

"Maybe we're making more headway with Sarah than we thought," DeAnn observed. "Sounds like she's suspicious of what her fiancé might give her."

"If Connie's right about Rod's aunt, it's with good reason," Harriet said.

Connie's husband Rod parked their car three spots over, and their trio joined the group.

"What did we miss?" Connie asked, and Harriet filled them in on what had been discussed. Robin suggested Harriet and Lauren start with a visit to Sarah, to be followed by Mavis and Beth and then herself and DeAnn.

Aunt Beth pulled her plastic rain hat from her purse and put it carefully over her hair.

"Let's go in before the rain decides to get serious," she said.

The first thing Harriet noticed when she and Lauren came through the front doors of the Foggy Point Senior Center was Aiden, standing at the reception desk deep in conversation with the young blond woman who had taken Sarah's place. The second thing was that all the chairs and side tables on both sides of the large entrance area had been replaced with rows of folding chairs facing a podium. Bouquets of silver and blue helium-filled balloons were tethered to large Chinese ceramic vases on either side of the podium, creating a stage-like space.

A tall man in a navy blue suit guided the Loose Threads to a row of chairs at the back of the audience area. Aunt Beth and Mavis removed their rain bonnets, shaking them out before folding them and stowing them in coat pockets then settling on chairs.

"I didn't realize there was going to be a formal presentation," Mavis said in a quiet voice.

"Me, either," Connie said. "Sarah's mother said they were planning a welcome program, but she didn't mention anything like this."

Harriet nodded toward the front rows of chairs. Silver ribbons with bows on each end were draped across the first two.

"I guess the VIPs will be sitting there."

Lauren looked where Harriet indicated then back at their own location.

"I guess we know where we rank."

"I think we already knew," Harriet said with a chuckle.

The center was an X-shaped building with a large square in the middle. The legs of the X were the resident rooms, with the reception area, offices and dining rooms located in the center square. The leg to the right and rear of the reception area was the one that had been remodeled to create the memory care unit.

When all but the two front rows were filled, a single file of people came from the direction of the new wing and were guided by the usher to the two empty rows.

"That group is definitely overdressed for Foggy Point," Lauren whispered to Harriet, covering her mouth with her hand.

A blond man stood and went to the podium, introducing himself as Howard Pratt. He proceeded to introduce the luminaries who were financial contributors to the new wing. The reality TV star had a mother who would be moving into the facility, but the presence of the aged leading man was never explained.

Lauren leaned across Harriet to talk to Connie.

"Are all these people going to speak?"

"I don't know," Connie answered. "I wasn't expecting this."

The speeches began, and after the mayor and the Foggy Point PUD rep had spoken, Harriet turned to Lauren.

"I'm going to go to the restroom in the left-hand hallway. Give me a five-minute lead and then follow."

"Okay," Lauren agreed without looking at her.

Six minutes later, Harriet and Lauren had escaped and were on their way to Sarah's room.

Interior halls connected the outer ends of the legs of the X-shaped building, and Harriet led Lauren from the independent living hall restroom where they'd met to the skilled nursing area at the end of the adjoining corridor.

"Wow, I didn't know this hallway existed," Lauren said. "I've always come in through the reception area."

"I think they keep the doors closed most of the time, but I saw a nurse go this way when I was leaving Sarah's room one time, so I followed her."

"Did she say anything?"

"No, I acted like I belonged, and she didn't challenge it." Harriet crossed the larger hallway to Sarah's room and stopped so abruptly Lauren bumped into her back.

"What's wrong?"

"She's not here." Harriet stepped into what had been Sarah's room. "Looks like she's moved out."

She opened the closet; it was empty. The bed had been made with fresh sheets and looked ready for a new patient.

Lauren went into the bathroom and opened the medicine cabinet.

"No toiletries or anything in here."

"Maybe she moved to the independent living area."

Lauren came back.

"Wouldn't we have walked past her room? That was the hall we started in."

"Let's check the rest of the rooms in this section to make sure they didn't just move her."

"I didn't think she was ready to be on her own. Her arm is still a mess with that contraption sticking out of it. That can't possibly feel good."

Harriet led the way back into the hall and began peering into rooms.

"I thought Sarah might tell one of us if she was going into the shelter."

"Really? This is Sarah we're talking about."

"You're right. I hope she's at the shelter. They aren't going to tell us if that's the case. If she doesn't call, we aren't going to know, unless we can come up with an excuse to visit."

The two women reached the end of the hallway with no sign of Sarah. Harriet opened the door to the connecting hall.

"Shall we go see if the speeches are done? I still want to talk to the rest of her family."

"Which one of them do you think is most likely to tell us where she went?" Lauren asked.

"Let's start with the boyfriend and go from there."

Harriet turned and headed down the hallway back to the reception area.

"How's Sarah?" Aunt Beth asked when they'd rejoined their group. "I assume that's where you two sneaked off to."

"She's checked out," Harriet replied. "Or at least, she's vacated the room she's been in."

"Did any of the caregivers know anything?" Robin asked.

"Everyone must be working on this shindig," Lauren said and gestured to the podium, where many of the guests were now surrounding the VIPs. "We didn't see anyone in the hallways."

"They told us they're starting tours of the facility in ten minutes," Mavis reported. "They have snacks set up in the main cafeteria and suggested we go there before they start."

"I think the family members are leading the tours," Carla told them. "Maybe we should divide up so we get different guides."

"Good idea," Harriet said.

Carla looked down at her feet, letting her hair fall over her face.

"We better get moving," Mavis said and led them out of the seating area toward the dining room.

"Wow, they spared no expense on the snacks," Harriet said, pointing at a tray of chocolate truffles. "Those are a specialty of Chef James at the Cafe on Smugglers Cove. He handcrafts them himself."

Mavis leaned in for a closer look.

"Those are handmade?"

"I'm not sure it still counts as handmade when you're a trained chef and own a restaurant," Lauren said.

Harriet picked one up.

"Whatever you call them, I'm having one." She took a bite and closed her eyes. "He hasn't lost his touch."

The rest of the Threads each took one.

DeAnn tilted her face up and sniffed loudly.

"Smells like someone's been baking bread all day."

"That's an old realtor's trick," Mavis said. "People will overlook some of the flaws in a kitchen if it smells of fresh-baked bread or chocolate chip cookies."

Lauren smiled. "I don't think it's the smell of kitchen flaws they're covering up."

"Be nice," Harriet scolded.

"Don't tell me you couldn't smell the place when we weren't in the cafeteria or lobby," Lauren said.

"Only in the nursing wing and memory care area," Harriet said.

Two tables away, Aiden sat across from the blond receptionist, their heads nearly touching as they spoke in low tones. Harriet stared as they laughed, the blonde reaching across and playfully punching Aiden on the arm.

Aunt Beth wiped her hands on a cocktail napkin.

"That was amazing," she said in a louder than normal voice.

"We better start going on tours." Robin put her arm on Harriet's shoulder and gently turned her away from Aiden and toward the new wing.

A group was gathering around Howard Pratt at the entrance to the memory unit.

"Mavis and I have this one," Beth said and headed toward the group. A moment later, they disappeared down the hall, the receptionist stepped into the same space, and a second group assembled. Aiden got up with her and joined the group. The blonde led them toward the independent living hallway.

"DeAnn and I will take blondie," Robin told Harriet. "See if you and Lauren can get the boyfriend. Connie and Carla, see if you can find Sarah's mother and ask her where Sarah went. She must be here somewhere."

"Rod, would you mind doing some snooping?" Harriet asked Connie's husband.

"That's why I'm here. What did you have in mind?"

"There have to be some nurses' aides or caregivers in the other wings. With the family busy giving tours, it's the perfect chance to grill them."

"Say no more." He picked up a plate and put a selection of chocolates on it then filled another plate with small cookies. He covered both plates, picked them up and headed for the assisted-living wing.

A dark-haired man in an expensive-looking suit appeared at the intersection of the assisted-living unit and the main dining hall.

"Come on," Harriet said to Lauren. "Our guide is in position."

Seth introduced himself as Howard's son and the company pharmacist. He had the rich sort of voice opera singers and television news anchors possessed. Harriet wondered if it was natural or something he'd cultivated with years of practice.

When the group got to the memory unit, he explained how the entrance hallway was crisscrossed with motion sensors and monitored with security cameras. In addition, residents would be given a difficult-to-remove bracelet with a microchip embedded in it that would set off an alarm if the resident tried to escape the area without checking out. It also had GPS capabilities. It was all very state-of-the-art.

Lauren leaned toward Harriet.

"Somebody donated a pile of money. I installed the software on that baby—it has some customizable parts. It's an expensive system."

Harriet had tuned out what Seth Pratt was saying as she studied him. He was aware of his audience. His jokes were well-timed, but his smile never quite reached his eyes. It was clear to her he saw tour guiding as beneath him.

She looked surveyed the group around her. They seemed to be mesmerized. He probably got that a lot.

When the group broke up to look into one of the four empty rooms that had been staged for the tours, Harriet used the opportunity to speak to Seth.

"Do you know where Sarah is?" she asked without preamble.

"Who?"

"Sarah. You know, your fiancé."

"This is not the time nor the place for this discussion."

Lauren joined them, blocking Seth's path back to the group.

"We're friends of Sarah's, and we want to know where she is."

"She's in her room. Not that it's any of your business." He started to turn away, but Harriet stopped him with what she said next.

"No, she's not. Her room is empty and has been cleaned out."

Seth stared at her. She could tell this was news to him.

"Who did you say you are?"

"We're friends of Sarah's, but I think you already know that. She used to quilt with us before you stopped her from coming to our group."

"I have no idea what you're talking about. As for Sarah—not that it's any of your business—I'm sure she just changed rooms. She probably got tired of having so many visitors."

So, he did know who they were.

"You must have a record on your intranet," Lauren said.

"As I said, this is not the time or place for this." Seth turned his back on them and continued his practiced speech about the activity room that included dolls and stuffed animals and a variety of sensory activities designed to stimulate the brain.

"That's interesting," Lauren murmured. "He has no clue where she is."

"Let's hope the rest of the group has had better luck," Harriet replied.

✂ - - - ✂ - - - ✂

Aunt Beth and Mavis were sitting opposite Robin and DeAnn at a six-person table in the cafeteria when Lauren and Harriet returned from their tour.

"Any sign of Carla and Connie?" Harriet asked as she pulled out a chair and sat down.

"Or Rod?" Lauren added.

Mavis looked toward the front of the room.

"Here come Connie and Carla."

Lauren collected two chairs from a vacant table and fit them between hers and Harriet's.

"Have a seat and tell us what you learned."

"Sarah's mother didn't seem to know she's not here anymore," Connie reported. "And I don't think she's lying. She's very mousy. And she seemed very nervous. She kept looking past us while we talked, and she jumped when a door slammed. Something or someone has her spooked."

"She blamed Sarah for her own injuries, too," Carla added.

"That's terrible," Harriet said. "Her boyfriend claimed not to know she'd left, but he seems slick. I couldn't get a good feel for his truthfulness."

"Me, either," Lauren agreed. "My money's on him being a liar, but he did seem surprised when we said she was gone."

Robin took a sip from her paper cup of coffee.

"The sister was seriously perky. She was lobbying Aiden for an internship at the vet clinic, so she gave us the bare minimum information."

"Her tour consisted of a brief introduction and then 'look at stuff when we go by and ask if you have any questions,'" DeAnn said. "She was a walking blonde joke."

"We didn't get an opportunity to ask her about Sarah. She was so completely ignoring our group it would have drawn too much attention if we'd tried," Robin added.

"Beth and I had the same thing happen," Mavis said. "Daddy Pratt was so busy sucking up to his investors we were invisible."

Carla got up and went to the buffet table. She came back carrying a tray laden with cups of coffee and tea and a plate of cookies. Rod arrived as she was unloading her treats.

"The mystery deepens," he said and took a cup of coffee. "The aides are suspicious of the drugs that are being dispensed at this place. Given the pay here, many of them work off-shift jobs at other care places in neighboring areas. They say the labels on the drug-dispensing bottles are sometimes written in foreign languages and other times missing altogether. And the drugs don't look the same.

"They did allow that sometimes that's the case with generic drugs, and when they asked Seth that's what he told them.

"I didn't see any sign of Sarah and none of the aides I talked to had any knowledge of whether she was still here or gone or had just changed rooms."

"That could be why Sarah doesn't appear to be taking her pain meds. Good work," Harriet said. "Anyone have anything else?"

Aunt Beth pulled her rain bonnet out and gave it a shake before putting it on.

"All we can do is wait for Sarah to surface. Mavis and I will go home and work on our quilts for the shelter. The sooner we finish one, the sooner one of us will have an excuse to check to see if Sarah's there."

"We can finish them by Sunday," Mavis said. "I'd be surprised if we can arrange to deliver them before Monday or Tuesday, though."

Robin pulled her coat on and stood up as well.

"Beth's right. If we come on too strong, the family is likely to close ranks, and we won't get any information from them about Sarah."

"I'll run background checks on all the family members and dig around more on the Internet," Lauren offered.

Harriet sighed. "Thanks for the effort, everyone." She picked up a small cookie and popped it into her mouth. Aunt Beth glared at her, but she ignored her aunt and led the way out to the parking lot. Harriet's weight was a long-running point of contention between the two women. "I'll be at my machine stitching. Call me if anything comes up."

The Threads returned to their cars and drove home. Harriet's group was subdued, speaking only when it was time to say good-bye.

Chapter 8

Harriet changed into her running outfit when she returned from the open house.

"You are not allowed to go running," she explained to Scooter. "And don't get any ideas about those little front packs people carry their therapy pets in. You are not getting one, and I am not wearing one, especially when I'm running."

Scooter gave a little yip and went to his fleece bed in the corner of the kitchen, where he circled three times, plopped down and shut his eyes.

Harriet ran a zigzag pattern up and down the hill below her house. She mentally reviewed everything they'd heard and seen at the senior care home, but nothing new had revealed itself by the time she went back into her house through the studio door.

She looked at the quilt loaded on her machine. Fred meowed from the kitchen.

"Be right there."

✂- - -✂- - -✂

She woke the next morning to the sound of the phone ringing. She grabbed the cordless receiver from her nightstand and cleared her throat before pushing the on-button. The display read eight am.

She'd stayed up past midnight machine stitching the intricate pattern her customer had specified, so she'd turned her alarm off before going to bed.

"Hey," a male voice said.

"James?" she said with a yawn when she realized she was talking to the chef of the Cafe at Smugglers Cove.

"I'm sorry to bother you, but I'm in a bit of a bind. Is there any chance you could help me with something today? I know it's short notice, but it's sort of an emergency. It's going to take a few hours, too."

"Perhaps you could tell me what 'it' is?"

"It's my dog Cyrano."

"Shouldn't you be talking to Aiden if there's something wrong with your dog?"

"Cyrano's fine. I mean, he will be after he wins his race."

"His race? What sort of dog is he?"

"He's a wiener dog. He has a qualifying race for nationals this afternoon on Bainbridge Island. My sister was supposed to be our support team, but my niece woke up with a hundred-and-two-degree fever. She'll be fine, but Sis can't leave her with the babysitter she'd arranged for, and her husband has to work."

Harriet did a quick calculation in her head. After her previous evening's stitch-a-thon, she could take the whole day off and still be ahead of where she'd planned to be by the beginning of the week.

"I'd love to come," she said. "Wait, before I agree—what do I have to do?"

"Thank you, thank you, thank you. They won't let him compete unless he has two humans on his team. It's easy. One person—that's you—holds him at the starting line, keeping him pointed toward the finish line. The second person—me—waits at the finish, waving Cyrano's favorite toy and a dog treat and screaming his name, looking like a total fool and trying to get him to cross the finish line before the rest of the dogs."

"Sounds like I've got the easy job."

"I wouldn't ask, but like I said, this particular race is a qualifier for the national race. There are a few more qualifiers between this one and the finals, but this is the first step."

"Does he *want* to be a race-dog?" Harriet asked.

"It's his passion," James said in a serious voice then laughed.

"When do I need to be ready?"

"Can I pick you up in a half-hour?"

"Yikes!"

"Is that too soon?"

"No," Harriet said and jumped out of bed.

"Good, we'll pick you up at your place in thirty minutes."

"Wait," she said with a giggle. "What do I wear?"

"I'll have a team T-shirt for you."

"Perfect, I'll see you in thirty."

Fred began weaving through her legs the minute she stood up.

"Watch out, Mama's in a hurry this morning."

She ran downstairs, grabbed Fred's and Scooter's cans of food and scooped globs for each into their respective dishes before running back upstairs. She returned fifteen minutes later, showered and dressed in jeans and a white tank top.

"Come on, Scooter, you need to get busy outside." She dialed Aunt Beth on her cell phone, holding his leash in her free hand and wriggling into a green fleece jacket at the same time.

"Aren't two men enough for you?" Aunt Beth asked after she agreed to stop by to take Scooter out in the afternoon.

"This isn't like that." Harriet tugged on Scooter's leash, pulling him away from a blackberry bramble that threatened to swallow him whole. "James is in a bind, and he *was* helpful when Aiden stood me up that time."

"That was different. You were stranded at his restaurant, so he couldn't help it. It was his job."

"He didn't need to sit with me. He could have stayed in the kitchen and let the wait staff deal with me."

"My point exactly. He's interested in you."

"No, he's not. Believe me. He is well aware I have a very complicated love life."

"Whatever you say, honey. I'm guessing you would have mentioned it if you'd heard from Sarah."

"Unfortunately, no, I haven't heard from Sarah or anyone else. I'm worried about her. Anyone who could put her in the hospital like Seth did could go a step further if he was mad enough."

"Let's not go there yet. We need to concentrate on finding Sarah before Seth does. By the way, Mavis and I had been working on our dog quilts for the shelter, but since the pet room isn't done yet, we were afraid they might not be enough to get you into the shelter right away.

"So, we put them aside and worked on the bathroom curtains last night. We got three sets done. We thought that might be enough for you and Lauren to take and hang. You can install curtain rods, right?"

"Yes, I can install curtain rods. I'm sure Lauren can, too. I'll call Georgia first thing in the morning and see if she'll go for it, assuming Lauren's available."

"I'll call her while you're gone dallying with the chef and make sure she is."

Harriet sighed but heard the crunch of gravel at the bottom of her driveway before she could muster a protest.

"I've got to go. James is here." She pushed the off button and slid the phone into her jeans pocket.

James parked his brown BMW SUV and got out.

"Thank you so much for doing this."

"No problem. Let me get this little guy inside and grab my purse, and I'll be ready."

"Here." He handed her a red T-shirt emblazoned with the wiener dog race logo. "If you don't mind, I'm going to let Cyrano out for a quick break while you lock up." He picked up a bag from the seat of his car and held it up. "I made us chocolate croissants for the drive, and I have a thermos of coffee. I hope you haven't had breakfast yet."

"I haven't, and for a chocolate croissant, I'll follow you anywhere."

The sun was peeking out from behind the clouds and reflecting off the raindrops that had fallen earlier that morning, causing the grass and the tree branches to shimmer. During the drive, Harriet learned James had lived an ordinary life up to this point.

Based on the success he'd enjoyed in every sport in which he'd chosen to participate during his childhood, his parents had expected him to accept one of the several sports scholarships he was offered at the end of his high school years. They were mildly surprised when he chose instead to work his way through culinary school and then accepted an apprenticeship with a New York chef before returning a little over a year earlier to open his own restaurant.

She attempted to convey the whiplash she'd grown up with, shuttling between a series of mostly European boarding schools and the cozy warmth of her aunt and uncle's home in Foggy Point, with the occasional command appearance for a photo op wherever her famous-scientist parents were plying their trade at the moment. An hour and a half was nowhere near long enough for that story.

"Wow, this is more hoopla than I expected for wiener dog races," she said as James navigated the car to a parking lot next to the soccer fields.

"That's because the races are just a part of the Wagfest. The local animal welfare organization puts on this event to raise money for its various programs."

He parked and got Cyrano out of his travel crate.

"We need to take our star here to the veterinary check station before we can pick up his race packet." He snapped the harness into place and set the chocolate-and-tan dachshund down on the grass to attend to his business.

Picking him up again, he led the way to a path that wound through the park.

"I don't believe this," Harriet said as they came to a clearing.

The veterinary check station was in front of them, and standing behind it, examining a black-and-tan dachshund, was a familiar tall, dark-haired figure with unusually light blue eyes.

James sighed, his shoulders sagging.

"Is this going to be a problem?"

Harriet stiffened and strode toward the table.

"Not in the slightest."

Aiden finished checking the dog then copied some numbers onto a form and handed it back to the woman who accompanied the entrant.

"I have to say, I'm surprised to see you here," he said.

"I could say the same," Harriet replied in a tight voice.

"Not really. I *am* a veterinarian, and you know I volunteer for dog welfare events all over the Puget Sound area."

Hannah Pratt walked up to the trio and handed Aiden a printout of names and numbers.

"Here's the list you wanted," she said. She looked at Harriet. "Am I interrupting something?"

Harriet looked her over for some sign she was something other than a wide-eyed schoolgirl in awe of her mentor, the good doctor Jalbert, but she didn't see any.

"Have you met Sarah's sister Hannah?" Aiden asked. "She's taking classes at the community college and is going to do an internship with me for the next six weeks."

Hannah beamed at him as if he'd just presented her with the tiara and cape at the Miss America pageant.

"I'm so excited for this opportunity." She smiled her megawatt smile again.

"Have you seen your sister?" Harriet asked.

Hannah's eyes narrowed, and the sunshine left her face.

"She's not my sister. My dad is married to her mother, but we're not related in any way."

"Okay. Do you know where your dad's wife's daughter is?" Harriet shot back.

Hannah took Cyrano from James, the sunny smile back in place.

"I have no idea where she is, but that's not unusual. Sarah doesn't have time for her family."

Aiden took Cyrano with one hand and handed the dog's paperwork to Hannah with the other.

"Let's see how this little fella is," he said and pressed his stethoscope against the dog's chest.

"I take it you know the blonde," James muttered to Harriet as Aiden performed Cyrano's pre-race physical.

"Her stepsister's in my quilt group. She's currently missing in action, after having been beaten within an inch of her life by her fiancé, who coincidentally is the bimbo's half-brother."

"Yikes! Can I do anything to help?"

"Thanks, but I can't think of anything." Harriet explained what she and the Threads had done and were planning to do. "If you can come up with something else for us to do, let me know."

"All done," Aiden said, interrupting their conversation. He handed Cyrano back to James. "He seems healthy. Make sure he drinks water before and after each heat he runs." He handed Cyrano's signed entrance papers to Harriet, brushing her hand with his as he did. "Good luck."

She blushed. "Thanks," she said and turned away to follow James and Cyrano back to the main trail and on to the field where the race course had been set up.

James stopped and greeted friends and customers along the path as they made their way to the field. Where Aiden had the terrible beauty of a brewing storm, James was a perfect summer day. Everyone smiled as he left them, some of his sunshine lingering with them after he moved on.

"There's going to be a police K-Nine demonstration and then the All-Breed Canine Search and Rescue group is going to do a demo." James snapped Cyrano's leash onto his harness and set him down. "The wiener dog races start after that."

"Should we be doing anything for the star athlete?" Harriet asked with a grin.

"All he needs is to put his colored shirt on, and he's ready. If you wouldn't mind holding him for a minute, I'll go back to the car and get a waterproof blanket for us to sit on and his water dish and bottled water."

Harriet took Cyrano's leash and watched James jog back down the path and out of sight.

"I have to say, I was surprised to see you here," Aiden said from behind her. She turned and saw that he was alone.

"So you said."

"I didn't know you were seeing—what's his name—James?"

"I'm not seeing him, unless you consider eating in his restaurant seeing him. His sister's child got sick at the last minute, so he asked if I could sub for her. As it turned out, I could."

"You can tell a lot about a person from his pet," Aiden said cryptically.

"And?"

"Okay, he has good taste in dogs and obviously takes very good care of this little fellow." He reached down and scratched Cyrano's ears.

"What's the deal with Sarah's not-sister?"

Aiden smiled his lopsided grin.

"Would *you* claim Sarah if you could help it?"

Harriet couldn't argue when he smiled at her like that. She smiled in return.

"No, I guess not. I feel bad that she got hurt, but she's still the most annoying person I've ever met."

"I read a statistic that narcissism is on the rise in the current generation compared to our parents. They blamed it on parents who gave participation trophies to their kids every time they turned around."

"After meeting Sarah's parents at the open house, it's hard for me to believe they overdid it on her self-esteem."

"They aren't your average family, that's for sure."

Harriet sighed. "I just wish I knew Sarah was safe. Even she doesn't deserve what that guy did to her."

"That's actually why I came to find you. Is there anything I can do to help find her?"

"Lauren and I are going to see if we can go to the women's shelter tomorrow to install some of the curtains Aunt Beth and Mavis made. That'll give us an excuse to look around and see if she's there."

"Let me know if you have any trouble getting in. I can take you if the curtain scam doesn't work."

Harriet laughed. "We really do have curtains to put up."

Aiden put his hand on her arm and squeezed gently.

"I have no doubt." He smiled at her. "I've got to get back to work. And I won't embarrass you with a PDA."

Harriet raised her left eyebrow.

"Public display of affection," he translated with a laugh as he turned and went up the path to the activity area.

✂- - - ✂- - - ✂

"Wow, he really does like to run, doesn't he?"

Cyrano was licking James's face and wagging his tail for all he was worth as James tried to wipe the mud off the dog's belly. Harriet reached out, and Cyrano lunged into her arms, licking her face as he came.

"I told you it was his passion. I know you didn't believe me, but it is." James smiled as he finished cleaning the dog's paws. "And he's good at it."

"I guess so. He won all his heats and the finals by a wide margin."

"If all the dogs were as focused on the finish line as he is, it might be a different story." James looked up at the now-cloudy sky. "We should get going before the rain starts."

Harriet set the dog down to pick up the picnic blanket and dog dish while James gathered Cyrano's racing shirt, towel and toys. They let him lead them back down the trail to the parking lot.

Cyrano started barking as soon as they reached the paved edge of the car park.

"Hush," James said, but that just seemed to make the dog redouble his hysterics. "I don't know what his problem is."

He picked the dog up and held him close to his chest, muffling the noise slightly.

"Oh, no!" Harriet pointed as they approached the car. Someone had smashed the driver's-side window.

"Darn it." James picked Cyrano up to prevent the dog from stepping in broken glass.

"Something wrong?" Aiden asked. He was in the next row up, loading his supplies into the back of his vintage Bronco.

"Someone broke into James's car," Harriet called back. "They broke the window."

Aiden joined them in examining the damage. Hannah followed him.

"The CD player and GPS are gone," James reported.

"Do you have a car alarm?" Hannah asked.

"I do. I'm guessing whoever did this timed it for the height of the dog races. With all the crowd noise, no one would notice a car alarm going off."

"Look." Hannah pointed several cars away to another broken window.

"Can we do anything for you?" Aiden said. "I can wait until help comes, or we could give you a ride back to Foggy Point, if you want."

Hannah looked at him, her eyes wide.

"Do you need to be back?" he asked her.

"I have to work at the senior center tonight. I suppose I could call if we need to stay," she added with obvious reluctance. "I'm sure they can find someone to cover for me if they have to."

"Thanks, but that won't be necessary. I'm sure my car's drivable. I can tape plastic over the window." James looked at Harriet. "Do you want to go with them?"

She glanced at Aiden, who waggled his eyebrows up and down, then turned back to James.

"I'll stay and keep you company while you call the police and the insurance company."

"Do you want me to walk Scooter when I get back?" Aiden offered.

"Thanks, but I already have Aunt Beth on Scoot-duty. I'll just give her a call and let her know I've been delayed."

"Okay, if we can't do anything for you, we're going to get Hannah back so she can go to work." Aiden put his hand on Hannah's back and guided her to his car.

Harriet watched until they were in the car and driving out of the lot. By the time she looked back at James, he had Cyrano in his travel crate in the back seat and was talking on his cell phone. He smiled when he noticed her.

"The adventure continues," he said. "Lucky for you I never go any-where without food." He opened the cargo door and brought out a cooler. "I have sandwich stuff and some drinks."

The food turned out to be a lifesaver; the police took their time investigating the crime scene. It turned out that seven cars had been broken into. If it had only been James's car, they could have filled out a report and been done with it, but because of the scope of the damage, the local police were out in force.

"I'm going to call my aunt again." Harriet pulled out her phone. "We're finally done and headed home," she said when Beth answered. "The police helped James tape plastic over his window; we should get there in about an hour and a half."

"Don't worry, honey, I went to your house when you called before, and I'll go again on my way to meet Mavis for dinner. Tell James to drive carefully."

Harriet assured her James was an excellent driver and promised to call when she got home.

"I guess I better make the most of the trip home," James said when the car was ready to drive and they'd been cleared to leave. "You're never going to want to go anywhere with me again." A wry smile crossed his lips before he became serious again. "I had really hoped this was going to be a fun day for you."

She reached out and put her hand on his arm. "Hey, this was fun. I've never been to a wiener dog race before, much less gotten to hold the star athlete in his starting gate. You had no control over someone breaking into your car."

"If you say so."

The drive back was a quiet one, and it was full dark by the time James dropped her outside her studio door.

"Don't worry," she said one last time before getting out of the car. James rolled down the passenger window.

"I'll make this up to you," he said.

Harriet waved at him, and he closed the window and drove away.

Chapter 9

"Where have you been?" Lauren asked when Harriet opened her studio door. "I've been trying to get you all afternoon. I finally called your aunt, and she told me you went to Bainbridge Island with that cook."

"Did she tell you what we were doing?"

"Ewwweee, too much information."

"Don't be silly. I was holding his wiener…"

Lauren covered her ears with her hands.

"La la la la—don't tell me anymore, I can't take it."

"Oh, stop it. I was helping him race his dog. There was a wiener dog national qualifying race on Bainbridge Island, and his sister was supposed to help, and her kid got sick, and so he asked me to stand in."

"Your aunt didn't say anything about dogs, except Scooter. She mostly said she thought you needed to settle your business with the two men you already have before you added another."

"She's imagining things. Besides, Aiden was at the races, too."

"Did you know he was going to be there?"

"No, and he wasn't alone. Sarah's stepsister is interning with him, and she was there helping him."

"Did you ask her where Sarah is?"

"Of course. She made it a point that Sarah isn't her blood sister and said she had no idea where she is."

"Connie checked at the senior center, and she still hasn't shown up there."

"Aiden said he would help us get into the shelter if our curtain ruse doesn't work."

Lauren took her fleece jacket off and threw it onto one of the chairs in the reception area.

"Are you going to ask me to stay for tea?"

"Where are my manners?" Harriet led the way into the kitchen and started getting out mugs and tea. "Did you come over for a reason? I mean, I'm happy to have the company, but you don't usually drop by unannounced for tea at seven-thirty on a Sunday night."

"Really? I need an invitation? Or now that you're juggling three men, I need to call first. Is that it?"

Harriet put her hands on her hips and stared at her.

"It's only two, and I'm not even juggling them at the moment."

Lauren laughed. "Okay, you got me. I do have an ulterior motive." She paused.

"Hmmm, I'm getting the feeling I'm not going to like this plan, whatever it is."

"Give it a chance." Lauren paced across the kitchen and back.

"Spit it out. The tension is killing me."

"Okay, I say after we have our tea and whatever treat you're going to dig out of that cabinet, we go to Sarah's cabin."

"I knew I wasn't going to like it."

Lauren took the mug Harriet handed her and dipped the teabag up and down.

"Do you still have the key from the other night?"

"No, I gave it back to her while she was at the senior center."

"We could go have a look anyway. If she's there, she'll let us in. If not, we could poke around a little."

"I'm not going to break into Sarah's house. She's just the sort that would press charges against us, even though we were trying to help her."

"You think?"

"I know. Besides, what if Seth is there with her? He's not dumb enough to fall for our lame excuses. He already knows we don't like him. What if he takes it out on her? We could be making things worse."

"I guess." She took a sip of her tea. "Don't you have anything tasty in your snack cupboard?"

"I haven't had time to snack shop." Harriet pulled out her nearly empty box of gingersnaps. "This is as good as it gets." She rattled the box.

Lauren reached out for it.

"Better than nothing."

She took the box and her cup of tea to the kitchen table and sat down. Harriet joined her.

"I wish I could think of something we could do for Sarah that didn't involve kidnapping or breaking-and-entering, but with her family so firmly in place, it's going to be hard."

"I got nothing, if we can't bend the law a little."

"Are you making any progress on your Pratt family background checks?"

"Howard seems to have had several ex-wives who are curiously dead before their time. I'm still digging on Seth, but I think he's running an internet discount prescription drug business. Based on Connie's suspicions, he may be getting his drugs from illicit sources, but I can't make a direct connection on that yet. I'll keep digging until I can prove it one way or the other."

Fred came into the kitchen and meowed loudly.

"Don't even try it. Aunt Beth told me she fed you at five o'clock. And she gave you some bites of sliced chicken as a treat, since you had to spend the day alone."

Fred poked his nose in the air, swished his tail forcefully and left the room.

"He's got an attitude prob—" Lauren was cut off by the kitchen phone ringing.

"Hello?" Harriet said. "Hello?" She looked at the caller ID and flicked the speaker phone button so Lauren could hear the conversation. "Sarah? What's wrong?"

"Help me," said a rasping voice. "Help me."

The phone went dead.

"Come on."

Harriet hung up and grabbed her fleece, purse and keys from the kitchen closet. Lauren jumped up and pulled her jacket on, slinging her messenger bag over her shoulder.

"Did she say where she is?"

"According to caller ID, she's at the cabin.

Lauren veered toward her car. "I'll drive."

Harriet got in the passenger seat, and Lauren tore out of the driveway like her hair was on fire.

"It won't help Sarah if we end up in the river," Harriet protested.

"Oh, hush. I took the adult race-driving course at the speedway in Monroe. I'm certified."

"If you say so," Harriet said, grabbing onto the edges of her seat.

"Do you think we should call nine-one-one?"

"Let's wait until we get there and see what's going on. If Sarah's been attacked but was able to call me, she'd be able to call the police or an ambulance."

"Do you think she would, though? She seems weirdly protective of that creep."

Cloud cover meant the night was dark, and as they sped away from porch and street lights, it got even darker. Lauren slowed to a crawl as she approached the road that led up to the cabin.

"I'm going to pull off at the bottom of the drive," she whispered.

"I don't think they can hear us in the car," Harriet whispered back.

"I'm getting ready. We don't know what we're going to face."

"Sarah sounded really desperate. I hope Seth took off."

"People like him are usually cowards. They never pick on someone their own size."

Harriet opened her door as Lauren stopped the car. She pulled a penlight from her purse and flicked it on. Its weak light did little to illuminate the night.

Lauren came around to stand by her.

"Do you think we should we go around the back and look in the windows first?"

"No, she called us asking for help. We're going in the front door."

With that, she led the way up the drive and onto the cabin's porch. A dark-colored cat jumped from the bench and slithered away into the night.

"I hope that was a cat and not a skunk or possum," Lauren whispered.

Harriet tapped on the door; when no one answered, she knocked again, harder.

"Sarah?" she called then listened. "Did you hear that?"

Lauren leaned past her and pounded on the door. They listened.

"Help," cried a weak voice.

Harriet opened the unlocked door and went in.

"Sarah?"

No one was in the living room. Lauren stepped toward the kitchen then shook her head.

Bedroom, Harriet mouthed.

An unearthly wail came from that direction, and Harriet dropped all pretense of stealth and ran the last few steps to the room. Lauren slammed into Harriet's back as she followed; Harriet stood frozen in the doorway.

"Sarah, what happened? Are you okay?"

"What's wrong?" Lauren asked. "Why aren't we going in?"

Harriet leaned to one side, and Lauren gasped.

"I think we better call the police." Harriet finally moved into the room, stepping carefully to the end of the bed.

Sarah was lying beside Seth, leaning over his lifeless body, tears falling onto his limp form. He lay on his back with his arms flung wide—not a position someone would ordinarily choose for sleeping. But with the amount of blood soaked into the Baltimore album quilt underneath him, there was no possibility of his being asleep—or alive.

"Sarah," Harriet said softly. She reached out and put her hands on Sarah's shoulders, examining her for evidence of injuries. "Come on," she said and pulled, trying to get her away from the lifeless body beside her.

"What happened, Sarah?" Lauren asked in a surprisingly gentle voice. She moved to the other side of the bed, carefully avoiding the body, and pushed Sarah toward Harriet. "I've called the police, so you need to tell us before they get here."

"You called the police?" Sarah cried. "They'll arrest me!"

Harriet eased her into sitting on the edge of the bed—she couldn't tell if Sarah was able to stand on her own. She looked at the nearby chair and gauged the distance but wasn't sure she could get Sarah that far away from her fiancé's body.

"Did Seth hit you again?" A purple bruise was blossoming across Sarah's left temple, a large lump forming under the bruise. The hardware sticking out of her cast was twisted at an unlikely angle. Sarah nodded and cried out in pain at the movement.

"I didn't kill him," she whispered.

"Can you tell us what did happen?" Harriet asked her.

Sarah shuddered.

"Lauren, see if there's ice in the refrigerator."

Lauren returned a moment later with a blue ice pack wrapped in a kitchen towel.

"Here." Harriet held it gently against Sarah's temple. "Now, can you tell us what happened?" She tried to keep her focus on Sarah so she didn't have to look at Seth.

"I don't know."

"What do you mean, you don't know, Sarah? If we're going to help you, you need to tell us exactly what happened. And if I'm not mistaken, that's a police siren we're hearing."

Sarah sighed and began to cry. Harriet rubbed a hand in circles on her back.

"I was going to go to the shelter, but I needed to get a few things from here, in case I didn't get to come back. I called a cab to bring me here. I had some pain pills from before, so I took two—my hand hurt so bad. I got sleepy, and the next thing I knew, Seth was waking me up. I'd slept for hours.

"He made me a smoothie, and then he brushed my hair." She glanced at his supine body. "Seth could be really sweet. He said we could start over, forget about all this." Sarah looked down at her damaged arm.

Lauren rolled her eyes skyward but kept quiet.

"Go on," Harriet encouraged.

"I need a lot of help right now. It's hard to take a shower or button a blouse or open food containers. And it was impossible to cook."

"He expected you to cook?" Lauren blurted.

Harriet held her hand up.

"Go on."

"Tonight, he was tired. My injury, his job, everything. He came home in a bad mood. Nothing made him happy. He said he couldn't sleep here. He said I cried in the night. He said he was going somewhere else, and he wouldn't tell me where. He told me I better not try to call him.

"I just asked him if he could help me wrap my arm in plastic before he left so I could shower. He said that was the straw that broke the camel's back, and then he...he...he must have hit me. He was yelling, and then the next thing I knew, I woke up, and he was..." She looked back at his body.

The sirens were getting louder. The police had to be climbing the last part of the hill.

Harriet stood up. "Do you own a gun?"

"Or does Seth?" Lauren added.

"No," Sarah said with a sob. "Why would you even think that?"

The dead body lying beside you, Harriet thought, but she didn't say it out loud.

"Was anyone else here? Or did anyone else ever come here while you lived here with Seth?"

Sarah shook her head slightly as she cried.

"He wasn't big on friends. He said we didn't need anyone but each other."

"If you didn't kill him, someone else must have been here," Harriet insisted, but Sarah was spared having to reply by the arrival of the police.

She stood up and walked around the bed to the spot where Seth must have been standing before he'd fallen on the bed. She looked around while Lauren sat beside Sarah.

She pulled the curtain aside with her flashlight, being careful not to touch anything, and exposed a broken windowpane. Glass littered the floor. She coughed, and Lauren made eye contact then looked at the window.

"Sarah, honey." Lauren gently rubbed Sarah's uninjured hand. "How did your hardware get so mangled? Did Seth push you into the window?"

"No…yes…I don't know what happened." Sarah started crying again.

Harriet came back around to Sarah's side as someone came in the front door.

"We're back here," she called out, and two paramedics she didn't recognize came into the bedroom. She moved out of the way so they could verify Seth's demise and tend to Sarah.

Lauren had called nine-one-one, but she'd also called Jane Morse. Detective Morse arrived at the same time as the uniformed officers.

"You two, outside," she ordered. "Wait for me on the porch. Don't touch anything or go anywhere. And please tell me you didn't touch anything in the house."

"We touched Sarah," Harriet said.

"I got an ice pack from the kitchen for the bump on Sarah's head."

One of the paramedics hustled out, returning with the gurney from their ambulance.

"We need to transport the woman," he said to Morse as he passed her. True to his word, a few minutes later, he and his partner wheeled Sarah out the front door.

Lauren zipped her fleece and sat down on the porch bench.

"What do you think happened?"

Harriet joined her, sitting on the other end of the bench.

"That is the sixty-four thousand dollar question, isn't it? We better tell the rest of the Threads what's happened." She pulled her cell phone from her pocket. "I've got a couple of bars. I'll call Aunt Beth and Mavis. You start with Robin and Connie. They can all spread the word."

She touched the phone icon and started dialing.

Chapter 10

S o, where has Sarah been all this time?" Mavis asked when the majority of the Threads were assembled around the table in Harriet's dining room. Jorge came from the kitchen, a coffee pot in one hand and a teapot in the other, followed by Aunt Beth carrying a tray of mugs.

Lauren leaned toward Harriet, who was sitting beside her at the table.

"Did Jorge become a Loose Thread while we were gone?"

"I heard that, señorita," Jorge said and poured tea into the mug Beth set on the table in front of Robin. "If you must know, Beth was helping me laminate the pages of my new menu. The pages lace into the covers and some of the laces were broken. She found some gold cord to replace them, and we were at the restaurant putting them back together when Harriet called, so tonight you get the two for the price of one special."

"You should be happy he's here," Beth told them. "He's been experimenting all day with a new tres leches cake recipe, and he brought three of the test cakes with him."

Lauren leaned forward. "Welcome to the Loose Threads, Jorge. You need me to get plates?"

"That would be very helpful," he said with a smile.

✂ - - - ✂ - - - ✂

"I'm going to have a heart attack right here at this table if somebody doesn't tell us something right now," Mavis said when everyone had a piece of cake and a mug of their chosen drink in front of them. Harriet noted that even the diet-conscious Robin had accepted a sliver of cake.

She stood up behind her chair.

"We found Sarah, and it's not good. She was at her cabin—with a very dead Seth."

Connie gasped, "Diós mio."

Carla put her hand over her mouth.

DeAnn set her mug down on the table after taking a sip.

"What happened?"

"We're not sure," Harriet said. "Sarah was a mess, as you might expect. She says she doesn't know what happened. She has a big knot on her temple, and that hardware in her hand was all mangled. Seth was mad at her, he probably hit her hard enough to knock her unconscious. Then she woke up with him bleeding out next to her."

"Where is she now?" Robin asked, all business.

"They took her to the hospital," Lauren said.

"Has she been at the cabin all this time?" DeAnn asked.

Harriet walked from one end of the dining room to the other, carrying her mug with her. She was much too wired to sit quietly and talk about what had happened.

"According to her, she left the senior center while we were at the open house. She had Joe's Taxi Service drive her to the cabin, where she says she took some pain pills she had stashed there and went to sleep. Seth found her hours later and has been taking care of her ever since."

"Until he got tired of being a nurse," Lauren added. She took her stress out on her mug of tea, stirring her spoon in time with Harriet's pacing.

"You two stop that," Mavis told them.

Harriet froze in mid-stride.

"Sorry," she said and sat down at her place at the table.

"Sarah must have thought her drugs weren't safe at the senior center if the first thing she did when she got back to the cabin was to gobble down a double dose of pills she knew were good," DeAnn said.

"Yeah, that's what I was thinking," Harriet agreed. She stood up again as car lights flashed past the dining room window. "Someone else is here."

"Everyone's here who belongs," Aunt Beth observed.

"Aiden's home watching Wendy for me," Carla told them, eliminating the only other person who came to Harriet's mind.

"I'll go see who it is," Jorge said and left the room.

He returned a few moments later with Detective Jane Morse. He had led her through the kitchen, where he'd given her a cup of something warm and a plate of experimental cake.

76

"I thought I might find you all here," Morse said when she was seated in the chair Jorge pulled out for her between Harriet and Lauren. "You seem to gather whenever there's trouble involving one of your own."

"And your point is?" Lauren prompted her.

"Let her have her cake first," Aunt Beth said with a stern look at Lauren. "It's been a long night for her, too."

Detective Morse gave Aunt Beth a weak smile and dug into her cake.

Morse's plate was clean and her mug had been refilled with coffee before she spoke.

"Thanks, Jorge, that was dinner, and it was wonderful. I'm sure you're all wondering why I'm here at nearly midnight. It's not to try to pry information out of you, if that's what you think."

Harriet looked around the table. Judging by the expressions on everyone's face, that was exactly what most of them had thought.

"I talked to Mavis and Beth last week, and they filled me in on what's been happening with Sarah."

Harriet and Lauren both turned to look at the older women.

"Don't blame them for anything. They were asking me if I knew of any options you all hadn't thought of. I couldn't think of anything you weren't already pursuing. That's beside the point now. I came to give you some advice. That is, if I can count on your discretion."

"Of course," Connie said.

"Keeping in mind I'm an officer of the court," Robin reminded her.

"Join the club." Morse picked up her story. "I shouldn't be here, but I feel like the good old boys' club is coming into play.

"Howard Pratt is very well connected in this community. He's going to want someone to pay for the death of his son, and it's not clear to me that he cares if it's the actual person responsible or not. I could see in the faces of the uniforms and first responders that they're looking at Sarah like she's a perp instead of a victim."

"What's that mean?" Aunt Beth asked.

"It means Sarah is not his blood relative, and in spite of the evidence against her being the killer, Howard could blame her and pull in favors to make sure everyone else blames her, too. At this point, I'm not sure why he'd want to protect the real killer, but my gut is telling me that's exactly what he's going to do.

"As if that weren't enough, there's been so much crime in Foggy Point lately the chief is going to want to put someone away quickly, too, so he'll go along with Pratt just to close the case."

"Are we sure she *didn't* do it?" Robin asked. Connie glared at her, and she shrugged. "Someone has to play devil's advocate, and you know I believe everyone deserves a competent defense, no matter what."

Morse gave Robin a withering stare and then continued. She was showing a side of herself Harriet hadn't seen before.

"There aren't any witnesses to the shooting that we know of, but Sarah would have to have gone outside, aimed and fired a gun with one hand, come back in, and then beaten herself up, mangled her orthopedic device and passed out on the bed. All of that is possible but unlikely."

"So, what are you suggesting?" Harriet asked.

"Sarah's going to be in the hospital for a day, at least. I know you were working with Georgia at the women's shelter. I do some volunteer work there, and I know they're good at getting people from the hospital to the shelter under the noses of abusers. I think she could help you get Sarah out in the same way and hopefully before anyone can bring charges against her."

Harriet looked intently at the detective.

"Is Sarah in danger?"

"I can't say. That probably depends on who really killed Seth and why. I've probably said too much already." She looked intently at Har-riet and then the rest of the group. "Out of sight, out of mind is sometimes the best way to handle a situation."

"Got it," Lauren said.

Harriet leaned back in her chair.

"I'll call Georgia first thing in the morning."

Morse reached into her pants pocket and pulled a card out.

"Here's the twenty-four-hour number for the shelter."

Harriet took the card and stood up.

"I'll call her now," she said.

Aunt Beth stared into her coffee cup.

"I knew I should have tried harder to talk some sense into that girl."

Jorge reached over and took her hand.

"You can only help someone if they want to be helped. I heard her refuse to listen to you. Don't blame yourself."

Harriet cleared her throat, breaking the silence that had fallen over the group.

"Moving forward, Georgia is going to go talk to Sarah at the hospital once she gets out of surgery. We're assuming they're going to have to cut into her arm again to replace the damaged hardware. When she's in a room, Georgia's people will arrange to have her moved. She said they have nursing staff they can call on. They've worked with the hospital before, apparently."

"I'd have hoped this was an unusual enough case they wouldn't have medical staff in place already," Lauren said. "I guess not."

"Back in the nineteen-nineties, the surgeon general ranked abuse by husbands to be the leading cause of injury to women aged fifteen to forty-four," Morse said. "I don't know what the current statistics are, but I can tell you, it's way too common."

"What else can we do?" Mavis asked Morse.

"If you know anything else about Seth Sarah may have told you, now would be a good time to share it."

"Sarah had stopped coming to quilting, so she didn't tell us much of anything," Mavis told her.

"We might be able to find out for you," Harriet said thoughtfully.

"I can't ask you to do that." Morse sighed. "I hate to sound like a broken record, but in spite of what I said earlier, you need to let the police do the police work."

Lauren leaned across her to speak directly to Harriet.

"What did you have in mind?"

Morse shook her head, but she didn't stop Harriet from speaking.

"When we were touring the senior center the other day, I talked to some of the women in the independent living section about quilting. They were saying they missed their old quilting groups but many of their members had passed away and those left had trouble getting to the fabric store or their families had left their sewing machines behind when they moved them to their smaller quarters. One of them showed me the appliqué she still did, but she has no way to assemble it into a finished quilt."

DeAnn smiled.

"We could volunteer to start a quilting group there."

"I like it," Robin said. "I bet those women know everything that goes on in that place."

Harriet got up and started pacing again.

"Marjory has a couple of loaner sewing machines. I've got two six-foot folding tables."

"There are a bunch of folding chairs in Aiden's basement I could bring," Carla volunteered.

"This is perfect," Lauren said. "We can get the old ladies to help us make quilts for the women's shelter and kill two birds with one stone."

Detective Morse tore a strip off her napkin and twirled it into a rope.

"I hate to say it, but it might work. You have to promise you'll just quilt with them and let them talk. No snooping. No going into Seth's office or room or anything like that."

Harriet smiled at her.

"We would never do that."

Lauren held her two fingers up in a scout salute.

"On our honor, we promise."

Detective Morse shook her head.

"I may live to regret this, but I'm going to have to take your word for it."

"You're a quilter," Aunt Beth pointed out.

"Go on," Morse encouraged.

"You could come and quilt with us after we get set up," Beth said. "Then you could keep an eye on those of us inclined to stray, and you could hear stuff firsthand."

"Just let me know if and when you get things set up," Morse said. "And seriously, as far as your friend Sarah is concerned, don't take any chances, but time is of the essence."

"Is there something you aren't telling us?" Harriet asked. "You seem sure everyone is going to go after Sarah."

"Let's just call it a feeling." Morse stood up. "Thanks again for the cake. I didn't taste the other options, but I vote for this one." She pointed at her empty plate.

Jorge rose. "Would you like to take a piece with you?"

"I would love it," she said with a smile.

He led her back to the kitchen, and a few minutes later the others heard the door in Harriet's studio open and close. They watched the lights on Detective Morse's car move down the driveway and disappear.

Chapter 11

C an you meet with the new group on Thursday afternoon?" Harriet asked Lauren over cups of hot cocoa two days later. The two women were sitting in The Steaming Cup.

Since Lauren did her computer programming from her home, she met clients at the Cup when they wanted to meet away from their own offices. She came so often she'd developed the habit of starting most days there.

Technically, it was spring in Foggy Point, but it was coming in like a lion at the moment. Rain slashed at the windows, and although it was eight o'clock in the morning, the pendulum lights that hung over each seating area were on.

Lauren touched the face of her phone, opening her calendar.

"What time?"

"Two o'clock."

"I can do that. Is everyone else on board?"

"The activities director at the center was all over it. She's one of the first people I've met there who isn't a family member—at least, as far as I can tell without asking her directly. As for our group, Robin can't make it, and of course Jenny's still gone, but everyone else can come.

"Once we get the groups going, we may not want to have all the Threads there every time. It might overwhelm them. They would like to expand the group to include some of the early dementia residents, too."

"Good idea. Do you need me to bring anything?"

"Do you have any of those little cameras people use to spy on their nannies?"

"Bugging the place is not only illegal but I have a strong suspicion it falls into the 'don't do anything else but listen' category Detective Morse was talking about."

"I wasn't thinking about leaving them there. Do they make wireless versions? I was thinking we could have them on one of our sewing machines. Or even on our person. Is that possible?"

Lauren sighed. "Anything is possible, but I will *not* agree to leave anything on their premises, not even if it's on a sewing machine we leave behind. One of my clients has used a wireless micro-camera that's mounted in a pendant necklace. It produces surprisingly clear pictures."

"That would be a good start."

"I can imagine a few things you might be looking for, but what are you hoping to get a picture of?" Lauren picked up her cup and took a long swallow.

"I've been thinking about this since we found Sarah. We know she didn't kill Seth, so we have to consider who else might want him dead. Since he was the team pharmacist, and there has been some suspicion raised about the sources of the drugs being used there, it's possible someone blames him for the death of their loved one and decided to seek revenge."

"You think Connie killed him?"

Harriet laughed out loud and then looked around to be sure she hadn't attracted attention.

"Of course not. I don't think Rod did it, either. But if Connie and Rod suspect the senior center killed his aunt, maybe someone else has had a similar experience."

"Except Seth's dead."

"Yeah, but his drugs are still there. They aren't going to throw away his drugs, at least, not until they can bring in replacements. If Seth was running the cut-rate drug business by himself, the others might not even know about it yet."

"That's whole bunch of ifs and buts."

"It can't hurt to snap a few pictures of the drug dispensing operation at the place. We should be there long enough on any given day to see someone get their meds."

"I suppose it couldn't hurt."

Harriet swished the last of her cocoa in the bottom of her cup.

"Have you heard anything about Sarah from anyone?"

"No, but then, I didn't expect to. Have you deployed the curtain-hanging team yet?"

"No, I thought it might be a little too obvious right after Sarah moved in, but maybe by the end of the week, we could approach them about it."

"It would be worth it to see if she has anything else to say."

"I don't know. I don't think we should badger her while she's so injured and probably drugged to boot."

"Whatever."

✂- - - ✂- - - ✂

"Should we bring the tables and chairs in right away?" Carla asked when Harriet had parked in front of the senior center.

"Let's wait and see what the activities coordinator came up with. She had several possible spaces we could use, but it was going to depend on how many residents signed up. They have a small dining room in the middle of the building that has its own tables and chairs, and then there's a living room-type area off the hall where the independent living people have their rooms. If we use that space, we'll need our tables and chairs."

The two women were met in the lobby by a heavyset woman with brown hair who looked to be in her thirties.

"Hi, Harriet," she said and shook Harriet's hand. She turned to Carla. "I'm Sabrina Winthrop, the activities coordinator." She stretched her hand toward Carla, and after a brief hesitation, Carla shook it.

"It turns out your idea is a very popular one," Sabrina continued. "Before we look at the spaces, tell me this. What would you think of doing two groups, one in each space? It seems like you have enough people in your group to do that. We could put the people who are fully functional in the common area of that wing, and the dementia people in the small memory-care dining room." She stopped to take a breath. "I'm sorry, I'm getting carried away. I haven't given you a chance to say you can do both groups."

Harriet smiled. "I think that would work fine. What if we staggered the time so we'd be sure we could cover things when we get busy with other projects?"

"That's a great idea," Sabrina said. "I apologize for being so enthusiastic, but it's a rare day when someone volunteers to do an activity of this magnitude with our residents. Usually, we're scrambling to get people who are willing to come in and work with our folks."

Harriet and Carla followed Sabrina as she led the way down the independent living hallway and into the common space.

"We're happy to come quilt with your people," Harriet told her. "They'll probably teach us some new tricks."

"I gathered a few extension cords and power strips, and I'm hoping you were serious about bringing a few folding tables." Sabrina pointed to a pile of wires and electrical equipment sitting on a coffee table pushed against the wall in the large rectangular room. "I moved the upholstered chairs to the other end of the room, as you can see, and I'm hoping you can put your folding tables in this area." She spread her arms to indicate the empty end of the space. "If this takes off, I'll order folding tables that can stay up permanently."

"This looks great," Harriet said.

"Oh, good. While you're getting set up, I'll go talk to the supervisor in the memory care unit and tell her we'll put her people in the dining room a little later. I asked our receptionist, Hannah, to come help you." She looked toward the interior hallway. "And here she is now. Hannah, this is…"

"Hi, Harriet," Hannah said, interrupting Sabrina. "This is so nice of you. Can I help you carry anything?"

"Thank you, but I think we can get it. We're used to lugging our quilting supplies around. Besides, we didn't bring too much today. We mostly wanted to meet everyone and see what they're interested in doing."

Sabrina looked down the hallway behind Hannah.

"Maybe you can spend an hour with each group today, since you weren't expecting to have two. Then we can plan a longer time for your next visit."

"That will work fine. As I was saying, we need to assess things and see what materials they have and what they need," Harriet said. "We can do that today and then get serious about sewing next time."

"Just let me know if you need anything else from us," Sabrina said. Then to Hannah: "If anyone is looking for me, I'll be going between here and the memory unit for the next hour or so while we get these two sessions going."

"I'll make a note," Hannah said then followed her out of the independent living wing.

Lauren was waiting by the car when Carla and Harriet returned to the parking lot.

"What's the plan?" she asked.

Carla quickly explained while Harriet opened the hatch and began pulling folding tables and chairs out.

"Even though we aren't going to be sewing today, I'm going to go ahead and set up a couple of tables and chairs. I'll leave them here until they get their own. I have a loaner sewing machine Marjory donated to the cause. We can leave that set up so the people can sew when we aren't here if they want to."

"Good idea," Lauren said. "On the spy front, I rigged two supply bags up with lipstick cameras that look out from the end of each one. If we set them at either end of the room, we should be able to catch all of the action." She handed Harriet a necklace. "This has an embedded microphone. If you want to record someone, just fiddle with the pendant. It has a small contact switch on the back. It looks flat, but if you squeeze it, it will engage."

Harriet took the gold, rhinestone-encrusted heart.

"Kind of gaudy, isn't it?"

"But totally you," Lauren shot back with an evil grin. "I wanted it to be big enough that you would naturally need to fiddle with it."

Carla started loading tables onto the fold-up flatbed hand truck Harriet had pulled out after the tables were unloaded.

✂- - - ✂- - - ✂

"Let's give a warm senior center welcome to the Loose Threads quilting group," Sabrina said when the room was set up and all the participants in place. One small white-haired woman clapped vigorously, but the rest of the group either patted their hands together politely or ignored Sabrina completely.

"That's not necessary," Aunt Beth said. "I think I can speak for our whole group in saying we're happy to come spend some time with you all."

"Not likely," a skinny bald man said in a stage whisper everyone could hear.

"We really are," Harriet said. "I'm guessing you all have plenty of quilting experience to share with us. We may be good with the new techniques and machines, but I, for one, could use help with the basics. I'm an absolute disaster at hand quilting."

"And I'm just learning to quilt on a sewing machine," Mavis said. "I've always hand-pieced, so I need help with how to do more efficient machine work."

"I won the blue ribbon in the hand quilting division of the Jefferson County fair a few years ago," a plump woman in a flowered cotton dress volunteered. She had on a name tag that said *Violet*.

Harriet pulled out a fabric sandwich made of two layers of plain muslin with a piece of wool batting in between that she'd prepared for hand quilting practice. She crossed the room and sat beside the blue ribbon winner. Carla picked up her bag and moved to the seat on the opposite side of the woman. She pulled a similar blank quilt piece from her bag.

"I'm Harriet, and this is Carla." She held her hand out.

"We all know who you are," the woman whispered.

Sabrina surveyed the room.

85

"If you're all squared away, I'll just go make sure the dining area is ready for the next group." She turned and left without waiting for agreement from anyone.

Violet followed Sabrina with her eyes until the activities director had turned the corner and disappeared. She turned to Harriet.

"Okay, tell us why you're really here. It's to investigate the murder, isn't it?"

"Umm," Harriet stammered.

The small white-haired woman held her hand up, shushing Harriet before she spoke.

"Mickey?" She pointed toward a boom box sitting on a built-in bookshelf beside the sofa.

The bald man got up, shuffled over to the player, and turned it on then adjusted the volume to a level loud enough to make conversation difficult, although not impossible. He pointed toward the side of his head.

"The walls have ears," he said before returning to his seat.

"We all know who you are," the small white-haired woman said. "I'm Josephine, by the way, but you can call me Jo. That tall drink of water over there is Mickey." She pointed at the man. "Don't let him fool you—he's very handy with a needle."

"And that's not all," said a woman in a wheelchair. Her hair was black with a few wisps of gray, and she appeared a decade or two younger than the rest of the residents. "I'm Janice."

Harriet looked at her aunt and then Lauren. Beth's eyes got wide, but she remained silent. Lauren shrugged.

Violet followed Harriet's gaze then looked back at her.

"Am I being too forward? I suppose you didn't think we'd figure out why you're really here."

"We don't mind," Jo said. "When we saw you at the open house, and you came into our wing and talked to some of us, we were hoping that meant you were going to investigate."

"We've all heard about your involvement in the murders that happened this past year. Sarah *is* part of your group, after all, isn't she?" Janice asked.

Harriet stood up.

"Okay, you got us. This is our fumble-fingered attempt to get inside the center and find out what's going on. I'm sorry we were going to use you. We can pack up and be out of your way in a few minutes. I'll think of something to tell Sabrina."

"Hold your horses, dearie," Mickey said. "We can work something out here. We want to know who killed Seth ourselves. We know Sarah didn't do it, but we're fairly sure Howard is going to set her up to take the fall."

"We really could use someone to help us get fabric and thread for our quilting projects," Jo said. "Buying fabric off the Internet isn't all it's cracked up to be."

Aunt Beth looked at Mickey.

"How do you know Sarah didn't do it?"

"Come on," he said. "You do know Sarah, don't you? If she were capable of killing him, she wouldn't have waited until he'd beaten her within an inch of her life. She was convinced till his dying breath that he was going to change. She was sure he was going to take her away from all this, too."

"Maybe she just snapped," DeAnn suggested. "Everyone has a breaking point."

"And who are you, dear?" Mickey asked.

DeAnn told him her and her husband's names.

"Your family has the video store?" he asked.

"Yes, do you know my parents?"

"Your grandpa—we were business associates, of a sort."

"Mickey was a bookie in his younger years." Violet beamed like the proud mother of a precocious first-grader.

"Getting back to Sarah," DeAnn continued. Her face had turned scarlet. "Why couldn't she have just snapped?"

"These things are familial, if you know what I mean," Mickey said. "Have you met the mother?"

"We have," Harriet interrupted. "But we do need to talk quilting before we move on to the other group. Also, you need to know, the police have specifically warned us not to interfere with their investigation."

"Come on, that's exactly why you're here," Mickey countered. "Don't try to kid a kidder, Miss. We both want the same thing. Plus, we know you have at least thirty more minutes with us before Sabrina will have the memory people ready. The point is, we want to know who really killed Seth and so, it appears, do you."

"And we want to make sure Howard doesn't convince the police it was Sarah," Violet added.

"Why would Howard want to do that?" Harriet asked them.

"So the police won't know what's going on here," Janice told her.

"Which is?"

"That's what we need you to help us find out," Janice said.

"I'll also note that if those cameras in the corners of your quilting bags are the best you've got, you're going to need our help, too," Jo added sweetly.

"Jo used to be in the CIA," Violet told them. "And Mickey—"

"Mickey has prior experience with the Foggy Point police," he interrupted her.

87

"This is a bad idea," Lauren said and shook her head.

"I agree," Mickey said. "But, as you can surely see, our options are a bit limited."

"I think our group needs to talk this over among ourselves," Mavis said. "We need to let whoever wants to opt out do so before we go any further."

Mickey shook his head.

"Yeah, sure. Go talk. I told the girls you were lightweights. It's been nice knowing you."

"You stop that," Violet scolded. "We've taken them by surprise, and now we need to let them process what we've told them. I'm sure they'll do the right thing."

"Maybe you can pick me up a package of crib-size wool batting at Marjory's store and bring it by tomorrow?" Janice suggested. "Will that give you enough time to decide what you're going to do?"

"Sure," Harriet said.

"I see you've all gotten to know each other a little better," Sabrina said brightly as she reentered the room a short while later.

"Indeed, we have," Harriet agreed. "Indeed, we have."

✂ - - - ✂ - - - ✂

Thankfully, the people from the memory care wing were exactly as promised. All of them were in the early stages of dementia, and none appeared to have an agenda other than quilting.

"These ladies need to go back to their rooms and begin getting ready for dinner," Sabrina said when an hour had passed. "Thank you so much for spending some time with us."

Aunt Beth turned off the sewing machine she'd been using to repair the binding on a tattered quilt one of the women had brought with her from her room.

"Thank you for letting us spend an enjoyable afternoon at your lovely facility and allowing us to meet these wonderful women," she said.

"I hope you'll be able to come back again next week." Sabrina's barely disguised look bordered on desperation.

Harriet stood up and went to her side.

"You can count on it. Lauren and I are going to come by tomorrow with some supplies for the other group, if that's okay with you."

"You don't need my permission," Sabrina assured her. "The independent living seniors are free to come and go as they please and to entertain whenever and whomever they choose."

"Good to know," Lauren said.

"We'll see you next week, then," Mavis said as the residents filed out of the room, led by an aide who had materialized outside the door to the small dining room. She picked up the foot pedal to the machine Beth had been using and wound its cord around it before setting it on the base. Beth removed the power cord and tucked it into the pocket on the machine cover then snapped the cover onto the base.

"I need something to eat," she said. "Let's grab a bite and mull this over."

"Should we go to Tico's?" Harriet asked. Tico's Tacos was centrally located in downtown Foggy Point, making it a little closer than her house for the people who lived on either of the coves.

"I'll call and give Jorge a heads-up," Beth said.

Carla put her coat on.

"Is it okay if Wendy comes?"

"I'm sure she's welcome," Connie said. "But let me call Grandpa Rod. I'll bet he'd love to pick her up from play group and bring her to our house until we're done. We made tamales this morning; you can pick up Wendy and take some home for dinner. Then you won't have to cook for Aiden."

"That would be great," Carla said. "Are you sure it's not too much trouble?"

"I wouldn't offer if it was, chiquita."

"Everybody else good?" Harriet asked.

"I'll call Robin and see if she can join us," DeAnn offered.

"See you at the car," Harriet said to Carla and left, followed by Lauren. "I want to swing by the lobby a minute."

Hannah was back on duty at the reception desk, if you could call polishing one's nails while listening to a music player "on duty." Harriet had to stand directly in front of her before Hannah noticed her and pulled an earbud out.

"Do you need something?" Hannah asked without taking her gaze off the pinkie finger of her left hand. She stroked bright pink polish neatly on its surface then held her hand out to inspect the result.

"I was just wondering if you could tell me something about the residents in the independent living wing."

"You want to know if Mickey really is a prize-winning boxer and if Jo won the gardening prize at the state fair three years running?"

"Something like that."

"It's probably confidential, but I say 'Who cares?' I have no idea if their stories are true, but they have so many, it isn't likely anyone could do that much in a lifetime."

"How long have they lived here?" Harriet asked.

"I don't know. I only work here summers, usually." She began painting the next nail on her hand.

"Can you look it up?"

"No, my nails are wet."

"Really?"

Hannah sighed. "Mickey's been here since his daughter got tired of him drinking whiskey on Friday nights. That was while I was still in high school. Jo's been here since the doors opened, and Janice moved in after all the rehabs got done with her after her accident.

"Those are the ones I remember, and that's only because Dad talked about them at dinner. And I'm really not allowed to give out information from the computer. Dad has strict rules about stuff like that."

"Thank you, you've been *so* helpful," Harriet said.

Lauren took her by the arm and turned her away from the desk.

"Don't bother, it goes right over her head. Besides, you should have asked. I can get you the information. If you weren't afraid Blondie is trying to move in on your man, you'd have realized that."

"He is not my man," Harriet sputtered. "Not right now, anyway."

"Yeah, keep telling yourself that," Lauren said and guided her out the door.

✂- - -✂- - -✂

"Thoughts anyone?" Harriet asked when she was seated at the large table in the back room at Tico's Tacos. Jorge had placed several baskets of warm tortilla chips on the table, along with queso dip, guacamole and several styles of salsa. She dipped a chip into the queso and waited for someone to speak.

"Let me see if I understand," Robin began. "The independent living group at the senior center is asking us to investigate the killing of Seth Pratt and have offered their help. Their special skills include being a former bookie and a retired CIA employee of some sort as well as at least one prize-winning quilter."

"That's it in a nutshell," Lauren confirmed.

"We're not seriously considering taking them up on it, are we?" Robin asked, looking around the table at her friends.

Jorge came in with a pitcher of lemonade in one hand and a pot of hot coffee in the other.

"I would not reject them out of hand just because they are old and live in a center," he said and set the drinks on a side table next to an assembly of glasses and mugs. "You ladies can help yourselves to drinks.

"I can tell you Mickey used to be a real player in this town, according to some of my customers. I got a group of old guys who play poker here on Wednesday nights. They still talk about him."

"What about Josephine?" Harriet asked.

Jorge shook his head. "Her, I don't know."

"Don't get too excited," Robin cautioned. "Most of the people the CIA employs are accountants and lawyers."

"What about Janice?" Mavis asked. "She's younger than the other two and wheelchair-bound. Do you know her?"

Jorge looked at the ceiling in thought for a moment.

"I think I remember something about that. If I'm thinking of the right person, it was very hush-hush, something about a scorned lover seeking revenge. There was a suggestion her car had been rigged to crash; then, all of a sudden, someone squashed the story. No one talked about it, nothing. Months later, she showed up in the Foggy Point Senior Center." He shook his head. "It was all very mysterious."

"They seem to want to help Sarah," Carla suggested in a quiet voice.

"Carla's right," Harriet said. "They mentioned that they thought Howard would try to make Sarah a scapegoat. They didn't really say why they thought that, though."

Mavis got up and went to the drinks table.

"I can see why they wouldn't think Sarah was a killer." She poured coffee into two cups and set them on the table in front of Connie and Beth. "Anyone else?" Robin raised her hand, and Mavis poured another cup. "The real question is why they think Howard would want to frame his own daughter for murder."

Harriet joined her and started pouring and handing out glasses of lemonade.

"The obvious reason," she said, "would be to avoid any negative publicity for the senior center and its new, probably expensive, memory care unit. Is that enough of a reason to sacrifice your own daughter?"

Lauren twirled a chip into the guacamole and paused before popping it into her mouth.

"Let's keep in mind that Howard isn't Sarah's dad, he's her stepdad. Big difference."

"True," Harriet said. "She referred to him as her father, but when she told us about Seth, she made it clear they weren't blood relatives."

"The residents probably know the most about what goes on at that place, next to the family," Aunt Beth pointed out.

"And they can move around more easily than we can," Mavis added. "If they get found where they shouldn't be, they can always blame it on confusion."

"They're also more vulnerable," Robin cautioned. "Remember, the center controls their food and drugs. If whoever killed Seth works there, it would be easy for him to kill those old people if he becomes suspicious."

"If the killer does work at the center, they're all in danger anyway," Harriet said. "The killer might not be done yet."

Connie stood up.

"For all we know, Seth might have figured out who killed Rod's aunt and others. If he was murdered for that knowledge, the killer might go back to his angel of death activities."

"We need a little more information before we go down that path," Robin said. "It hasn't been confirmed that Rod's aunt was murdered yet, has it?"

"No, but we've hired a private pathologist to investigate our suspicions."

Harriet cleared her throat.

"Let's deal with one case at a time. I agree we don't want to put our new quilting friends in danger, but on the other hand, they do have a lot of information. I think we should at least talk to them. Before we go any further, though, I'd like to talk to Sarah. She should be able to answer a few questions."

"I think that's a good idea," Aunt Beth said with a smile for her.

"We have all the curtains finished, too," Mavis added. "Now you have a real reason to go."

Lauren sighed and looked at the ceiling then pulled out her smartphone and opened the calendar app.

"I know, Kemosabe, checking my schedule as we speak." There was a pause. "I've got a nine o'clock conference call, and then I'm free. Not free free—I have to work sometime—but I can go with to the shelter and to take batting to the batty, I mean, the seniors."

"While you all are doing that, I'll research the newspaper archives for stories about Janice and Mickey," Aunt Beth offered.

"You go, girl," Lauren said.

"Anyone want to quilt at my house tomorrow?" Harriet asked. "We all should know more by then, and I don't know about you all, but I need to work some more on my bed quilt for the shelter."

Mavis took a sip of her coffee.

"Sounds good to me."

The group agreed to meet in the afternoon to give everyone time to do their various tasks.

Chapter 12

I can't tell you how much the women here will appreciate your gift," Georgia Hecht said to Lauren and Harriet as they installed the last rod and straightened the curtain hanging from it. "The rooms look so much brighter already."

Harriet stepped down from the ladder she been on so she could reach the top of the bathroom window.

"Would it be appropriate for us to provide some coordinating paint for the walls? We'd be sure we got the kind that was safe to use around babies."

"I think that would be wonderful," Georgia replied. "As you can tell, we had a large batch of commercial paint donated by a contractor who was working on our original remodel. She had it left over from another job. It was good to have, but pale gray is a bit monotonous."

"Great. I'm happy to buy a few gallons, and I'm sure my aunt will donate some, also."

"Me, too," Lauren said with a small sigh. "A little color on the walls will show our quilts to their best advantage."

"I can't thank you enough. I'm sure our residents will be happy to do the actual painting, so don't worry about that." Georgia stepped back to look at the curtain as Harriet tugged again at its bottom edge.

"My aunt said to tell you the wrinkles will disappear on their own, but if you want to speed the process, you can spritz the curtains with a little water."

"Good to know," Georgia said. "Tell your aunt I appreciate the tip. Before you go, your friend Sarah asked if you could come up to her room for

93

a few minutes and talk to her. She'd come down, but the doctor doesn't want her going up and down stairs until her knee injury is more healed."

"We'd love to see her," Harriet said.

"Especially since that's the whole reason we're here," Lauren murmured so only Harriet could hear.

"I think she could use the support," Georgia said. "She's having a pretty hard time. No one comes here in great shape, but—and believe me, I wouldn't be talking to you about this if we weren't seriously worried about Sarah— she's not doing well.

"Even though her fiancé was her abuser, she's grieving his loss. When someone comes here, our staff and the other residents make an effort to let the new person know they aren't alone, and that they've all had a similar experience.

"Sarah won't talk to anyone. She just insists no one could possibly understand what she's been through, and then she goes off by herself. We hear her crying during the night. She hardly eats, and she can't possibly be healing properly without adequate nutrition and enough sleep."

Harriet took a deep breath.

"We'll see what we can do."

The Sarah Harriet and Lauren found in the upstairs bedroom bore no resemblance to the young woman they'd been quilting with for the last year or more. She looked like she'd lost thirty pounds. Her previously rounded apple-cheeks were now sharply angled, her face gray and sunken, making her bloodshot eyes look larger than normal.

She sat up in her bed, her ratty quilt clutched to her chest with her good hand, her mangled arm on a pillow lying on her belly. Her hair looked like it hadn't been washed since they'd seen her last.

"Sarah?" Harriet said in a hushed voice.

Her eyes jerked toward the sound of Harriet's voice, but she didn't move.

"May we come in?"

When she didn't reply, Lauren and Harriet eased into the room, shutting the door quietly behind them.

"Is he really dead?"

Harriet looked at Lauren and then back at Sarah.

"Do you mean Seth? Yes, Seth is dead. Someone shot him at your cabin."

A strangled sob escaped Sarah's lips. Harriet moved closer to the bed, but Lauren stayed by the door.

"Georgia said you wanted to talk to us?" Harriet suggested.

"She told me Seth was dead, but I needed to know from someone I could trust." Tears ran down Sarah's hollow cheeks.

"You know he was shot. You were there. You called me and told me you woke up beside him, and he was dead," Harriet reminded her. She wasn't sure if she should press the matter at this point, but she didn't know what else to do.

Sarah sighed and dropped her good hand to her lap.

"I was hoping it was all a bad dream. They've given me so much pain medication since I've been here, it's been hard to tell what's real. For a while, I wasn't sure I'd ever left the hospital. I thought maybe I'd imagined it all."

"That's magical thinking," Lauren said. "Not only is Seth dead, we're fairly sure you're suspect numero uno."

"Lauren, stop," Harriet said.

"She needs to know what she's up against. We don't have time for this psycho business."

Harriet glared at her.

"She's right," Sarah said. "I have to figure this out. I don't remember much, but I'm sure I could never have hurt Seth. We were going to be married."

"Give it up, Sarah," Lauren said. "You weren't going to be married. He was going to kill you. If you did kill him, he had it coming."

Sarah began to cry again.

"Lauren, this is not helping."

"I was hoping to shock her out of this." She gestured toward Sarah. "Whatever this is."

"It's not helping, so lay off."

"Fine. Why don't you show me how it's done, then?"

Harriet moved to the edge of the bed and put her hand gently on Sarah's shoulder.

"I know this is difficult, but we need to figure it all out. We know you didn't shoot Seth, if for no other reason than your arm was too injured for you to have done it. So, we need to know as much as you can remember so we can help the police find the real killer. Unfortunately, your stepdad is not going to help you."

"Howard is an evil man. Seth was going to leave the senior center because of him."

"What did he do?"

"Seth wouldn't tell me. He said he was gathering evidence. He said if anyone found out what his dad was doing, it could implicate him and he could lose his license."

Lauren came closer.

"And you have no idea what he was talking about?"

"No. Seth didn't want to say anything until he'd gotten evidence to back up his suspicions. He said he couldn't risk having me blab to Howard if his suspicions turned out to be not true."

Harriet looked at Lauren, and Lauren pulled a small notebook from her bag and made a note.

"Can you think of anyone else who would want Seth dead?" Harriet asked.

"I don't know." Sarah twirled the torn edge of her quilt into a tight spiral. "Joshua, maybe."

"He's your stepsister Hannah's brother?" Harriet asked.

"Her half-brother. Howard adopted him when his mom Jill died. He's a little younger than Seth. He never got what Seth did, though. Howard wouldn't pay for Joshua to go to college. He wouldn't even pay for him to play sports or do activities in high school, even though he paid for Seth and Hannah. I'm not really sure why he adopted Josh other than to please Hannah."

"Josh and Hannah are close?"

"Not really." She hesitated. "I'm not sure. Maybe they were when they were younger. I don't think Josh likes any of us now. I can't say I blame him. He's always been a sort of indentured servant. Howard would make him do the jobs no one else wanted."

"That sounds grim." Lauren looked up from her notebook, where she was making additional notes.

"Ours isn't the traditional family unit," Sarah stated.

"Does Joshua live in Foggy Point?" Harriet asked.

"Of course. He works at the senior center. That was why I said Howard could make him do whatever he wanted."

Under normal circumstances, Sarah's sarcastic remarks got on Harriet's nerves, but today she was happy to see a glimpse of the old Sarah. She pulled the desk chair to the bed and sat down.

"If Josh is so abused, why doesn't he just leave?"

"Seth and I couldn't figure that out. I mean, Howard made it clear to Seth that he had to stay because he'd gotten a 'free' education, even if he didn't get to choose what to study. Josh had gotten nothing. We assumed Howard had something on him—Howard is that sort of person. He's got something on about half the people in town. No one likes him, really, but they can't afford to be anything but nice to him."

Lauren looked up from her notebook again.

"If Howard is so awful, why did your mom marry him?"

Sarah slumped back against her pillows.

"That would be the question, now, wouldn't it?"

Harriet stood up.

"Anyone else?"

"Detective Morse keeps asking me that, but I don't know what to say. Everyone loved Seth." Tears started trickling down Sarah's cheeks again.

Harriet picked at a piece of lint on her pants leg and glared at Lauren and the response she knew was lurking in her friend's mind. Lauren put her hand up in surrender.

"Sarah, can you tell us anything about the group of seniors in the in-dependent living hall at the center?" Harriet asked finally.

"Like what? Their medical records are confidential."

"I was thinking more like what their backgrounds were before coming to the center."

"Violet claims to be a prize-winning quilter. There's a faded blue rib-bon hanging on the wall in her room, so I suppose it's true. Everyone knows Mickey used to be a bookie and who knows what else."

"What about Jo?" Harriet asked.

"What about her?"

"Is she really a retired CIA operative?"

"How should I know?"

Harriet sighed and pressed her lips together to avoid saying what she was thinking.

"You don't have to look at me like that," Sarah said. "Yes, I overheard Jo say she worked for the CIA, but we hear all kinds of crazy things, espe-cially in the memory care area. Those people were normal once, too—right up until they weren't. I haven't been in Jo's room, and short of calling up the CIA for a job reference, there's no real way to know. Could be true, could be the wild imaginings of a deteriorating mind."

"She's got a point," Lauren said.

"Rule of thumb is fifty-fifty," Sarah offered. "People change memories every time they take them out and talk about them. By the time you've told a story for fifty or more years, it probably has lost half of its original truth. That doesn't just start when you're old. We all do it. Think about it, and you'll see I'm right."

"Good to know," Lauren said.

"I did go to school, you know. I've got a masters in psychology."

That was interesting, Harriet thought. Robin had told her one time that three-fourths of the people who studied psychology did so to try to solve their own problems.

"The director here is worried about you. She says you aren't letting them help you."

"I don't have anything in common with these people. They say our situations are the same, but how many of them had their fiancé, who they'd grown up with, murdered, probably by one of their own relatives?"

"Sarah, no one is going to have exactly the same story, but you all have experienced violence and loss."

"You don't understand."

Harriet had an idea.

"You're probably right, but could you do something for me?"

Sarah wiped her nose with a tattered tissue and then looked at her for a moment.

"What?"

"The rest of the Threads and I are working on a quilting project with some of the residents at the senior center." Harriet looked at Lauren, daring her to contradict her. "We were thinking we could do a joint project with the women who live here. We could teach these women to quilt, and they could make some squares for a quilt the senior women could finish and raffle off to make money to buy things the shelter needs."

She continued to look at Lauren. It took a moment for Lauren to realize Harriet was waiting for her to say something.

"We thought we'd have both groups make grandmother's flower garden blocks. They can either do English paper piecing or freehand it, but in either case, they would be hand sewing, so we wouldn't need much equipment."

"We realize you can't sew yet, but we thought you could watch them and give them pointers," Harriet added.

"None of them know how to quilt at all?" Sarah asked.

"Not that we know of." Harriet hoped it was true.

"I suppose as long as I'm stuck here, I could make sure they don't mess their blocks up. And they certainly could use the money. Did you know they make grocery store coffee in an electric percolator? Can you imagine? It's undrinkable.

"Can you make sure Detective Morse keeps looking for Seth's killer? I know you've helped her before."

That's one way of putting it, Harriet thought. Sarah apparently didn't realize Lauren hadn't been lying when she'd said Sarah was Morse's number-one suspect.

"We've got to go," Harriet said. "Can we get you anything before we go? They have some magazines downstairs."

"No." She raised her injured arm with its fiberglass-and-wire casing. "I can't really do anything but lay here and think about Seth."

Lauren and Harriet picked up their purses and coats from the floor beside the door.

Sarah sniffed. "There is one thing."

"Sure, what can we do?" Harriet asked.

"Could you check on Rachel? I haven't heard anything about her since I took her to Aiden."

"I'm sure Mavis is taking good care of her," Harriet assured Sarah. "But I'll ask her for a report when I see her this afternoon. We'll let you know the minute we can."

Lauren pulled the door closed behind them and turned to Harriet.

"Does she not get that being battered is what she has in common with the rest of these women?"

Harriet started for the stairs.

"She's not ready to face the truth about Seth yet. When she's healed a little, and they've figured out who killed him, she may be more willing to get some counseling to help with that. Who knows? If she's here long enough, maybe one of the other residents will get through to her."

They found Georgia in the kitchen.

"Everyone's working on quilts, so we'll have those soon, and in the meantime, we'll let you know when we have paint for you."

"I could pick it up from you after work someday, but I'm sure you want to deliver it yourselves so you can check on your friend."

Harriet had the good grace to blush.

Chapter 13

avis came into Harriet's kitchen and set two pink boxes tied with string on the counter.

"I brought two coffee cakes from the new bakery that went in at the opposite end of the block from Annie's coffee shop downtown. One is almond and the other is Marion berry."

Harriet filled first the teakettle and then the carafe to the coffee maker and then set them on their respective heat sources.

"Sounds great. I'll get hot drinks ready. Do you know if Wendy is joining us?"

"Yes, she is," Mavis told her.

She took a sippy cup from her cabinet and filled it with chocolate milk.

"Sarah asked how Rachel is doing. I told her I was sure you were taking good care of her."

"She doesn't like having that cast on her leg, but she's otherwise good. Curly is a good nurse," she said, referring to her little rescued dog. "They've started taking naps side-by-side on the sofa when the curtain is open and lets the sun shine on it."

"I'll let Sarah know. I'm sure that'll make her feel better."

Aunt Beth came into the kitchen carrying a large flat box under her arm.

"Do you want us in the studio or in the dining room?"

"Since we're having coffee cake, we'd probably be better off in the dining room," Harriet told her. "What do you have there?" She indicated the mystery box.

"I got a tabletop flipchart holder for us. It's hard for everyone to see Robin's legal pad when we're making group notes. I figured we could use

100

it when it's our turn to present our block for the guild quilt-along project, too. I ordered it from the office supply store in Seattle."

Mavis came over for a closer look.

"What a great idea."

"It came with plain paper, but I ordered a pad of the sticky note pages also so we can tack them to the wall if we get multiple pages going," Aunt Beth said.

Harriet pulled a stack of saucers from her kitchen cupboard.

"Well done, Auntie. That's really cool."

Beth tugged on the bottom hem of her cardigan and stiffened her spine.

"I haven't been cool in decades, if you don't count last month's festival, that is."

The rest of the Loose Threads trickled in, removing their coats and grabbing their drink of choice before settling in their favorite spot at the table. Carla pulled a portable DVD player and a set of headphones from her tote bag. She popped an educational cartoon into the unit and put the pink earphones on her toddler's head.

"We need to be careful what we say around her. She asked me if Michelle was a witch the other day. If Aiden hears her saying that, we'll be out on the street."

Lauren laughed. "She really said that? Good for her."

Carla's face turned pink, but for once she didn't retreat into silence.

"It isn't funny. She has to learn proper behavior."

"But the woman *is* a witch. And she wasn't nice to Wendy. The child is learning to call a spade a spade," Lauren countered.

"Not on my watch," Carla said.

Aunt Beth opened her portable flipchart and set it on the table between Robin and DeAnn.

"Let's get busy before Wendy's show is over," she suggested and handed Robin a brand-new black marking pen.

Robin wrote *Seth Pratt Murder* at the top of the first page.

"Let's start with what we know," she said.

"Seth's dead," Lauren offered with a barely contained snicker.

"Don't make me send you to time-out," Connie scolded.

Harriet leaned back in her chair.

"We know for sure Sarah was there. She says she was unconscious when he was killed, and evidence points to that being true, but the only certain part is her being there."

"The window glass was broken," Lauren said, serious now. Robin wrote *broken bedroom window.*

"Were the glass shards inside or outside?" DeAnn asked.

"Good question," Robin said. "Harriet?"

"There was glass on the bedroom floor. I didn't look outside, since it was dark."

Robin wrote "glass inside" under the *broken window* line.

"Sarah showed evidence of a recent and brutal beating," Harriet said. "Not only was her face a wreck, the orthopedic contraption on her broken arm was all mangled."

Robin made a note.

"What else do we know for sure?"

"Sarah's not in jail," Lauren pointed out.

"Good one," Robin said and wrote it down. "That tells us the police don't have enough evidence against Sarah to arrest her. Anything else?" She looked from person to person. When no one spoke up, she nodded to Aunt Beth, who got up and pulled the paper from the flipchart and stuck it to the glass front of the side board.

Harriet's eyes got big.

"Don't worry, honey. It said on the package that it doesn't leave a residue," Aunt Beth assured her.

Robin drew two vertical lines down the fresh page then wrote at the top of the three sections *means, motive,* and *opportunity.*

"Anyone could have had the opportunity," DeAnn said.

Carla twisted her napkin then tore little bits from the end of the paper rope she'd made.

"Not really," she said quietly. "I mean, I guess that's true, but if the cabin belonged to Sarah's mother, Seth probably used the senior center as his legal address. Didn't Sarah say he slept there most nights? And he worked there during the day. To kill him at the cabin, someone needed to know he'd be there and not at the senior center."

"That's a good point," Harriet said. "It had to be someone close enough to the situation that they would know when Seth would be there, which wasn't all that often."

"Unless it was a crime of opportunity," Mavis suggested. "Maybe someone else was beating Sarah, and Seth arrived unexpectedly. I know it sounds farfetched, but we're supposed to write down all possible options at this stage of the process. We can eliminate stuff later."

The group fell silent. Robin flipped the current page up and wrote on the third piece of chart paper "Random Ideas" and then wrote "Seth interrupted a crime of opportunity."

Harriet took a sip of her tea.

"While you have that flipped up, put 'Howard wants to blame Sarah.' That's what the seniors we met at the center believe."

"Why do they think that?" Robin asked when she'd made the note.

"Apparently, they think he'd throw anyone under the bus to have this end quickly, before it can taint his business and his expensive new memory care unit."

"Sarah also suggested there was no love lost between Joshua and the rest of the family," Lauren told them.

"Who's Joshua?" Robin asked.

"He's some sort of adopted former stepchild," Harriet told her. "He's Hannah's half-brother. I think."

Robin pulled the two pages she was writing on off the chart.

"I think we need a family tree. Since your loved ones are usually suspects in this sort of thing, maybe we should start there."

Harriet's dog Scooter ran into the dining room from the hallway, barking as loudly as his six-pound body could manage.

"Hey, little guy, what's wrong?" Harriet soothed. Scooter buried his head in the cleft under her arm.

"What's got into him?" Aunt Beth asked.

"And him," Mavis added and pointed to Harriet's cat. She was the only one who had noticed Fred come into the room behind the dog. Fred's tail was puffed to three times its normal size, and his back was hunched, causing him to appear to be tiptoeing.

Beth attempted to pat his head, but the cat hissed and continued on to the window.

"Look," Harriet said and pointed to Wendy, who was looking out the dining room window, her pink earphones around her neck.

Before anyone could get to the window, they heard a series of explosions. Carla leaped up and swept Wendy to the floor, enclosed in her arms. Everyone else scrambled out of their chairs and retreated to the kitchen.

Harriet stared out the window as she dialed 911 on her cell phone. Her driveway was filled with smoke like it was ground zero on the Fourth of July.

Then, as suddenly as they had started, the explosions stopped. Harriet scooted out of the dining room and across the foyer to a window that gave her a view of the entire circular driveway. There were flames coming from all the cars she could see.

"Someone just firebombed our cars," she said to the dispatcher.

Chapter 14

What's going on out there?" Beth whispered when Harriet joined the rest of the Threads in the kitchen. The women were huddled on the floor space between the island and the counter.

Connie made the sign of the cross.

"Diós mio, the terrorists have arrived in Foggy Point."

"I doubt that," Lauren whispered.

"I'm guessing we whacked the wrong hornet's nest." Harriet held her phone out. "Does anyone want to use my phone to call their husband?"

Lauren was the only other Thread who had her phone with her. Connie, DeAnn and Robin called their families. Aunt Beth took Harriet's phone when they were finished.

"Jorge," she said, "we've got trouble at Harriet's."

"Should I call Aiden?" Carla asked.

Harriet handed her the phone.

"We're likely to be here a while, and if you're late coming home, he'll worry. If Terry is around you might call him, too. I suspect he knows more about explosives than anyone on the Foggy Point police force."

Carla's boyfriend Terry Jansen was a career Navy SEAL who did some sort of investigation for his branch of the military. It was all very hush-hush, so no one was ever sure where he was or what he was doing. He just showed up when he was able to. With her nomadic upbringing, it seemed Carla was used to people coming and going in her life.

She took the phone and dialed a number then hung up. A moment later, it rang.

"Someone blew up our cars at Harriet's...We're fine, we were in the house...Okay, see you. He'll be right over," she said to Harriet. "He said to stay in the house until he gets here."

She dialed a second number and repeated the same information to Aiden, adding that Terry was on his way.

Robin rose into a crouch then shifted over next to Harriet.

"Do you really think someone did this because we're looking into Seth's murder?"

"Don't you? The Small Stitches might steal our quilt pattern ideas, but I can't see them doing something like this."

Robin didn't smile.

"Sorry," Harriet continued, "that was my lame attempt to lighten the mood. Can you think of another reason anyone would attack us as a group? We must have been getting too close to something. I just wish we knew what or who it was."

"You and me both."

A knock sounded on the door that led to the garage. It opened before Harriet could say anything, and Detective Morse came in, her expression grim.

"Oh, thank heaven," Connie whispered.

Harriet stood, and the rest of the women followed suit. She moved out of the small space where they'd been huddled. Lauren eased toward the dining room.

"Anyone care to explain why there are bombed out cars sitting in your driveway? I just got a call telling me a military bomb squad was arriving and the FPPD aren't to touch anything." Morse turned to look into the face of each woman. "Anyone want to tell me anything?"

"We know almost nothing," Harriet turned to block Morse's line of sight into the dining room. "We were in the dining room having coffee and cake when my driveway blew up."

"Why were you all here?"

"Lauren and I went to the women's shelter to hang curtains my aunt and Mavis made. The rest of us are all working on quilts and pillowcases for them, too."

Lauren had made her escape, and Harriet could only hope she was concealing the flip chart and its pages.

Morse's radio crackled. She took it off her belt and turned a knob on its top, adjusting the volume so only she could hear it. She listened with it pressed to her ear for a moment then clipped it back on her belt.

"We'll be here for a while so they can clear your driveway. The men in your lives have been stopped at the bottom of the hill. They expect us to be in here for at least an hour, so you all have plenty of time to explain to me what's really going on."

Mavis cleared her throat.

"Before you start accusing Harriet of bombing our cars or, at the least, causing them to be bombed, let's take a look at the facts. Someone killed Sarah's fiancé and possibly beat her up in the process. We're all friends of Sarah's. Naturally we're interested in what happens to her, but we haven't done anything to warrant this sort of treatment."

Morse closed her eyes and took a deep breath then let it out.

"I'm sorry if I came on too strong, but since I've been in Foggy Point, every time there's been a major crime, you all have been in the middle of it. You've been lucky so far, but if you keep this up, someone is going to be hurt or even killed."

"So you're saying it was our fault a storm knocked out the power and the road last winter, trapping us in town with a killer?" Mavis asked. "That wasn't our idea of a good time, you know."

"We're not reading the crime page of the local paper looking for opportunities," Aunt Beth added. "Each time we've been involved in something, it's because we couldn't avoid it. For instance, when your best friend is murdered, it's hard not to ask a few questions."

"I get it. I really do. These are people you know. You want to help them. What I want is for you all to not be the next victims. Let the police do their job. It's what you pay all those tax dollars for."

Harriet went to the sink and filled the teakettle.

"Can you get paper cups from the garage shelf?" she asked her aunt. "Our mugs are still in the dining room..." She looked at Morse. "...and I'm guessing you don't want us near that big window."

Carla went to the refrigerator, found the carton of chocolate milk and refilled Wendy's sippy cup. Wendy had been clutching the cup when Carla had scooped her up and brought her to the kitchen.

"You guess correctly," Morse said. "Now, let's get back to why you're really here."

Lauren had returned; she gave Harriet a slight nod.

"We *were* talking about what happened to Sarah," Robin admitted finally. "We don't have any insider information, so it was all speculation. We're worried about our friend. Surely, you can understand that."

"None of us believe Sarah killed Seth," Connie offered. "Even if she was there when he was killed. She could never have killed him."

"Why do you say that?" Morse asked.

"You saw her, didn't you? She was beaten nearly senseless, and her arm is in that contraption. If she would let him do all that, why would anything change?" Connie finished with a sigh.

"Everyone has a breaking point," Morse told her, echoing what DeAnn had said previously.

"When we spoke to Sarah in the hospital the first time, she was still talking about getting married to him," Harriet said as she put teabags into the paper cups her aunt had brought in. When the water boiled, she poured it into the cups. Mavis handed the first round to Robin, Connie, DeAnn, Lauren, Aunt Beth and Detective Morse while Harriet refilled the kettle and set it on the stove to heat again.

Morse dropped a spoonful of sugar into her cup.

"Can any of you think of anyone else who would want Seth Pratt dead?"

Harriet turned from the stove.

"We don't know Seth Pratt. He kept Sarah isolated from us. Most of us wouldn't have known the man if he passed us on the street until the Foggy Point Senior Center open house; and we didn't exactly have deep personal conversations there."

The rest of the Loose Threads nodded as she spoke.

"He used to come into Tico's," Beth told Morse. "Jorge has talked to him, as a customer only. Naturally, when Sarah was in the hospital the first time, we asked him a few questions, but Jorge didn't know anything useful."

"Let me be the judge of what's useful," Morse said.

"You'd do better to talk to him directly," Beth said.

Morse stirred her tea.

"Whether you know something or not, someone's clearly worried about you."

Harriet poured the next round of tea water.

"I can't imagine we're that much of a threat to anyone."

Morse's radio crackled again; she adjusted the volume, listened then said, "Put him in a patrol car at the bottom of the driveway for now. I can't leave until the bomb squad gives the all-clear."

The Loose Threads looked expectantly at her as she turned her radio down.

"They found a blond guy lurking in the bushes out by the street when they were evacuating your neighbors. That sound like anyone you know? Patrol says he's mid-to-late twenties, slight build."

"Possibly Sarah's..." Harriet paused. "...whatever he is. Adopted step-brother—Josh? He's blond, isn't he?"

"There was a blond boy at the senior center open house," Mavis suggested.

Morse looked at Harriet.

"And you have no idea why he'd be lurking in your bushes?"

Harriet held her hands up in front of her. Morse's gaze shifted to Lauren.

"Don't look at me," Lauren protested. "I never met any of Sarah's family other than at the open house, and I didn't speak to any of them personally. Him being the bomber does come to mind, though."

Morse glared at Harriet.

"If you women know something, I *will* find out."

"Okay." Connie stood to her full five feet to emphasize her point, "I know you're just doing your job, but I speak for the group in saying we've had enough," she said in her best schoolteacher tone. "We just had our cars blown up in the driveway and aren't allowed to see our husbands or find out how bad the damage is. We've answered your questions to the best of our ability. If you can't stop harassing us, you're going to have to go sit in the other room."

Morse pursed her lips but didn't say anything. She topped off her cup of tea and sat down at the table.

"Anyone have any show-and-tell?" she finally asked.

Harriet had to turn back to the sink to avoid making eye contact with Lauren and bursting out laughing.

Lauren pulled her tablet from the bag she'd rescued from the dining room.

"I have pictures of the curtains we hung," she said with a straight face.

The group crowded around and watched as she flipped through the pictures. They were carefully shot so as to not include a view of the outside or any other identifying information.

"They look real nice," Mavis commented when they were through.

"It's kind of you to help the shelter out like that," Morse said.

"We're kind people," Lauren told her.

"Speaking of the shelter," Harriet said with a glance at Lauren, "we're going to do a joint quilt project with the women there and the people at the senior center." She explained the plan she'd made up on the fly when they visited Sarah. "It was all I could think of to try to get Sarah involved in something."

"I have to admit, it was ingenious," Lauren said. "Sarah took the bait—she can feel superior to the others and she's behind helping make money to buy more creature comforts for the place."

"I guess we can make that work," Mavis said.

"Anyone need a ride to go car shopping tomorrow?" Harriet asked. "Mine is safe and sound in the garage," She looked at her aunt. "I started Uncle

Hank's truck last week. If you want, I can drive that, and you can take my car."

"That's very sweet of you to offer. I may take you up on it, though I hate driving something that big."

Morse looked around the kitchen table at them.

"I'm sure anyone who had a car out in the driveway is going to be car shopping tomorrow. One of you should probably call Bill Young and warn him he's about to get a bunch of insurance claims."

Harriet held up her cell phone.

"Anyone?"

Aunt Beth took the phone and called Foggy Point's most popular insurance agent to tell him to brace himself.

✂ - - - ✂ - - - ✂

It was another forty-five minutes before Terry entered from the garage, followed quickly by Aiden, Jorge, Connie's husband Rod, and Robin's and DeAnn's husbands.

"Your driveway and yard are clear," Terry said. He stood with his arm around Carla. "The forensic people are collecting samples and fingerprinting what's left of your cars, so they're off-limits for a little while longer. We'll know more when the lab guys are finished, but it looks like someone put a pipe bomb made from fertilizer and motor oil under each car."

"So, they weren't trying to kill us?" Harriet asked.

"Doesn't look like it. They could have waited to detonate until you were in your cars if they'd wanted to hurt you. They could have built bigger bombs or filled them with nails or other shrapnel, too, but they didn't. If I had to hazard a guess, I'd say they were trying to give you people something else to think about besides the murder of Seth Pratt."

Robin threw her paper cup into the wastebasket under the sink.

"I'd have to say they succeeded. All I'm thinking about right now is how I'm going to get my kids to school and practice until I can replace my van."

"You and me both," DeAnn agreed. "My SUV was our only vehicle big enough to carry our whole family."

The rest of the Threads lamented the hardship their lack of a car would create.

Harriet took the wastebasket from under the sink and carried it to the garage to empty into her larger trash can. Aiden followed her out and, the instant the door was closed, pulled her into his arms.

"Are you okay?"

"I'm fine. My car was in the garage. I feel bad for everyone else. If they hadn't been at my house, they'd still have cars."

"I doubt it. The police would just be going to a lot more houses to pick through the debris." He rubbed her back as he held her body against his. "This isn't your fault."

"It's all such a mess. My friends are car-less, and meanwhile, Sarah is hidden away by herself, mourning the death of the guy who beat her senseless on more than one occasion while her loving stepfather is by all accounts willing to let the police believe she did the killing, just so he doesn't lose any business."

"Where did you hear all that?" Aiden asked. He held her at arm's-length so he could look at her face while she answered.

"Lauren and I talked to Sarah when we were at the shelter hanging curtains. The rest I got from people who live at the senior center."

"Sarah's going to need major league therapy no matter how this all sorts out," Aiden said and pulled her back into an embrace. He rested his chin on her head. "Are you sure you can believe what the people at the center are telling you? They might have their own agen-da."

"I'm sure they do, but I'm not sure why they'd lie about Howard's treatment of Sarah."

"Be cautious," he warned her. "Listen to what they have to say, but don't take it as gospel. I've made a few house calls in the independent living wing, and some of the residents say they feel like they were forced by their family to move there. I'm sure they see Howard as a coconspirator."

"I'll keep that in mind. By the way, did you see a young man being held in a squad car at the bottom of my driveway or the bottom of the hill?"

"Yeah, it's Hannah's brother Joshua. He brings her to work sometimes. Do they think he had something to do with this?"

"No one said that, exactly, just that he was lurking around in the bushes at the bottom of the drive. Morse had him held for questioning. What does Hannah say about him?"

"Not much. I get the feeling he's here because he has to be, not because he wants to be. I don't know if he's on probation or some sort of diversion program or what. Like I said, she doesn't talk much about her family."

Harriet tightened her arms briefly around his waist then pushed away from him.

"We better go in before they send a search party."

Aiden followed Harriet to the door.

"How did Scooter handle the noise? Do I need to check him?"

"I'm sure he'd love a checkup from his favorite doctor, but I think he's fine. He might make a watchdog yet—he barked just before the explosions started."

"We were about to send the detective after you," Mavis said as they came back into the kitchen.

Jorge loudly cleared his throat.

"You ladies won't be able to rescue any remains from your cars for a while, and some of you are going to need rides home. How about I treat you all to pizza at Mama Teresa's? Maybe the good detective can join us, too."

"It might be a while, but I'll try," Jane Morse said before leaving the kitchen and going outside.

DeAnn looped her arm through her husband David's.

"Thanks for the offer, Jorge, but we've got to pick the kids up from my mom's. We're going to have to make two trips, so we need to get started."

"I'd like to go home and hug my kids, too," Robin said. "Thanks for the thought, though."

The rest of the group decided that a nice gooey pizza with a side of cheesy bread was just what they needed to return some normalcy to their lives.

Chapter 15

Harriet wheeled her Honda MVP to the curb in front of Lauren's apartment like a seasoned school bus driver. She felt like one, too; it seemed like all she'd done for the last few days was drive between Mavis's cottage on the strait, Lauren's place on the cove and Aunt Beth's in the middle, with a few cycles to Robin's and DeAnn's thrown into the mix.

Connie's husband had a hobby car he'd restored but not yet traded for a new project, so Connie was able to use his truck while he drove his baby. Aiden simply picked another of the many cars he'd inherited from his mother for Carla to drive. Driving vintage luxury cars was one of the perks of her job.

Lauren opened the passenger side door and got in.

"When does your aunt get her new car?"

"Not sure. They had to order it, which means she has to wait until they have enough cars to fill a truck to come to Foggy Point. When do you get yours?"

"The broker hasn't found one yet. He said it could take a couple of weeks. Don't worry, one of my clients has a company car they're willing to loan me. They said I could pick it up in a few days."

"That's lucky. DeAnn and Robin get their new cars today."

"I guess." Lauren stared out the window as they headed for Mavis's cottage. "What are we doing at the senior center today?"

"Sabrina called and said she talked to Josephine and Violet, and then they talked to the others about making a raffle quilt in conjunction with the shelter to raise money. They suggested the two groups share the profits. She'd like to use their cut to buy a few used sewing machines they can keep set up permanently. She told me she realized they wouldn't be able to keep Marjory's loaner forever."

"Good to know, but I was thinking more in terms of what are *we* doing there today."

"We don't have a plan," Harriet braked at a red light and turned to look at Lauren while they waited. "If the residents are right about Howard wanting to blame Seth's death on Sarah, I'd like to know the real reason. I mean, I'm sure Seth's death isn't something they'll put in their marketing brochure, but he wasn't killed on the premises, so I doubt it would cause anyone to move out, or even to not move in."

"Do you believe the old people? About him blaming Seth's death on Sarah, I mean."

"I don't know why they'd make something like that up. And they may be eccentric, but these folks seem pretty sharp, especially compared to the memory care bunch. If they think Howard is going to blame Sarah, they've got some reason, and it's probably a good one."

"So, back to my original question. What're we going to do?"

"As much as I'd like to get into Howard's offices and take a look around, I'm not going to do anything but quilt."

"Really?"

"Really. If someone is willing to blow up our cars, what else might they be willing to do? I don't want whoever it was to get ideas about doing anything to our senior citizen friends."

The light changed and Harriet pulled away from the intersection.

"You think they would hurt the geezers?"

"I don't know, and that's the point. I wouldn't have guessed someone would blow up the Loose Threads' cars in my driveway, but they did.

"Connie and Rod are convinced someone at the center killed his aunt. It's within the realm of possibility that a medication mistake happened. Since Seth was in charge of medications, Howard might have blamed him. Maybe he's that intolerant. On the other hand, Rod's aunt might have discovered something else going on there and been silenced for it."

"Hard to believe he'd kill his son over a medication mistake," Harriet argued. "Or for that matter, that something worth killing Rod's aunt over was going on. And in that case, why is Seth dead?"

"I didn't say it was a perfect theory. Someone wants to keep us from digging into Seth's death. The car bombs are proof of that. They tell me there's something to be discovered."

"Maybe there was something to be found, and the bombs gave someone the time to bury it."

"That might be, but it's up to the police to figure it out. I just worry they're going to be looking for the easy answer—Sarah killed Seth because he beat her. And if the senior center bunch is right, Howard is going to encourage them to believe it."

"Seth may have been a creep, but no one deserves to die like he did. If we want to have any hope of getting the old Sarah back, we need answers. I worry, too, that if she moves out of the woman's shelter and avoids getting arrested, someone may come after her. Whoever needed to shut Seth up might worry that Sarah knows enough to be dangerous, too, and if they were willing to bomb our cars just to distract us, who knows what they might do to Sarah."

"Do you think?" Lauren asked.

"I don't know, but Sarah was unconscious when Seth was shot. She thinks Seth hit her, because Seth always hit her. But what if the killer is the one who knocked her out? What if they think she's dead and then find out she isn't? She wasn't in the hospital very long, but I'm sure the nurses aren't going to tell anyone she was there or where she is now. I really do believe she could be in danger."

Lauren leaned back and ran her hands over her hair.

"Maybe we should let the police handle this one."

"I plan on keeping a low profile." Harriet's grip tightened on the steering wheel. "I just wish we had an idea of which direction the danger is coming from."

"What are you going to tell the rest of the group?"

"I'd like them to keep their eyes and ears open, but that's all. Personally, I'd like to know if the police found out why Joshua was hanging out in my bushes. I'm assuming he wasn't the bomber, or he'd be in jail, and I haven't heard that anyone's been arrested."

"I haven't done a background check on him; I've been working on Sarah's mom and stepdad and her biological father. I can check him out and see what comes up."

Harriet pulled up in front of Mavis's cottage.

"Let me know if you find anything," she said and got out to fetch Mavis.

✂ - - - ✂ - - - ✂

"Is everyone else coming on their own?" Aunt Beth asked when she was safely belted into the middle row of seats, next to Mavis.

Lauren recited the Loose Threads' car status as Harriet drove toward the senior center. Mavis turned slightly to face Beth.

114

"Did you ever get a chance to do the research you were going to do on our new friends at the center?"

Beth pulled a small notebook from her purse.

"As a matter of fact, I did. I went to the library and the newspaper and read a ton of old documents, all of which were on microfiche."

"I would have thought that would all be on computer by now," Mavis commented.

"That's what I thought, and I said as much to the librarian, but she just sighed and said the library would be happy to update its system and if I wanted to bestow a large grant on them, they'd get right on it."

Lauren leaned into the space between the front seats.

"That's all very interesting, but could we get to the point before we arrive? What did you learn?"

Beth looked at Mavis and then cleared her throat.

"To start with, there was absolutely nothing in the paper or anywhere else about Josephine. I checked the old phone books, church registries, every community organization that had filed their annual directory with the library and came up with a big zero."

"I suppose that makes sense if she really is ex-CIA," Harriet said.

"Mickey, on the other hand," Beth continued. "He was all over the legal section of the paper. He was also all over the charitable page and in their newsletters. Several generations of district attorneys attempted to make their career by busting Mickey Brown, none successfully. At the same time, numerous defense attorneys owe their expensive educations to his scholarship fund."

"That's interesting," Harriet said. "Not sure how it helps, but good to know."

"There's more," Aunt Beth said. "The most interesting information I found was about Janice."

"Do tell," Lauren encouraged.

"She was not alone when she had her car accident. She was a passenger in a car driven by none other than Howard Pratt."

"Whoa, that was worth the price of admission," Harriet said.

"Or a day spent in the musty basement of the library," Beth said with a grin. "It seems like it was quite the scandal."

"Which was when?" Lauren interrupted.

"September fifteenth, nineteen ninety-seven."

"So, how old is she?" Harriet asked.

"It says she was twenty-one at the time of the accident, so she's not forty yet," Beth told them.

Lauren leaned back in her seat.

"Wow, I wouldn't have guessed that. I'd have put her at least ten years older."

"So, what was she doing with Howard?" Harriet asked. She did a quick calculation in her head. "He was at least twice her age but probably older than that, judging by Seth and Sarah's ages. I wonder what their relationship was."

She pulled to a stop in the senior center parking lot and undid her seatbelt.

"Wait," Beth said, "there's more. Nineteen ninety-seven was a busy year for Mr. Howard Pratt." She paused for effect. "His wife Jill died under mysterious circumstances earlier that same year."

"Wow," Harriet said and looked at Lauren. "That is a bombshell."

Beth gathered her purse and quilting bag and opened her car door.

"We'll have to mull over what this all means later."

Sabrina was waiting for them in the lobby. Her hair was piled on top of her head and held in place with a clip. She blew at a strand that had fallen over her eye then swept it back with her hand.

"I hope you don't mind, but we've changed the order of things. We're going to have you working with the memory care folks first. Mr. Pratt has reporters from AARP coming to tour in an hour and a half.

"I thought you could work there for forty-five minutes or so, and then we can clean up the quilting supplies and get the residents back to their rooms so the aides can get them ready for prime time." She laughed. Harriet wasn't sure what was supposed to be funny, but she smiled.

✂ - - - ✂ - - - ✂

Violet met Harriet at the junction of the memory care hallway and the main lobby forty minutes later. The rest of the Threads were helping the nurse's aides clean up the quilting debris and load the sewing machine and supplies onto a wheeled cart to take them to the other side of the building.

The dementia quilters had been surprisingly proficient at cutting the required hexagons from the flowered fabric once the Threads got them started, and the time had passed quickly.

Violet glanced left and then right.

"Hurry," she whispered. No one was in sight, so she grabbed Harriet's arm and hustled her across the dining room and then the lobby and back to the independent living common room. "We don't have time to wait for the others." The thick soles of her flesh-colored oxfords made a squeaking noise as she hurried across the linoleum. "We need to talk before the others get here."

Mickey and Jo stood on either side of Janice's wheelchair in the middle of the room as Harriet and Violet approached.

"We need you to search Howard's office," Mickey said.

"Mickey," Janice scolded, "we agreed we were going to lay out our facts in a logical fashion."

Jo held her hand up.

"We don't have time for argument. We have a key to Howard's office, and we have reason to believe he's doing something to the drugs that are being given to the patients in the other wings. We think Seth suspected the drugs weren't right and confronted his dad. You need to go into his office and find proof."

Harriet held her hands up in front of her.

"I'm not a detective, and I don't know if you heard, but my friends' cars were all blown up in my driveway a few days ago. Someone was sending me and my group a message. I received it loud and clear."

"I don't believe it," Jo said.

"It was in the paper," Harriet protested.

"Not that. I don't believe you could be frightened off that easily. The fact that someone is trying to put you off just means they think you're the person who is most likely to find them out. Now is the time to press your advantage, even if you can't see what it is yet."

Mickey leaned toward Harriet.

"Unless you're chicken, that is."

"I can't go wheeling in there, or I would," Janice said in a low voice. "Seth's death is related to something that's going on here. We know it, and you know it. We aren't physically capable of doing a proper investigation. We thought we could count on you."

"Janice was an investigative reporter in Seattle," Violet added, ever the proud mother figure. "She was nominated for a Pulitzer Prize."

Jo's shoulders drooped.

"Forget it, guys. We can't ask a civilian to take a risk she doesn't want to take. She's right. What we're asking her to do is dangerous; the car bombings prove that."

Harriet took a deep breath.

"Okay, I'll do it."

"Do you know how to pick locks?" Mickey asked her.

"I thought you said you had a key." Harriet wiped her palms on the back of her jeans.

"We do," Jo said in a hushed tone. "We have a door key, but if there are records of what he's doing, they're likely to be in a locked file."

"And his office has a private conference room and bath attached," Violet added.

Mickey led the way to the hall.

"I'll stroll over to the memory care unit and keep an eye on Howard. He'll stay over there until the reporters arrive—I heard Hannah say he was meeting them there. But he may decide to bring them to his office, maybe even before they tour.

"If he finishes early or heads to his office before the tour, I'll signal Janice in the dining area, and she can create a distraction. Violet will keep eyes on Janice and will signal Jo so she can warn you.

"I got a guy in the assisted living area who's going to get Hannah off the front desk—they have video monitors up there. We can count on Syd, though, he'll keep her busy. He worked forty years on the carnival circuit; he can con anyone."

Harriet took another deep breath and let it out slowly.

"You guys have thought of everything."

Mickey stopped and looked back to her.

"Get going. You only have fifteen minutes for certain."

Lauren joined Violet and Janice as Harriet went with Jo toward Howard's office and Mickey went to his post as lookout.

"What's going on?" Harriet heard her ask. A moment later, she appeared at her side.

Harriet slid the stolen key into the lock on Howard's office door.

"It appears we're going to search Howard's office after all."

Howard had spared no expense when it came to his surroundings. Harriet imagined Donald Trump's must look something like this—with a million-dollar view added, of course.

The two women stepped into a lush leather-and-brass living room setup. A sofa, love seat and two side chairs surrounded a black glass coffee table. Behind this reception area was a heavy wood desk with a top-line leather chair. A smaller secretary's desk and chair sat to one side. Doors opened off either side of the area—the aforementioned bathroom and conference room, no doubt.

Harriet crossed to the desk, but there were no papers on its surface and a quick check showed the drawers were locked. A credenza behind the desk revealed a row of unlocked horizontal file drawers.

"Take a quick look at these," she said and gestured to the files. "I'm going to check out the conference room, or whatever is behind this door." She stepped toward the door to the right of the desk.

Lauren stood in front of the files.

"You can pretty well guess that if he leaves these unlocked, there isn't going to be anything worth finding."

"Let's look anyway," Harriet said and disappeared into Howard's private conference room. She closed the door behind her.

A large conference table dominated the space. The usual oversized commercial art offerings adorned the walls—pastel squares on an off-white background and a yacht-racing scene done in pale blues. But something was missing. More than one something.

For starters, there were only three chairs, and they were all on one side of the table. And the buffet didn't hold a pitcher and glasses. There were no tablets of paper, no teleconferencing equipment. Instead, the buffet held a precision scale and a bowl of empty capsules. Did they have it wrong? Was *Howard* dealing illegal drugs?

Before she could ponder the answer, the door was flung open.

"Someone's on their way in," Lauren said. "I don't know who, but their key was in the lock." She held her hand to her beating heart. "I thought you had a lookout."

"I do," Harriet whispered. "I did."

"You can come out," said an unfamiliar voice from somewhere near the floor. Harriet's eyes followed the baseboard around the room until she found an old-fashioned speakerphone on the floor. She looked at Lauren, but Lauren shrugged.

"Come on out," the voice said again. "Or else I'm coming in."

Harriet didn't recognize the voice, but it was hard to distinguish, coming from the tinny speaker. She looked at Lauren again then opened the door.

"My, my, who have we here?" said a small blond man. His curly straw-colored hair stopped just short of his shoulders. "Harriet Truman, isn't it? And, I'm sorry. You are?" He reached toward Lauren as if to shake hands. She stared at his hand, frozen.

"Well, never mind, friend of Harriet Truman. As I'm sure you've both guessed, I'm Joshua Pratt, Howard's adopted stepson."

Harriet stepped closer so she could look him in the eye.

"Did you blow up the cars in my driveway?"

The left side of his mouth lifted slightly.

"Of course not. Why on earth would you think that?"

"Maybe because the police found you in my bushes, right after the cars went boom."

Lauren followed Harriet's lead, joining her in front of Joshua.

"I'm going to go out on a limb here and guess that Howard didn't give you that key."

"And if he did?"

"But he didn't," Harriet said. "And we're wasting time."

A knock sounded on the door, followed by a loud whisper.

"Get out now!"

Harriet didn't waste any time. She grabbed Lauren by the arm and pulled her to the door, where they both slipped out into Jo's waiting grasp.

"Come on, Howard's coming."

The older woman led them across the hall and into what appeared to be a locker room for the nurses' aides. No one was sitting at the kitchen table. A door led from the back of the room to a dressing area complete with two showers. From there, another doorway led to a storeroom, which connected to a commercial laundry area and then a residents' laundry room. Finally, they went through a door that deposited them in the main independent living hallway.

"Come on," Jo said, but Lauren leaned against the wall.

"My heart can't take much more of this," she said. "I thought you were the lookout."

"I saw Joshua come into the hall, but we didn't realize he had a key. I can guarantee Howard didn't give it to him. They don't even have a copy of his key in the emergency access key box at the front desk."

Harriet started toward the common room.

"We need to get back to the group."

Jo left them and headed in the opposite direction.

"Do you think Joshua got out?" Lauren asked.

"I don't know, and at the moment, I don't really care, but I'm sure he's used to dealing with his stepdad if he didn't."

✂ - - - ✂ - - - ✂

Aunt Beth's head was bent over her work when Harriet returned to the group, some of whom were busy cutting hexagons from card stock then handing them across the table to other members, who laid them on fabric then cut the shape out again, this time from fabric, leaving a quarter-inch margin outside the paper. Dark spots of color marked her cheeks, the only indication that anything was other than normal.

She looked up at her niece. "Where have you been?"

Harriet could tell from her tone she wasn't making small talk.

Mavis stopped cutting and looked at Harriet as well.

"Violet wouldn't tell us anything, and she seemed to be the only one who knew where you were."

Harriet looked pointedly at a small woman she'd never seen before sitting to Mavis's left. She and another woman had joined the group today.

120

Mavis shrugged, but Harriet was reluctant to speak in front of the new people until they'd gotten some indication from Jo or Mickey whether the newcomers could be trusted to keep their mouths shut and neither one of them had returned yet.

Sabrina hustled in before the pause became awkward.

"How are things going in here? I'm sorry I couldn't check in sooner, but one of the residents from the assisted living area had a small accident in the lobby. He'll be fine, but as you can imagine, we were anxious to take care of him before the visitors came back out there."

"We're fine here," Mavis said. "We need to cut a lot of hexagons from both card stock and fabric. Next time, we'll iron the edges of the fabric over the paper pieces and then we can start whip-stitching the units together. It's all hand sewing, so everyone can work on it."

Sabrina glanced back over her shoulder.

"That's great. If you're sure everything's fine here, I'm going to go see if I can help with our guests."

"We're good," Harriet said and watched as Sabrina disappeared down the hallway.

A moment later, Mickey returned, pushing Janice in front of him. It appeared to Harriet that it was more a case of Mickey using Janice's chair as a walker than him pushing the woman, but she kept her observation to herself.

Everyone was sewing quietly when Jo finally reappeared.

"So, did you have time to find anything out?" she asked.

Harriet glanced again at the two newcomers.

"Don't worry about Eunice and Mary," Mickey told her. "They're part of this."

Aunt Beth set her scissors down on the table.

"If you don't mind, I'd like to know what you've gotten my niece into. I don't appreciate being kept in the dark about it."

Mickey struggled to his feet.

"We meant no offense, Ms. Carlson. We didn't have time to fill you all in. We saw an opportunity and took it."

"Apparently, you had time to tell Harriet and Lauren," Aunt Beth shot back.

Jo leaned across the table toward her.

"I'm sorry. Something terrible is going on here, not the least of which is the murder of Seth Pratt. It took us more than a week to secure a copy of Howard's office key. He guards the place like it's a maximum security prison. A rare opportunity to search it presented itself. As we told your niece, we aren't physically capable of doing some of this stuff ourselves or we would. We had safeguards in place so she wouldn't be caught."

"Except that we were," Lauren said from her spot at the end of the sewing table.

Janice wheeled across the room, looked into the hallway and, apparently seeing no one, wheeled back.

"Joshua isn't going to tell anyone Harriet and Lauren were there. He would have to confess he was there, too, and I assure you, he won't. I'm not sure what his agenda is, but very likely it's similar to ours. He definitely isn't in Howard's inner circle."

"Just because he doesn't like his stepdad, it doesn't mean he's on our side," Harriet observed.

Mickey walked to her side of the table.

"Enough with the chitchat. What did you find?"

Lauren looked at Harriet and waited for her to speak.

"Not much," Harriet finally said. "He has a lot of expensive office furniture. He had files in the outer office that were unlocked. Lauren can tell you about them. I had just gotten into the conference room when Joshua showed up."

"So all this effort was a big waste of time?" Janice asked.

"Let me finish," Harriet said. "We didn't have time to search, but the conference room isn't set up like any meeting room I've ever seen. The table only has chairs on one side, and the credenza has a precision scale and a slew of empty capsules."

"So, he's got an illegal drug operation?" Violet asked.

"Not necessarily," Harriet corrected. "He could be repackaging the drugs that are prescribed for the patients. If he was selling illicit drugs, he wouldn't have needed to send Seth to pharmacy school. Maybe they're diluting the drugs they give patients."

Connie looked up from her stitching.

"They could make a lot of money doing that. Rod's aunt had one prescription that cost seven hundred dollars a month. Her insurance paid for it, but if she was only getting half the dose and her prescription coverage was paying for it, Howard could pocket a really good profit."

She paused for a moment, looking thoughtful.

"Her doctor upped the dosage of her medicine when it wasn't working well enough in the beginning, until eventually her symptoms went away." She shook her head. "I remember him remarking at the time that people who'd never had the drug before usually had a better response to the lower dosage than she did."

Harriet picked up a pencil and a paper hexagon and started tracing more images onto blank card stock.

"If that's the game they're playing, Howard wouldn't have much of a motive to kill Seth. I mean, he was the one figuring out which drugs it was both safe and profitable to dilute. Seems like Howard needed him."

"Maybe the kid grew a conscience," Mickey said. "It happens, you know. I knew a guy once…" The Loose Threads stopped stitching and looked at the old man. "Well, never mind. Let's just say, people never cease to amaze."

Mavis started stitching again.

"So, where does that leave us," she asked without looking up.

No one spoke for a minute.

"I'd like to talk to Joshua," Harriet finally said. "I asked him if he bombed our cars, and he said he didn't."

"Did you think he'd tell you the truth?" Lauren objected.

"Maybe," Harriet continued. "In any case, I'd like to know what he was looking for in Howard's office. He may not be on our team, but I'm still curious. I'd be willing to bet he knows more about what goes on in this place than almost anyone else."

"He seems like a guy who has secrets," Lauren admitted. "By tomorrow, I should know what some of those secrets are. That might give us a little leverage when we talk to him."

Aunt Beth glanced at her watch and put her stitching down.

"I just want to go on record here. I don't think we should be sneaking around this place trying to act like we're the police—or the CIA." She looked directly at Jo for emphasis before continuing. "If we come across evidence in the course of things, fine, but we don't need to be breaking into someone's office or worse. Detective Morse is a competent investigator. If anything comes up, we need to call her."

Mickey shuffled over to Beth's side and stood looking down at her.

"That would be great if the world was a perfect place. I'm here to tell you, dearie, most days it's hard to tell the good guys from the bad guys. Howard has worked very hard to cover himself in a cloak of respectability. The cops are not going to look too hard at the number-one contributor to their charity programs. And you can take that to the bank." He went back to his chair and sat down.

Violet poured a glass of water from a pitcher sitting at the end of the table.

"Pass this to Mickey," she told Connie. "Don't get yourself worked up," she said to him. "You know your heart can't take too much excitement."

Jo cleared her throat.

123

"Can we talk about the business at hand?"

"I thought we were," Connie said.

"I mean the quilt. So far, we're doing scrappy flowers, but have you any idea about what the unifying background color will be? And shouldn't we have a common color for the center of each flower?"

"Jo's right," Violet said. "There are traditions about these things. The centers should be yellow to represent the center of the flower, and then the next row is any color to represent the petals of the flower. We'll have to decide if the flowers will be connected by white for a picket fence or green for a garden path."

"Diós mio," Connie whispered.

"How about we let you ladies decide about the green or white, and I'll come take you to the fabric store and you can pick out that color and whatever yellow you want for the centers," Harriet offered.

"Perfect," Jo said. "How about we go out to lunch, my treat, and pick up fabric on the way home?"

Harriet looked at Lauren, who raised her eyebrow and tilted her head slightly in assent.

"Sounds like a plan."

Chapter 16

Anyone want to come try Jorge's new recipe for Oaxacan grilled shrimp?" said Aiden's disembodied voice over the speaker of Harriet's phone as she began the drive to deposit Mavis, Lauren and her aunt back to their respective homes.

Mavis leaned forward between the front seats and said in a loud voice, "Sounds good to me." She looked back at Beth. "Beth's in, too."

Lauren picked up the phone.

"Sure, why not." She moved it closer to Harriet.

"What time?" Harriet asked.

After a little negotiation, they all decided six o'clock would give the women enough time to all take their dogs out.

"If no one has anything else pressing, it makes more sense for us to do it this way instead of making Harriet come back for us a second time," Mavis pointed out.

Beth pulled her own phone from her purse.

"I'll call Connie and see if she and Rod want to join us. I'll text Jorge if they say yes. They can give Mavis and I a ride home, too, if they come."

"Look at you, all high-tech," Lauren teased. "When did you trade in your Jitter-bug?"—referring to the simplistic phone that was often advertised in the AARP newsletter.

"I never had a Jitter-bug," Beth said when she had finished her call. "My old phone was state-of-the-art in its time."

"Yeah? And when was that? Cell phones aren't made to last more than six months, max. You must have had that one ten years," Lauren said.

Beth completed her text and dropped her smartphone back into her purse.

"They shouldn't punish a person," she said, "for taking proper care of her things. And it was only seven years."

Harriet laughed and glanced at Lauren.

"You'll never win that argument, so you might as well give up."

Lauren just shook her head.

✂ - - - ✂ - - - ✂

Harriet scooted her chair back from the table in the private room.

"I'd say that's a keeper. I can't eat another bite."

"You didn't save room for my flan?" Jorge asked in a hurt voice.

"I suppose I could squeeze some in," she answered with a laugh.

Aunt Beth set her napkin beside her plate.

"Maybe we can talk about what happened today while we let our dinner settle," she said.

Lauren filled the men in on the day's activity.

"Diós mio," Connie said and covered her face in her hands. "And we agreed before we left we weren't going to do anything else that might provoke the bomber."

"That would be easier if we knew who the bomber was," Harriet said. "And for the record, I had no intention of going into Howard's office. I wanted to, but I wasn't going to. That plan was all on the senior citizens who live there. They'd gotten a bootleg key and everything."

"Are you sure they're telling you everything they know?" Aiden asked.

"No, I'm not, but why do you ask? Do you know something?"

He slipped her hand into his.

"I wish I knew something for sure. I just have this vague recollection about the woman in the wheelchair. Janice?

"It was a big scandal in Foggy Point when she had her accident and it came out she was with Howard Pratt. Then it seems like it was all hushed up. My mom had heard some rumors at work."

He stared past her, trying to pull the memories from thin air.

"She wasn't from here. She was some sort of journalist, and she was investigating something or someone." He pressed his lips together. "I just don't remember. I was in high school." He grinned at Harriet. "Chasing girls."

Beth rubbed her hand across her mouth absently.

"I remember the accident was all over the paper when it happened, the part about the up-and-coming journalist being injured. I didn't remember Howard was in the car. You'd think I would have, too, since I think she was investigating the death of Jill Pratt."

126

"She was investigating his wife's death, and the paper didn't mention he was in the car with her?" Harriet asked. "That's rather fishy."

"I'm not sure many people knew what she was here for. I only knew because she came to Avanell's business to interview one of her secretaries. Jill's death was ruled a suicide. I don't know why Janice thought otherwise."

Aiden looked at Beth. "My mom told you and didn't tell me?"

Beth smiled sweetly. "She probably did and you just don't remember. You were fifteen at the time, and as I remember, you didn't listen to much of what your mother said back then."

"I wonder why she thought Howard's wife had been murdered," Harriet said. "I mean, if she wasn't living in Foggy Point, how would it even be on her radar. It wasn't exactly national news, I'm guessing."

Lauren took a sip of her water.

"I wonder why she got into a car with the guy if she thought he'd murdered his wife."

Jorge came in from the kitchen balancing a tray of dessert dishes filled with his creamy flan.

"Is it too obvious to just ask the señorita?"

Harriet put her hands around the dish he handed her as he made his way around the table.

"We could, but first, we don't know her very well, and second, with all the discussion about Seth's murder and the group's suspicion about Howard's involvement in that, she's never mentioned her relationship with him. It seems like if she suspected him of killing his wife, she'd have said something about that. Since she didn't, I have to wonder why."

Lauren took a bite of her flan.

"Mmmm, this is soooo good." She closed her eyes as she swallowed then opened them and looked at Harriet. "I'm with you. We need to find out a little more about her relationship with Howard before we ask her anything. Mickey and Jo seem to trust her, but what if they don't know she had a previous relationship of some sort with Howard. She could even be spying for him."

"That wouldn't be good," Harriet said.

Aiden took her hand again.

"Another reason for you all to back off."

"I'm taking Jo and Violet fabric shopping tomorrow. I'll see what they know."

Lauren turned toward Harriet.

"Are you sure Janice isn't coming with you?"

"I'll fold the back seat of my car up and throw something in the space; then there won't be room for her and her chair. And by the way, that's 'us.' Coming with *us*."

127

Lauren rolled her eyes but didn't say anything.

"That's not polite, excluding a handicapped person," Beth scolded.

Harriet looked at her aunt.

"Keeping secrets isn't polite, either. I get that maybe it's too painful for her to talk about her accident and the time surrounding it, but Sarah's in trouble. We don't have the luxury of being able to be considerate of everyone. If I can get the information from Jo tomorrow, Janice staying home will be a small price to pay for her not having to talk about it."

"My son is taking me car shopping in Seattle tomorrow," Mavis said. "I'll be back before dinnertime. Call me and let me know what, if anything, you find out."

"Are you getting another Lincoln Towncar?" Rod asked her.

"My boys want me to get a new car. They said they'd feel better if I drove something with all the latest safety features. So, no Towncar."

"Don't they make Towncars anymore?" Harriet asked.

Mavis sighed. "Sadly, no."

Beth reached over and patted her on the back.

"You'll live."

Chapter 17

Lauren set a paper cup of hot chocolate down on Harriet's cutting table.

"Here," she said, setting her cup of coffee next to it while she took off her black fleece jacket and tossed it onto a chair. "I figured we needed some fortification before we take on Violet and Jo. And we need a plan."

Harriet took a sip.

"My plan is to tell Jo what we've heard about Janice's past and ask her what the deal is."

"Do you think she'll tell you, just like that?"

"If she really is who she claims to be, she'll have done some checking up on her co-conspirators. If she claims no knowledge, then she either isn't an ex-spy or she has another agenda. I'm guessing she knows. Why she hasn't told us before now will be the interesting part."

Lauren pointed at the quilt top Harriet had spread out on her cutting table.

"Is that for the women's shelter?"

Harriet sighed. "It is. Or it will be, when I get the design worked out. The panel in the center is called 'The Healing Tree.' I've been trying out various pieced blocks to put around it, but I'm not sure any of them is going to work."

"Are you trying to soften the boldness of the tree image?"

"That was my plan, but I'm not sure it's possible. Maybe I'll just make a wall hanging from the panel and donate it at their next fundraiser. Then I can make something simpler for the shelter."

"We should get some of whatever fabric Jo and Violet choose and take it to the shelter for the flower blocks Sarah's going to do so they'll all co-ordinate."

"Good idea," Harriet said and took another sip of her hot chocolate.

"I do have one every now and then, you know."

"You know, I was thinking about Sarah. With Seth dead, I wonder how long she'll be able to stay at the women's shelter."

Lauren picked at a thread on the edge of one of the quilt blocks.

"Having her stepdad trying to blame her for her stepbrother's murder has to be some sort of mental abuse."

"If that's true," Harriet said. "We've been told Howard is going to blame Sarah, but I'm not sure we have any evidence that he is."

"Good point."

"I say we worry about one thing at a time. Let's go get Violet and Jo and see if we can figure out what Janice's deal is."

Lauren picked up her purse and messenger bag.

"Lead the way," she said.

Harriet's ruse to keep Janice from coming to the fabric store proved un-necessary. Violet and Jo were waiting alone in the lobby of the senior center, coats on and purses in hand, when she pulled into the pick-up/drop-off lane in front of the building.

"Are you two ready to go look at some fabric?" she asked when she joined them.

Violet smiled.

"Good morning, Harriet. I'm glad you decided we should go to the fabric store before lunch instead of after. I get sleepy after I eat."

Jo scanned the lobby.

"Let's get out of here before anyone sees us."

"Is there a problem?" Harriet asked as she pressed the blue handicapped button next to the door. The double glass doors swung open.

"You can't be too careful," Jo told her. "You never know who might be watching."

Lauren stood by the curb.

"That's what I always say. Here, let me hold your purse while you get in."

Harriet took Violet to the opposite side of the car and helped her in.

"Were there any repercussions after our last visit?" Harriet asked as she guided her car out of the senior center driveway.

"Pfft," Jo scoffed. "Howard is so sure he's smarter than everyone it doesn't occur to him that someone could get past his defenses. He put an expensive pickproof lock on his office door and then carried the key around on a monogrammed ring in his pocket. Mickey made an impression with a bar of soap and had the key back in Howard's pocket before he'd had a chance to miss it."

"Speaking of Howard," Harriet said, keeping her eyes on the road. "We've been doing a little research about Janice's accident."

"And you found out that Janice was investigating the death of Howard's second wife," Jo said before Harriet could continue.

"Was she?" Harriet shot back. "I was going to say he was driving the car when she had her accident."

Lauren turned and looked at Jo in the back seat.

"We do find it a little curious that now she's living at Howard's facility. I'd like to know if we're sure whose team she's playing on."

"Howard makes a big show of how guilty he feels," Jo said. "He refers to the 'terrible accident' that put her in that chair and fawns over her. For her part, she doesn't remember the accident or the time right before it. I tapped a few resources and did as much research as I dared do without raising suspicion, and here's what I know.

"Janice was a pretty, young investigative journalist who showed up in Foggy Point for no known reason. It's clear she entered into a personal relationship with Howard. What isn't clear is if she was doing it to get information from him about his wife's death or if she just succumbed to his charms. I'm sure, if he did have anything to do with Jill's death, he wouldn't be above using romance to throw her off the story."

Harriet made eye contact with Jo in the rearview mirror.

"I suppose she doesn't talk about it."

"She'd like to think she was working undercover, but she just doesn't remember."

"I never knew Janice back then," Violet said sweetly. "But Howard's wife Jill came to work at the hospital while I was a volunteer there. She was a nurse. I can't remember if she was an RN or an LPN." She thought for a moment then shook her head. "Well, that doesn't matter. What I remember is that she was very accident-prone, if you know what I mean."

Lauren turned to look at her.

"Just to be clear, why don't you tell us what you mean?"

"She ran into doorknobs and tripped on stairs—that sort of thing. Never at work, of course. She would come to work with a black eye or limping. I mean, really, how many people walk into a door more than once."

131

Harriet glanced into the rearview mirror.

"Did you ask her about it?"

"Of course we did. You know how that goes, though. She made excuses and assured us we were wrong. She asked us not to make any trouble for her. It went unsaid that she was worried how much worse it might get if we did."

"How did she die?" Harriet asked.

"We were told she committed suicide."

"Except you don't believe it?" Lauren said.

"What choice did we have but to believe it? I went to the hospital, and there was a sign at our station saying she'd died by her own hand and offering grief counseling to anyone who wanted it. They also had someone from the women's shelter come talk to us about recognizing the signs of abuse and telling people what their options were if they were the one being abused, but it was locking the barn after the horse was stolen."

The smile had left Violet's face, and she sagged back into her seat when she was finished speaking.

Jo turned to her. "This would have been useful information to know before now."

Tears filled Violet's eyes, and Jo reached over and patted her hand.

"It's okay. It wouldn't have changed anything we've done so far."

"Have you had any more thoughts about your fabric?" Harriet asked, ending the discussion about Howard and his dead wife.

✂ - - - ✂ - - - ✂

The quilters at the senior center had decided to set their blocks on a green background, and Violet found a perfect fabric at Pins and Needles. Jo selected a yellow for the centers, and Harriet had Marjory cut enough of each for both the senior center and the women's shelter and then had a yard and a half of each color cut for herself.

She wasn't sure how well the memory care folks were going to be able to do their share of the blocks and wanted to be prepared in case the Loose Threads had to make extra blocks to be sure they could make a full-sized quilt.

"Are you sure you don't mind driving to the Cafe on Smuggler's Cove?" Jo asked when the women were back in the car. "I made us a reservation, but I could cancel if you don't want to drive that far."

Lauren held her hand up, her first and second fingers twined around each other.

"Harriet and Chef James are like this."

Harriet turned in her seat and spoke to her back seat passengers.

"Don't listen to her. I'm actually a substitute on his dog Cyrano's support team. He is a racing wiener dog."

Violet smiled. "Does that mean we'll get chef's specials for lunch?"

"I don't know about that," Harriet said and pulled her seatbelt on, "but anything he cooks is going to be fabulous."

"Hey, Harriet," James said as she followed Violet, Lauren and Jo into the restaurant. "If I'd known you were coming, I'd have prepared something special."

She pointed at a small sign standing on the maître'd's desk.

"Looks like you did make something special."

"Of course, but I'd have made something extra-special. " James leaned in and gave her a quick hug.

"How's the racer?"

He picked up four menus and signaled the women to follow him.

"I got this," he said to his lunchtime hostess. "Cyrano is training hard and looking forward to his next set of qualifying races. I'll tell him you asked."

"Have the police figured out who vandalized your car?" Harriet asked.

"No. Not even a hint. Their best guess is random violence by disaffected youth."

"Did you hear about the bombing at my house?"

"Are you kidding?" James stopped at a table with a view of the cove and pulled out chairs for Jo and Violet. "Everyone in Foggy Point is talking about it. I heard your car was safely in the garage. That's good, at least."

"Mine was totaled, thanks for asking," Lauren said.

He smiled. "Sorry for your loss. I didn't realize you'd lost a car. If you'll allow me to, I'll make it up to you in chocolate."

"Say yes," Harriet encouraged her.

Lauren looked at her and then James.

"If you say so."

The four women were opening their menus when Hannah Pratt stopped by their table.

"Hey, Harriet, Violet." She gestured to include Lauren and Jo. "When I saw you at the dog races with that guy, Aiden told me he was a chef at the best restaurant in town. I thought I'd try it out."

Harriet smiled at her.

"What did you think? 'That guy,' as you call him, is not *a* chef here, he is *the* chef. And he owns the place. I've never been disappointed in anything he's prepared."

Violet set her menu down.

"He has a real gift for chocolate. His mousse is to die for."

Hannah grinned. "I had his Death by Chocolate. It was fabulous."

The hostess cleared her throat discretely. Hannah looked at her and realized she was blocking access to the next table.

"I guess I better go. Hope I don't fall asleep on the way back to work." She waved and left.

Lauren glanced at Hannah's back and then at the table she had just vacated. There were dishes for two people.

"I wonder who she was lunching with."

Harriet took her napkin from beside her plate and unfolded it onto her lap.

"Apparently, someone who left before her."

✄ - - - ✄ - - - ✄

An hour and a half later, Harriet again guided her car into the drop-off area in front of the senior center. Jo unhooked her seatbelt.

"I may never eat again," she said. "I've had lunch and dinner there more than once and never were we given so much food."

"That's the Harriet effect," Lauren told her.

Harriet opened her door.

"I know one of James's friends, and we went there when it first opened, before it was popular. He's never forgotten my loyalty."

"Yeah, right," Lauren muttered.

"I'm going to run in and talk to Hannah for a minute," Harriet told her.

"I'll help carry the fabric," Lauren said.

Jo and Violet thanked her for driving them then went with Lauren to their common room. Harriet watched until they were out of sight.

"Hey, Hannah, how's it going?"

Hannah flipped the wand microphone she was wearing away from her face.

"Peachy. Mr. Carrigan in the memory care unit broke out a window with a chair and tried to escape."

"Is he okay?"

"Yeah, the windows have safety glass, like in cars. It cracked into lots of little pieces, but the chair only made a small hole all the way through. The old geezer wore himself out swinging the chair, so he couldn't climb out."

"What will they do about it?"

"What they always do—up his meds."

"Can I talk to you about something else?" Harriet asked.

Hannah stood and looked in all directions.

"Sure, but if you see Howard coming, walk away."

"Okay…Are you not allowed to talk to the public? It seems like it would be part of your job."

"The public, yes. You? No. Howard's no fool. He knows you're not talking to me about a new place for your aunt to live. Anyway, you better get to the point before he shows up."

"I need to talk to Joshua."

"Good luck with that."

"Doesn't he live at your dad's?"

"Yes and no. He stays in a converted garden shed on the property, but he isn't there any more than he has to be. Personally, I think he's got somewhere else he crashes most of the time."

"Back to my question. Do you know how to get hold of him?"

"He doesn't answer his phone, and I don't know when we'll cross paths at home, 'cause, frankly, I try to spend as much time away from home as he does."

"So, what if it was an emergency?"

"I guess I could text him for you. He doesn't answer his phone," she repeated. She thought for a minute. "I could leave him a voice mail. Meet him in a public place."

"Why? Do you think he's dangerous?"

"I'm not convinced he isn't the one who killed Seth."

"Have you told the police that?"

"Of course not. My dad is the family spokesman. I keep my mouth shut, my head down, and look forward to the day I can live anywhere but Foggy Point."

"What makes you think he killed Seth? Do you have proof?"

"Joshua sees himself as Cinderella and Seth as an evil stepsister. He was always jealous of Seth and told anyone who would listen all about it."

"Was he treated differently?"

Hannah was quiet for a moment.

"I suppose. But he brought it on himself. He talked back to Dad all the time, and he got in trouble with the police. He wasn't grateful at all for anything Dad did for him. And he and Seth didn't get along at all." Hannah glanced at the security monitors then back at Harriet. "Where should he contact you?"

Harriet reached into her purse and pulled out a card for her long-arm business.

"Here's my business card. It has my phone number on it. He can call me."

"Okay. You better go now before my dad comes."

"Has he said something to you about me?" Harriet asked.

"Nothing specific. He's convinced you and your group know where Sarah is, and he's not thrilled that no one will tell him."

"Good to know. Thanks, Hannah."

"Sure," she said and repositioned the microphone in front of her mouth.

Harriet went back out to the car. Lauren was already sitting in the passenger seat.

"How'd you get out here without passing the reception desk?"

"Jo's room has a patio. Mickey called and said Howard was prowling the halls, so she let me out through her room, just as a precaution."

"I'll be surprised if she doesn't turn out to be ex-CIA. She certainly is paranoid."

"I wasn't eager to encounter Howard. If what Violet said about him abusing Jill is true, I don't want to run into him in a well-lit, antiseptic-smelling hallway."

"I got the same vibe from Hannah. She seemed really spooked when I stopped to talk to her. She checked the hallways and kept an eye on her monitors. She said Howard thinks we're withholding information about where Sarah is—which, of course, we are."

Lauren leaned her head back against her headrest.

"Maybe it's time for us to lay it all on the line to Detective Morse, let her deal with the crazy man."

Harriet sighed. "Yeah, maybe. Let's go talk to Aunt Beth and Mavis and see what they think."

Chapter 18

*L*auren swiped her phone and dropped it into the pocket of her messenger bag.

"Your aunt and Mavis aren't going to be available until dinnertime. One of them will arrange a dinner meeting for whoever is available and let us know. That being the case, can you drop me back at my place? I can get some work done between now and then."

Harriet turned in the direction of Lauren's apartment.

"Good idea, I can do some stitching, and we can both think about what we heard today."

The women spent the rest of the trip lost in their own thoughts.

"Hey, do you have company?" Harriet asked and pointed to the nondescript beige sedan parked in Lauren's designated spot as she pulled to the curb.

"Yes. I mean no. I don't have company, I do have a company car. Hallelujah, we have been loosed from our bondage."

Harriet looked at her.

"It hasn't been that horrible, has it?"

"Getting rides from you? No. Not being able to drive anywhere, ever? Excruciating. I actually had to dig out a coffee pot and make my morning coffee at home a couple of times."

Harriet laughed. "Oh, the pain of it all."

$\times$ - - - $\times$ - - - $\times$

Before the bombing, Harriet sometimes left her car in the driveway if she knew she was going out again. Since then, she locked it in the garage even if she was just going back into the house for five minutes.

She had barely secured the door into the house and taken her coat off when she heard a soft knocking on her studio door. Scooter ran to it before her, jumping up and down and barking. Harriet peeked out the bow window before opening the door.

"Joshua?"

"Don't act so surprised. Hannah said you wanted to see me. Here I am."

Not quite the public place Hannah had suggested, Harriet thought, but if she suggested meeting elsewhere at this point, she might lose him.

"Come in," She said and stepped aside. "Can I get you something to drink? Water? Soda?"

Joshua kept his hands in his jeans pockets, rhythmically jingling his change.

"Water's fine. Look, I'm here. Can we skip the happy hostess routine and jump to the part where you tell me why?"

Harriet led him into the kitchen, filled a glass with ice and poured filtered water into it from a pitcher in her refrigerator.

"What can you tell me about your mother's death?" she asked when he was seated at her table.

"She didn't kill herself, if that's what you're asking."

"Do you know who did?"

"Do you?"

"A woman I talked to today said an investigative journalist thought your father killed her."

Joshua took a sip of his water then set the glass back on the table.

"And look where that got her."

"Do you think he killed her?"

"What I think is Howard—who, by the way, is not my father—has a lot of power, and he'll use it against anyone who even suggests my mom was anything but a depressed drunk who died from an overdose after several failed attempts at suicide."

"Have *you* tried to prove otherwise?"

He studied her a long moment before speaking, as if he were choosing which version of the story he was going to tell her.

"I was in high school when my mom died. There were no other close relatives, so Howard adopted me. I'm not sure why, other than he was afraid I might ask awkward questions."

"Did you?" Harriet asked.

"When I graduated from high school, I made an appointment with the medical examiner. I just wanted to read her autopsy report myself. Before

I could meet with her, I was arrested on some trumped-up charge. Howard claimed I stole a gun from him and was carrying it around without a license, or something like that.

"It was completely bogus, but magically, a gun appeared in my car and, equally magically, a deal was struck and I had an ankle bracelet and was confined to home. My scholarship went out the window as well as any chance of getting a job in this town. I'm still on some never-ending probation, so I can't leave Foggy Point. Since no one will hire me for anything but the most menial of jobs, I have no chance of hiring my own lawyer to contest it."

Harriet leaned back in her chair, and Scooter jumped into her lap. "Wow."

"Yeah, welcome to my world. I should have killed Howard the first time he hit my mom—you know, kill the head, and the body will die; it would have saved the whole family. I would have been prosecuted as a minor. A few years in jail, and I would be free and my mom would still be alive. And Sarah never would have met Howard Junior—that's Seth to you outsiders.

"Instead, Howard's reign of terror continues, and the next generation is ruined. We're lucky Seth died before he and Sarah had a chance to procreate."

"Why *didn't* you kill him?" Harriet asked, watching his face for a reaction.

"Despite what you may have heard from Howard or Seth, I'm not that kind of person. Even knowing he was hurting my mom, I couldn't do something like that. I'd like to think that, if I'd known he was going to kill her, I'd have done something. I'll have to live with that guilt for the rest of my life."

"Is there nothing you can do about your current situation?"

"Like I said, short of Howard falling dead, I'm stuck here as long as he wants me to be. If I had any money, I could buy a fake identity and get out of here, but between my criminal record and Howard's connections, it's going to take me years.

"Howard is such a charitable guy, he charges me rent to live in the garden shed. He's making sure I can't escape. Personally, I think he's biding his time before he kills me, too. There will be some convenient accident, and that will be that."

"Do you seriously think he'd harm you?"

"Have you not been listening to me? The man has harmed me from the moment my mother took me to live with him. He's a sadist. He killed my mother. I don't *think* he'll harm me, I *know* he will. It's just a matter of when."

"Do you think he killed Seth?"

"I don't know, but I think it's possible. He and Seth were working some angle at the senior center. That place is way too profitable. I know he made Seth go to pharmacy school. I think maybe they're selling drugs on the Internet. I'm sure they're defrauding Medicaid and Medicare. Maybe Howard's fair-haired boy rebelled."

"Do you think they've killed patients?"

"Anything is possible, but if they did, I don't think it would be intentional. They need people in beds to rack up charges. If anything, they could be guilty of not sending a person to the hospital when the patient exceeded the level of care they can provide."

"So, what are you going to do about Seth's death?"

"It's not up to me to do anything. You act like Seth's a victim here. I realize he's dead, but he's not the hero in this drama, by any stretch of the imagination. He may have been planning to out Howard, but only if it meant he could take over the empire or inherit everything or gain in some other way.

"I know you're friends with Sarah. How can you feel anything for a guy who would do that to someone he supposedly cared about? Believe me, despite what Sarah says, the world is a better place without Seth Pratt in it. I'm spending *my* time trying to figure out how not to join him."

"If you didn't blow up our cars, do you think Howard could have?"

"He wouldn't get his own hands dirty, but I'd say yes, it's possible or even probable that he had someone bomb your cars. It's the sort of thing he does. He intimidates without ever rising to the level that the police would investigate too hard, and keep in mind he has half the force in his back pocket. He makes a point of having dirt on all his employees and what pass for friends in his world. He can always find someone to do that sort of thing for him."

"Are you sure you don't want something more than water to drink? I have some brownies my friend Mavis made, too."

"Do you have milk?"

Harriet smiled.

"Coming right up."

✂ - - - ✂ - - - ✂

Joshua stayed for another half-hour, eating brownies and talking about his life before his mother died. Two things were clear—Joshua had been a bright child. He'd earned a full scholarship to the University of Washington. And his mother had buffered him from Howard before her death.

Harriet was still sitting at her table pondering Joshua's visit when she heard another tap on her studio door. From Scooter's wiggling, yipping reaction, she was certain she knew who she'd find on her porch.

Chapter 19

iden." She stood aside so he could come through the open doorway. "Is anything wrong?"

"Can't a guy stop by to see his favorite…"

Harriet took a deep breath and was about to speak.

"…patient," he finished.

She smiled. "Nice recovery."

"I'm sorry. I know I'm not supposed to put any relationship pressure on you. My counselor reminds me every time we meet. But you *are* my favorite everything. When that's my reality, it's hard to keep it under wraps all the time."

"It's my reality, too, but that doesn't mean it's right. Until we figure out this…this…thing with your sister, we've got to keep our distance. We've tried ignoring it, and we both know that didn't work."

Aiden headed toward the kitchen, running his hand through his silky black hair as he went.

"Have you got any coffee?"

Harriet picked up Scooter and followed Aiden.

"I don't have any already made, but it will only take a minute. Do you have time?"

"Sure. My afternoon surgery got canceled, and appointments were light, so we drew straws. Mac is spending the afternoon catching up on the latest journals in the office, the techs are taking care of our current inpatients and the rest of us are having some well-deserved time off.

"By the way, speaking of my sister, she's getting better. You know she was in residential treatment for a while."

"Are you saying she isn't anymore?"

"She's living in a halfway house and doing work for the public defender's office."

"That was quick."

"While she was in the residential program, they put her on medication. I guess it's working. She seems really different."

"Bad different or good different?"

Aiden smiled. "Good, of course. And she's been talking to Pastor Hafer. He's setting up a meeting for her and Carla to talk. She really wants to make amends."

"Please don't tell me she wants to talk to me."

She set Scooter in his foam bed and picked an individual pod of coffee from a rack that sat next to her new individual-cup coffeemaker, popped it into the machine and put a cup under the spout before pushing the go button.

"Okay, I won't tell you, but she's going to want to talk to you. It's part of her therapy."

Harriet turned her back on him and rolled her eyes skyward.

"On a totally other subject, has Hannah said anything about her brother Joshua since the bombing?"

"I told you before, she doesn't usually talk about her family, but I did make a point of asking her after the police found him near your house when the bombs went off. She said he's a psychopath and can appear more normal than normal if you don't know him. She says he tortured small animals when he was a kid and set fires."

"Wow. Isn't that textbook psychopath-in-the-making behavior? That must have been tough to live with growing up."

"I'm getting the idea the whole Pratt family was tough to live with. Look at Sarah."

"She may be self-centered, but Sarah's not evil."

"No, but she definitely fell into the victim role easily enough."

"That's not fair."

Aiden drew back to look at her.

"Since when did you become a Sarah fan?"

She took his steaming cup from the machine and handed it to him.

"Since she's so hurt. She may be annoying when she's feeling well, but you should have seen her the last time we visited. She's a wreck, and I'm not sure she'll ever recover."

"That's too bad. At least Seth isn't going to get the chance to kill her. She should be thankful for that."

"I'm pretty sure she doesn't see it that way. In spite of everything, she still loves the guy."

"That's really sick."

Harriet picked up the now-cold cup of tea she'd been drinking when Joshua had been there.

"Joshua thinks Howard Pratt killed his mother."

"He could just be paranoid, or lying."

She sat down at the table opposite him.

"So, given all we know, who do *you* think killed Seth?"

Aiden leaned back, closed his eyes and ran both hands through his hair. After a moment, he blew his breath out.

"If you had asked me that question a year ago, I'd have said it must have been a stranger, because what upstanding citizen of Foggy Point could kill their own flesh and blood. After my uncle killed my mother, and my sister did...what my sister did, I was questioning whether I could trust myself around my loved ones."

Harriet started to protest, but he raised his hand to silence her.

"I've spent hours of my recent therapy talking to my counselor about the subject, and I accept that my uncle and my sister are responsible for their own actions. I even believe our bloodline isn't cursed—at least, most of the time."

He gave her the crooked smile that melted her heart every time she saw it. She reached across the table and took his hand.

"To answer your question, I don't know. Howard is an obnoxious self-promoter, and it seems like he's got half of Foggy Point in his pocket. On the other hand, he always talked about Seth like he was the anointed one. I assumed he was grooming him to take over the empire. It doesn't make sense that he would send him off to school so he could become his resident pharmacist and then turn around and kill him. Besides, shooting someone doesn't seem like Howard's style."

Harriet gave him a wry smile.

"And what, pray tell, *is* Howard's style?"

Aiden smiled back.

"Oh, I don't know. If we believe he killed his former wife—poison. Or maybe in a car accident, if we believe *those* rumors. He just seems way too sneaky to do something as straightforward as shooting someone himself."

"If not Howard, then who else?"

"Clearly, the psychopath brother has to be a candidate, but you know, it's still possible it's someone we don't know."

"I suppose, but if you believe all the true crime shows, you're more likely to be killed by one of your loved ones."

Scooter came over and put his front paws on Aiden's leg. He scooped the dog up with one hand and deposited him absently onto his lap.

"By all accounts, there wasn't much love to be had in that family."

"I just had a thought," Harriet said. "With the three wives we know about and the mix of half- and step-siblings, I wonder if there's an additional wife or kids we don't know about. There may be people who have either been driven away or escaped.

"I need to go check on Sarah again anyway. Maybe, if she's stronger, I can see if she knows. If Seth has always been the favored son, maybe there's a resentful sibling out there."

"I wouldn't hold your breath on that one."

"Have you got a better idea?"

He pressed his lips together.

"Hmmm, nothing really comes to mind, other than maybe letting the police handle this one."

"And let Howard railroad Sarah?"

"You don't even know he's doing that. I mean, I'm sure the folks at the senior center are wonderful people, but *they're* not the police, either. It might all be in their collective imagination."

"You're right. I need to talk to Detective Morse."

Aiden closed his eyes as if struggling for strength.

"You are impossible."

Harriet grinned. "Yeah, but that's why you like me."

<hr />

Harriet went directly to the big room in the back of Tico's Tacos. Aunt Beth had called to say she'd rounded up as many of the Loose Threads as she could, and that Jorge was fixing a special dinner for the group.

"Is that garlic bread I smell?" she asked her aunt.

Beth was already seated at the big table.

"Jorge had a craving for Italian food tonight, so he made us spaghetti and meatballs."

"You ladies are my trial," Jorge said as he came into the room with an antipasto platter arranged with slices of hard salami, cheese, and marinated artichoke hearts, sun-dried tomatoes and olives. "Depending on your reaction, I'm thinking I might have an international cuisine night once a month."

"I vote yes," Lauren said as she arrived. "We need a little more variety in this town." She turned to Harriet. "Do you have time to stitch on my quilt for the shelter? I finished the top this afternoon. Hopefully, they're not expecting fine art. This one's fairly simple."

145

"Simple and done is what they need," Aunt Beth told her. "I'm sure anything you made is going to look nice enough."

Lauren smiled at her.

"I guess."

"Do I smell—" DeAnn started.

"Garlic bread," Harriet finished for her. "Jorge's experimenting on us."

DeAnn sat down opposite Harriet and her aunt.

"Sounds good to me, I'm starving. I worked on my quilt for the shelter while the boys were at school and Kissa was at her play group. I think she looks forward to seeing Wendy there."

"It's wonderful that she's adjusted so well since you adopted her," Beth said.

Mavis and Connie came in, followed a few minutes later by Carla and then Robin. When the last two were seated at the table and Jorge had placed pitchers of iced tea and water on the table, Beth picked her flipchart up and set it in front of her place.

"Let's get started before Jorge starts delivering food."

Harriet stood up beside her aunt.

"It'll be easier if I just make notes on the chart of what I've learned this afternoon." She flipped pages until she came to a blank. She wrote *Howard, Joshua* and then a question mark across the top. Then, she wrote what Aiden told her Hannah had said about Joshua under his name and what Joshua had said about his stepdad under Howard's. Under the question mark, she wrote "possible other wives and children."

Lauren pointed to the last column.

"What's that supposed to mean?"

"When I was talking to Aiden today it occurred to me that, with the three wives and tangled collection of children and stepchildren Howard has had, it's possible there are more."

Lauren thought about that for a moment.

"I suppose that's possible, but given the ages of the children we know about, and the fact that he was married to all their mothers when they were born, it would be hard for him to have squeezed anyone else in. I'll dig around on the Internet and see what I can find."

Robin tilted her chair back.

"So, Joshua thinks Howard did it, and Hannah thinks it was Joshua. I wonder who Sarah suspects."

Mavis took a sip of her tea.

"Another way to look at it is who was abusing whom. Howard ab-used Joshua, may have killed his second wife, and, at the very least, has Sarah's mother cowed, but he's probably abusing her as well. Seth was abusing Sarah. I wonder if Howard was also beating Sarah."

"I'll ask Aiden to pay attention to Hannah and see if he thinks she's being abused. From what Georgia at the shelter told us, domestic violence tends to spread in a family."

Lauren pulled out her smartphone and keyed the notepad app.

"I think I'll do a little digging and see what happened to Seth's mother. No one has mentioned her. It would be interesting to see if she's dead or alive."

Carla twirled a strand of hair around her finger.

"If Seth's mother is dead under suspicious circumstances, would that move Howard to the top of the list?"

"Diós mio," Connie said. "If she's dead, too, it could make Howard a serial killer."

"Let's stick with what we know for sure," Robin cautioned.

Harriet rested her elbow on the table and her chin on her fist.

"We're missing something here, something big. We've got all sorts of clues indicating that Howard is a bad guy. If we believe Joshua—and I have to say what Lauren and I saw makes me inclined to believe him—Howard is cutting the drugs prescribed for the residents of the senior center then selling the excess on the Internet. Joshua says he's defrauding Medicare and Medicaid, also.

"Janice was investigating him for the murder of his second wife, and we've heard it suggested that Seth's mother was his first wife and she, too, died under mysterious circumstances. What we haven't heard is any real reason Howard would want Seth dead."

Lauren tapped the fingers of her right hand on the table.

"You know, to a lesser degree, the same could be said about Joshua. We've heard he's a psychopath and that he is, at the very least, on probation for some unspecified crime. He says he hates Howard and believes the man killed his mom—but again, no Seth tie-in."

"Hannah did say Joshua resented Seth for being the favored son." Harriet reminded her.

Lauren gave her a sarcastic look.

"Really? So he kills his brother because he got better toys when they were growing up?"

Aunt Beth smiled. "She's right, honey. That's not much of a motive for murder."

Harriet sat down as Jorge entered, setting baskets of garlic bread at each end of the table. She picked up a piece of the bread and used it to point at the flipchart.

"We need to find information—different information. We've established that Howard is probably a criminal, so we don't need more corroborating evidence of that. Same with Joshua. We need a motive for one of them or, failing that, someone else to commit murder." She bit into her bread.

"What about Janice?" DeAnn asked. "Could she be more than she appears?"

Lauren laughed. "Anyone could be. Janice could be lying about her memory loss. She could have been lying about her investigation of Howard. We could pick a name out of a hat."

Harriet accepted a glass of water from Jorge's waitress and took a sip.

"Maybe we're going about this wrong. Maybe what we need is more information about Seth. Why would anyone want him dead?"

"What are you thinking, honey?" Aunt Beth asked.

"We need to talk to Sarah again and maybe Joshua and Hannah. Maybe one of them would have an idea why he'd be a target. We've established he was abusive to Sarah, and that gives her a motive, but we need to find out who else might have wanted him dead."

"I could go talk to Sarah's mother," Beth offered. "Maybe I can get her to go out to tea. I may have to offer more bibs or lap quilts or something, but I think she'll go for it. Connie, maybe you can go with me, since you've had interactions with her, too. She probably won't confess if she killed him herself, but maybe she can tell us if Seth had conflicts with anyone else."

"Good idea," Mavis said. "My son went to school with the medical examiner's little brother. I could go see what she can tell me about Howard's first and second wives' deaths. I know that doesn't tell us anything about motives for killing Seth, but it could help us sort out who is lying to us and who isn't."

Robin wrote a note about the medical examiner at the bottom of the flip chart page.

"I think anything we can learn can't hurt," she said as she wrote.

Lauren pulled a stylus from the back of her smartphone case and tapped the face of her phone.

"I'm going to get some of my geek buddies working on Joshua and his criminal troubles. There's something fishy going on there."

Jorge had been making trips between the kitchen and the private dining room, carrying a big bowl of salad one time and a dish of grated Parmesan the next. He finally brought a large platter of spaghetti and meatballs and set it on the table.

"Has everyone got what they want to drink?" He looked around the table. The women nodded in assent. "I'd like to say one thing, and then

I'll keep my mouth shut." He paused to see if anyone objected then continued. "You need to talk to Detective Morse about your suspicions and let her handle it. It's her job. She's probably already interviewed the mother. Now, please enjoy your dinner."

Beth smiled at him.

"Can you sit and eat with us?"

"I think I can join you for a few minutes, if the rest of the group agrees."

"Of course we want you," Robin said. "We need someone to help keep us grounded—and if I keep eating here, I'll be grounded in more ways than one."

Jorge smiled as he pulled out a chair and sat down beside Aunt Beth.

"Let's eat," he said

Chapter 20

Words can't express how happy I am to have a car again," Aunt Beth told Harriet and Mavis as she slid into a chair at Harriet's kitchen table. "Would you like to come out and look at it?"

Lauren came in from Harriet's studio.

"I'm sure it's the most wonderful car ever made, but can we have some coffee first?"

"Of course. Have a seat—she doesn't really expect anyone here is going to pass up our coffee and muffins to look at her new car. I brewed yours when I heard you drive up."

Beth poured a dollop of half-and-half into her cup and stirred it.

"I still can't get used to the fact that my current car costs more than my first house, and I don't even have a luxury car."

Mavis took a muffin from a platter in the middle of the table and peeled the paper off before setting in on the small plate in front of her and then passed the plate to Lauren.

"I try not to think about it."

Lauren took a muffin and removed its paper. She blew across the top of her coffee mug and finally took a sip.

"This is surprisingly good," she said and set her cup down. "I wouldn't have guessed your new pod machine would be as good as your old Mr. Coffee."

She took another sip.

"It's taken a few days, but one of my guys has finally taken a peek at Joshua's criminal record. Or, I should say, lack of record."

"What are you talking about?" Harriet asked.

"The guys had to do some digging, but the only thing on Joshua Pratt's record is a footnote that he participated in a scared-straight program at the Foggy Point Police Department. It was a really special program."

"Let me guess," Harriet interrupted. "There was only one participant."

"Give the girl a Kewpie doll. There is no record of anyone else ever taking part in any program like that. For that matter, Foggy Point PD has never done anything of the sort before or since."

Aunt Beth broke off a bite of muffin and popped it in her mouth.

"So, the rumors about Howard Pratt having half the town in his back pocket are no exaggeration."

"That's so evil," Harriet said in amazement. "He's had Joshua wearing an ankle bracelet tracking his every move for years."

Lauren took a muffin from the platter.

"I'm not saying I believe this, but just to play devils' advocate, maybe it's like that serial killer show on TV. If Joshua is a psychopath, maybe Howard is doing him a favor. By making him think his every move is being watched, Joshua won't kill animals, much less move on to people."

Harriet sipped her coffee and studied Lauren.

"You're serious? You think Howard is the good guy here?"

"I didn't say that. I'm just saying maybe he's the lesser of two evils."

"None of this helps us narrow down our suspect list," Mavis observed. "I've got an appointment with the medical examiner tomorrow, so I can't add anything at this point."

Beth took another bite of her muffin and chewed.

"I have nothing new yet, either. I'm taking some bibs to Sarah's mother this afternoon, so hopefully, I can learn something."

Harriet tapped her spoon on the table beside her cup.

"I still say we're missing something." A knock on the studio door interrupted her. "I'll be right back."

Detective Morse stood on the porch, a folded quilt top clutched to her chest.

"I'm sorry if I'm interrupting. Do you have a minute, or should I come back later?"

"No, come in. My aunt and Mavis and Lauren are just here having coffee. Do you have time to join us?"

"That sounds great. Can I show you my project first? I've been working on this quilt for my niece's wedding this summer, and then they decided to save some money and elope. They get back from their honeymoon next week, and my stepsister is throwing together a reception."

She set her quilt top on Harriet's large cutting table and turned back the corner. She had made a traditional double-wedding-ring pattern in pastel colors.

"I was hoping you might be able to quilt it for me. I realize this is short notice, and I completely understand if you can't do it." She stopped talking and looked hopefully at Harriet.

"What were you thinking for a stitch pattern?"

"I was thinking whatever you can do in time for the reception."

Harriet spread the top flatter on the table, unfolding more of the fabric as she did.

"If you had a choice, what would you want?"

"Something simple—I'd like them to actually be able to use it. I don't want it so dense it won't drape."

"This is your lucky day. I finally finished the show quilt I've been working on for what seems like forever. I've had that thing on and off my machine at least four times. The woman kept changing her mind and adding more stitching, and the sad thing is, it still probably doesn't have enough stitch density to win in a major show. So, yes, as long as we can keep it simple, I can do your quilt."

"Oh, thank you. Do you still have that wide muslin available?" Morse meant the extra-wide fabric that was sold in off-white cotton and other basic finishes for the purpose of providing a seam-free back for large quilts.

"I do, indeed. I have wool or cotton batting on the roll, and if you want, Carla has a friend in her young mothers' quilting group who does binding for hire. Fifteen cents an inch, and she does really nice work."

"Perfect. Sign me up." She rubbed her hands together. "This might just work after all."

"Was there ever a doubt? And we aren't even going to have to tap into the Loose Threads. Now, how about some coffee and a cranberry-orange muffin?"

Harriet turned to lead the way back to the kitchen. Morse put a hand on her arm, stopping her.

"Wait. Before we go in, I want to apologize for my behavior the other day when the cars were bombed. I know you all aren't trying to cause trouble. I hope you can believe this, but I really do worry about your safety. You've been lucky so far. In the year or so since you've been back in Foggy Point, you've gone up against some nasty people and for the most part come out unscathed. I worry that your luck is going to run out. If I came on too strong, I'm sorry."

"I understand. It's just hard to stand around and do nothing when our friends are in trouble."

"Try to restrain yourselves. And it wouldn't hurt if you all didn't go places alone until we catch our perp."

"I promise," Harriet said and held up her two fingers in a Girl Scout salute. Even as she did it, she knew it wasn't true. She was sure Morse knew the same thing.

✂ - - - ✂ - - - ✂

"Good morning, Detective," Mavis said as Harriet and Jane Morse entered the kitchen. "Here, sit." She pulled out a chair.

Harriet refilled the water chamber, snapped another coffee pod into her machine and pushed the go button. Aunt Beth looked over at her.

"That thing is slick."

Mavis pushed the plate of muffins closer to Morse.

"Here, help yourself."

Beth handed her a napkin.

Jane selected a muffin and began peeling off the paper.

"I'm sure you are all anxious for an update on the bombing. Unfortunately, I don't have much for you. The bombs were made from a mix of fertilizer and motor oil with simple detonators activated remotely, probably by a cell phone. They didn't contain shrapnel of any sort."

"What do you mean?" Mavis asked.

"Often, in this type of bomb, you'll find that, besides the explosive materials, there will be nails or tacks or other small metal objects designed to cause as much damage as possible. There is no sign of that in your bombs.

"There were no large charges of material in the bombs, either. We think this person was trying to create a distraction—they were trying to damage the cars and nothing else, and they were successful."

Beth leaned forward.

"Were there any fingerprints?"

Detective Morse finished chewing her bite of muffin then brushed the crumbs from her mouth with her napkin.

"No, whoever made these was careful. They probably wore gloves."

"Do you have any suspects at this point?" Harriet asked.

Morse sighed. "Not really. We're interviewing all the people in our area that have shown a fondness for explosives in the past, but honestly, in this area that's mostly people we've had contact with over illegal fireworks."

Harriet took the finished cup of coffee from her machine and set it in front of Jane. She slid the sugar bowl to the detective before sitting back down.

"What do you think about Howard Pratt?"

Jane Morse stopped stirring her coffee and sighed. She pressed her lips together firmly, still not answering.

"I don't like the man. I don't like the way the upper level of the Foggy Point Police Department treats him like he's some kind of royalty. I'd bet he's abusive to his wife. I have no proof, so don't tell anyone I said that."

Mavis asked, "What about shooting Seth or bombing our cars?"

"He had solid alibis for both events."

"Could he have faked them?" Harriet asked.

Jane gave a forced laugh.

"Hardly. He was at a city council meeting when Seth was shot and playing golf with the mayor when your cars were bombed. And before you say it, yes, he could have hired someone to do it, but we have absolutely no evidence that was the case."

Beth looked at Lauren, Mavis and Harriet.

"We've been to the senior center quilting several times lately." She paused, giving the other three a chance to protest before she continued. "The people in the independent living section of the place think Howard is committing fraud involving medications and Medicare."

"Are you suggesting he might have killed Seth because Seth discovered what he was up to? Do they have any evidence to back up that theory?" Morse asked.

No one said anything.

"I didn't think so," she continued. "Seth Pratt was a pharmacist and probably took some sort of oath like doctors do, but everything I'm hearing is he was also egotistical and abusive, much like his old man. Everything points to him being complicit in whatever Howard is doing, not opposed to it."

"Can you investigate that?" Mavis asked her.

"No, not really. Medicare and Medicaid fraud are federal offenses. We can contact the FBI and tell them we suspect something, but we would need actual evidence to even do that."

Harriet took a bite of her muffin and chewed it slowly.

"What about Sarah?" she asked when she was finished.

"What about her? If Seth Pratt was her abuser, and we're sure he was, she should be safe now that he's dead."

"The seniors at the center think Howard will try to pin Seth's death on Sarah." Harriet told her.

"That doesn't make any sense. What would his motive be?"

Mavis stood up and went to Harriet's coffee machine.

"Do you care if I try this hazelnut pod?" she asked.

"Sure. Just snap it in and push the go button," Harriet instructed.

Mavis did as she was told and put her cup under the spout.

"For that theory to work, you have to believe Howard is the killer. He would blame Sarah to clear himself." She thought for a moment. "I suppose he could believe Sarah really did kill Seth."

"That's not what the seniors think," Harriet said. "They think Howard doesn't want any scandal to taint his business. Blaming Sarah would make it go away quickly."

Morse shook her head. "They're reaching. That makes no sense at all."

"I just had a thought," Harriet announced. "The senior center belongs to Sarah's mother, as far as we know." She looked at her aunt. "Didn't you tell me that when Sarah's parents divorced, they owned several health-related businesses? Her dad kept the medical supply business and her mom kept the senior center?"

"That's right."

Harriet stood up and paced across the kitchen.

"What if Howard wants to blame Sarah so he can secure the center for himself? He dominates her mother. And with the way his wives die, she may not be long for this world anyway. With Sarah in jail, he'd have full control of the place. If that happened, I'll bet he could talk her into turning it over to him."

Morse picked at her muffin.

"I hate to be a wet blanket, but all that supposes Howard is trying to blame Sarah for Seth's murder, and so far, I don't see anything but the suspicions of a group of senior citizens. And what are you talking about—'the way his wives die?'"

Harriet quickly explained what they knew about the untimely deaths of Howard's first two wives, including Joshua's suspicions.

"You must know all about that," Mavis said. "I mean, you've investigated Howard, right."

Morse looked at her.

"No, and before you say anything, he has an airtight alibi for both the murder and bombing, as I told you earlier. He also is very good friends with the movers and shakers in town. He's not someone you can casually investigate and expect it won't get back to him. Show me some concrete evidence, and I'm all over it, but until then, it's hands off Howard.

"Have any of you seen Sarah lately? Is she doing any better?"

Harriet sat back down. "We haven't seen her for a while. I haven't, anyway."

The other Threads murmured their agreement.

"We need to go check up on her and the quilting project they're working on." She explained the joint grandmother's flower garden activity.

"Let me know how she is when you do, okay?"

"Sure."

Morse ate several more bites of her muffin.

"I'll tell you what. I'll call my old partner in Seattle. *She* can dig around on Howard. If she ruffles any feathers, she can say she's investigating a complaint by one of the resident's families or something. You've got me curious about his dead ex-wives. One young wife dying is sad. A second young wife dying is a coincidence, and I don't believe in coincidence. Not when it involves dead people."

"Can you let us know what you find out?" Harriet asked.

Morse sighed again. "If I'm able to, I will, but no promises."

Harriet rolled a muffin crumb in her fingers.

"That's all we can ask."

Morse finished her muffin and folded the baking paper neatly on her napkin.

"These are really good. Where did you get them?"

"Would you believe it if I said I made them?" Harriet replied with a smile.

"Really?" Morse said.

Harriet pointed to an empty muffin mix box on her counter.

"Wow, did you add anything extra?" Morse asked.

"You really are a detective," Harriet said and laughed. "I added some fresh cranberries and freshly grated orange peel. Otherwise, they were straight out of the box."

Morse stood up.

"Speaking of detecting, I better go do some. Thanks for the coffee and muffin. They really hit the spot." She picked up her jacket from the back of her chair and put it on.

Aunt Beth stood up as well.

"Would you like to see my new car on your way out?"

Morse smiled. "I'd love to."

Chapter 21

Aunt Beth raised the presser foot on the sewing machine, picked up her scissors and clipped the threads on the senior bib she'd just finished.

"There, now I have a total of ten more bibs to take to Sarah's mom. Would you like to come with? I'll drive." She smiled.

"Can you give me five minutes to finish this section I'm working on?" Harriet had loaded Detective Morse's quilt onto her long-arm machine right after the detective left. Lauren and Mavis had followed shortly after, but her aunt had stayed and had been able to complete two more of the senior bibs she had cut out the night before.

"That's fine. I'll take the dogs out while you do that." Beth had brought her rescue dog along when she'd come that morning. "I'm going to bring the travel kennel in, too. Brownie's been getting into wastebaskets and chewing up tissues when I leave her unsupervised."

"We can leave them in the kitchen. I can shut the doors to the other rooms and put the gate across the stairs. That way, they can get in the back hallway and kitchen, but nowhere else."

Harriet finished what she was doing, and the two women headed for the senior center.

"Hi, Hannah," Harriet said as she approached the reception desk. "Is Elaine in?"

Hannah stood up.

"She's waiting for you in the small dining room. She had the kitchen people make tea and snacks. Could you tell her I'm leaving to go work with Aiden? Oh, and also that I put the phones on auto."

She set a desk phone onto the counter with a tent sign that instructed visitors to sign in or to dial 6745 to reach the nurses' desk if they needed help.

"Sure, no problem."

Hannah brushed by her and out the front door. Beth came up behind her.

"Where's she going in such a hurry?"

"Off to work with Aiden. She said Elaine is waiting for us in the small dining room."

"Hi, Elaine," Harriet said a few minutes later, after going to the memory care dining room first by mistake.

"I hope it's okay we're meeting back here. I asked the staff to make tea sandwiches for us so we could have lunch while we talk. I need to cover the front desk while Hannah's gone."

"Oh, yeah, I'm supposed to tell you she put the phones on auto. She put a phone and sign up on the counter, too."

Elaine pressed her lips tightly together and frowned.

"Is there something wrong?" Harriet finally asked.

"No, not really. Hannah was supposed to wait until we were done before she left. Howard doesn't like to have the front desk unattended."

"Would you like us to have our meeting out there?" Aunt Beth asked.

"It's okay. Howard is at a planning commission meeting. He won't be back for a few hours. It really doesn't hurt anything to leave the front desk empty once in a while. Howard just thinks it gives the wrong impression." Elaine stared at the door and then said, more to herself than anyone else, "If Sarah would just come back, we wouldn't be having all these problems."

Harriet looked at Aunt Beth, her eyes wide in disbelief. Aunt Beth moved her head back and forth in a barely perceptible negative, silencing any retort Harriet was about to make.

Aunt Beth held out the plastic bag containing the bibs she'd made.

"Here are some more of the adult bibs, as promised. Are they working out okay?"

Elaine took the bag and brought the new bibs out.

"These are lovely. They're working wonderfully. Unless you look closely, you can't tell the person is wearing a bib. It gives a much better impression to our visitors, and I'm sure it makes the residents feel better, too."

The bib conversation was interrupted by a small woman wearing a hairnet over her brown hair and pushing a cart laden with two teapots, two large platters full of crustless sandwiches and a smaller plate of cookies.

"Thank you, that will be all, Beatrice," Elaine said and unloaded the cart onto the table. She pulled three bundles of silverware wrapped in cloth napkins from the cart shelf along with three sandwich plates and three teacups and saucers.

"This is lovely," Aunt Beth said.

"And unexpected," Harriet added.

Elaine blushed. "Oh, it's nothing. We like to do this when prospective families come to tour."

Harriet hoped Elaine wasn't trying to make an impression on her regarding Aunt Beth. Beth had only just retired and when and if the time came, Harriet would move her back into her own home long before she'd let her come to the Foggy Point Senior Center.

Elaine set the table and poured tea before sitting on the opposite side of the table from Beth and Harriet. She was neatly dressed in an expensive navy blue skirt, plain white blouse and pale-blue cardigan sweater. Her makeup didn't quite conceal the dark smudges under her eyes or the purple bruise on her cheekbone.

"Have you seen my daughter Sarah?" she asked, looking at Aunt Beth as she spoke.

Aunt Beth paused, her cup almost to her lips, then went ahead and took a sip before answering.

"No, not lately."

"No one will tell us where she is, and Howard is anxious to have her back."

Harriet set the cucumber sandwich triangle she was eating back on her plate.

"I'd imagine she's convalescing somewhere."

"I can't believe that," Elaine said, her face turning pink under her makeup. "I mean, if she was sick or hurt she'd come here."

Harriet looked at Beth for help.

"I'm sure she's just staying with a friend," Beth suggested.

Elaine made a snorting noise.

"Sarah doesn't have friends. She has people who are kind enough to tolerate her. Why you all put up with her in your quilting group has always been a mystery to me. I'm sure you've seen her quilts. She never was willing to put in the effort it takes to make a fine one. Not like Hannah. That girl can do anything she puts her mind to. Not that she does. She's lazy, that one; but when she does make a quilt, her stitches are tiny and even and her points are always sharp."

It was hard to refute what Elaine was saying about Sarah, but Harriet couldn't let it go.

"All of us in the Loose Threads consider Sarah our friend," she said.

"Is Sarah staying with one of your group members?"

"No, she isn't." Beth answered for Harriet. "I'm surprised she hasn't called you to let you know she's okay."

"She always has been a difficult child," Elaine complained.

This wasn't going how Harriet had planned.

"Have the police told you anything about your stepson's death?" she asked.

Elaine's eyes filled with tears.

"You mean his murder? The Foggy Point Police Department has no idea. His father and I can't imagine who could possible want to harm him. He was such a help to his father in running this business. I hope Sarah isn't involved. The longer she's on the run the more I worry that she had something to do with it."

Aunt Beth reached across the table and patted Elaine's hand.

"I'm sure Sarah could never do such a thing. She loved Seth."

"Why won't she come home?" Elaine asked.

Neither Harriet nor Beth had an answer for that, so they ate their sandwiches in silence for a few minutes. Finally, Aunt Beth wiped her hands on her napkin.

"We're having fun quilting with the people in the memory unit and some of the independent living folks."

"We appreciate you coming to spend time with our people," Elaine said without noticeable enthusiasm.

"It's a pleasure for us," Harriet said. "And we're learning a few tricks from Violet."

Elaine set down her teacup.

"We're glad you're keeping that little group busy. They tend to stir up trouble here."

"How so?" Harriet asked.

Elaine looked at her hands, folded in her lap.

"They like to poke their noses in other people's business. And they get the other residents riled up. They put the other people up to things. I'd rather not talk about it. Thank you again for bringing the bibs, but I'd better go take care of the front desk. Feel free to stay a while longer if you wish." She dropped her napkin on the table, stood up and walked out, the door swinging shut behind her.

Harriet and Beth looked at each other.

"I think I just lost my appetite."

"You and me both." Beth stood up and gathered her purse and coat from a chair by the door where she'd left them. There was a knock on the door followed by Violet entering the room.

"Hello, am I interrupting anything?" She held two hexagons of a grand-mother's flower garden quilt block.

"Not at all," Harriet told her, coming over to join them. "We were hav-ing tea with Elaine, but she had to go back to work."

Violet's shoulders sagged with relief.

"Oh, good, then I don't have to pretend I have a quilting question. We saw you come in. Jo and Mickey wanted to know what was going on, but they thought it would be more believable if I said I had a question about our quilt project."

"I'm sorry you wasted a perfectly good pretense," Harriet said. "Elaine isn't here, and we didn't really learn anything from her before she left."

"She seems very meek, but I don't think she really is," Violet said sweetly.

"What do you mean?"

Violet wrung her hands.

"Oh, I don't know. It's just a feeling. She kowtows to Howard, but she rides roughshod over those two girls."

"They have a very strange family dynamic, it would seem," Harriet said.

"We'd better get moving," Beth said. "Tell Jo and Mickey we said hi and we're sorry, we don't know anything new."

✂ - - - ✂ - - - ✂

"Is it just me, or was that weird?" Harriet asked when they were back in Beth's new Beetle.

"She certainly doesn't seem supportive of the girls in the family."

"If she's also abused, maybe she doesn't have anything left for the girls."

Aunt Beth turned to look at her for an instant.

"Not that your uncle Henry would ever have done anything like that, but if he had, I would have protected you with my dying breath."

"And I love you for that," Harriet said with a smile. "But not everyone has a mother or aunt like you. Case in point, my own mother. She'd throw me under the bus at the first hint of trouble—and don't try to deny it."

"You're right. I can't explain your mother. And I feel sorry for Sarah. Her road to recovery will be that much harder without family to support her."

"Speaking of Sarah, I think I'll call Georgia and see if it's possible for me to pay her a visit at the shelter. I'd like to ask her a few more questions about her family."

"Mavis and I are working on our pet quilts this afternoon. She found a British TV mystery series we haven't seen yet and bought the first two sea-sons. We're going to have a marathon and try to finish as many small pet quilts as we can while we're watching."

"Sounds fun. I'll see if Lauren can come with me to the shelter. I'll let you know if we learn anything."

"We were thinking about making some animal blankets using a solid piece of flannel backed with fleece. What do you think?"

The debate occupied their conversation for the rest of the drive home.

Chapter 22

Lauren climbed into Harriet's car.

"Don't we need to take some quilts or pillowcases or something?"

Harriet, as was now her habit, looked underneath before sliding into the driver's seat.

"Logically, I know that no one sneaked into my garage and put a bomb under my car," she said in response to Lauren's raised eyebrow, "but I can't seem to stop myself from checking before I get in."

"I hear you. I do the same thing. It's just a little weirder in your case, since your car didn't get bombed."

"To answer your question," Harriet said after a long moment. "I decided to be straight with Georgia, and she was okay with us coming to see Sarah. She said Sarah is making a little progress, and she thought it would be good for her to have visitors.

"If you have time, I thought I'd swing by Walmart and pick up a new coffeemaker for the shelter. I was thinking about it while I was stitching and decided it was ridiculous for Sarah to have to go without good coffee until they finish a quilt and then sell it to raise funds for the purchase. I mean, it's maybe a hundred dollars."

Lauren pressed her lips together and was quiet for a moment.

"I'll pay for half," she said finally. "You're right. I thought about that myself. Not buying her a coffeemaker, but I did think she might feel a little like she was in prison without a good cup of coffee. You're thinking one like yours with the pods, right?"

Harriet turned toward the highway.

"That's the plan. And if you're paying for half the coffeemaker, maybe I'll get them an electric teapot, too."

Lauren looked out her window at the light rain that was starting to fall.

"Have you ever been with anyone who got physical with you?"

"No. My husband was a liar, as it turned out, but he never tried to hit me. Given his health, he might have hurt himself if he had—but he wouldn't have. It wasn't in his makeup. We had a really good relationship, right up until he died and it turned out he'd been conspiring with all our friends to keep me in the dark about his medical problems."

"That must have been weird. Was he afraid you wouldn't marry him if you knew or something?"

"Yeah, something like that. What I realized was that, the whole time we were married, it was all about Steve's friends and Steve's activities and what Steve wanted. I guess I wanted the relationship to work so bad I was willing to set aside my own needs. The sick part is, I probably *would* have married him anyway."

"That so doesn't sound like you."

"We were young when we married, and he was very charismatic. People were drawn to him without him even trying. He had the perfect parents—Dad was middle management, Mom a homemaker. They'd lived in the same house his whole life.

"After spending most of my life at boarding schools, I guess I bought into the whole white picket fence thing. I wanted a normal home and family. When we were first married, we were both busy starting our careers, so I guess I was too busy to notice if things were less than perfect."

She shook her head and glanced at Lauren.

"What about you?"

"I dated a guy in college who punched me and everyone else in the shoulder when he was joking around."

"What did you do?"

"I didn't have to do anything. One of his buddies had his fill and beat him to a pulp after he'd punched him in the bicep one too many times. He never did it again. Said he didn't realize how annoying it was."

"That's crazy."

Lauren laughed. "That's college."

✂ - - - ✂ - - - ✂

Georgia filled the water chamber of the new coffee pot and plugged it in.

"Who wants the first cup?"

Harriet passed a large sampler box of coffee pods to the shelter residents, who were standing in the kitchen, their coffee mugs in their hands.

Sarah stepped forward and set her cup under the spout.

"I want the plain coffee. Can someone get it out for me?" The fingers of her right hand were swollen, and she still had the cast with its accompanying hardware covering most of her right forearm.

Harriet popped a Starbucks coffee pod from the box and snapped it into place. She aligned Sarah's cup under the spout and pushed the brew button.

"Thank you for doing this," Sarah said quietly.

Lauren and Harriet looked at each other.

"We figured your arm would heal faster if you had good coffee," Harriet told her.

Georgia filled the new electric tea kettle.

"And the tea drinkers here thank you for their pot, too."

Harriet's cheeks turned pink.

"It's the least we could do."

"I'm sure you want some time to talk to your friend," Georgia said when Harriet, Lauren and Sarah all had steaming mugs in their hands. "Sarah can show you to the library."

She nodded to Sarah, encouraging her to lead the way. Sarah opened a door at the back of the kitchen, revealing a flight of stairs that led to the basement. They passed a laundry room then Sarah stopped and opened a plywood door, flicking on the light as she entered. The floor was concrete. Brick and board shelving held a row of tattered paperback books. Webbed lawn chairs provided the seating.

Lauren sat carefully in one of the insubstantial chairs.

"'Library' is a bit of a stretch," she said as she looked around.

Sarah followed her gaze.

"It grows on you," she said in a flat tone. "Don't get me wrong, these people are doing a good thing here, but let's be real. I'm a prisoner."

Harriet started to protest, but Sarah held up her left hand to silence her.

"I know I agreed to be here. I don't like it, but I get it—out of sight, out of mind and all that." She sighed. "Anyway," she said in a softer tone. "Sometimes it's good to get away from everyone and just think." She looked around the room. "This room is good for that."

Harriet pulled chairs closer for herself and Sarah. Lauren squirmed in her seat.

"Besides the prisoner part, how are you doing?"

Sarah hung her head.

"I don't know. We have a lot of group therapy here. And they have a counselor who meets with each of us one-on-one. They're trying to tell me that Seth couldn't love me and hit me at the same time."

"Sounds reasonable," Lauren observed.

"I *know* Seth loved me. We were going to be married."

"Yet, he did that." Harriet pointed to Sarah's arm.

"He said he was sorry." Sarah sighed. "It's all so confusing. Seth and I had plans. How could he make plans with me if he didn't love me?"

Because he was a sociopath, Harriet thought, but she kept that opinion to herself.

"After my birthday, he said I could quit my job," Sarah added. "He said he'd build me a studio, and I could quilt full-time if I want."

"What happens after your birthday?" Lauren asked.

Sarah picked at the padding of her cast with her good hand.

"It's a few months after we were supposed to be married."

"Why wouldn't you quit when you got married," Harriet asked. "I assume you were going to go on a honeymoon. The senior center would have to get a substitute while you were gone. Why go back for those few months?"

A tear slid down Sarah's right cheek.

"Oh, what difference does it make. It's how Seth wanted it, and I didn't care. Besides, we weren't going on a honeymoon. We both had to work, and we didn't have any money anyway."

Harriet reached over and patted Sarah's knee.

"I'm sorry we're asking you all these questions. I'm trying to find out what happened to Seth."

"Do you know any reason anyone would want Seth dead?" Lauren asked. "Like Howard, maybe?"

Sarah sniffed. "I know you're trying to help, but you didn't know Seth. Everyone loved Seth, especially his dad."

"Let's talk about something else," Harriet said. "Do you know anything about Howard's first two wives?"

Sarah stared at her.

"You mean did he kill them? I know that's what people think."

"Yes. Do you know anything about their deaths?"

"The only thing I know is Joshua believes Howard killed his moth-er."

Harriet and Lauren exchanged a glance.

"Are you and Joshua close?" Harriet asked.

"I don't think you'd call it close, but I let him stay at the cabin with me when Seth was sleeping at the center. That shed he lives in at Howard and my mom's is pretty awful. He doesn't even have a color TV."

"Did Joshua ever hurt you?" Lauren asked.

Sarah jerked her head toward Lauren.

"Are you kidding? He said he used to be Howard's punching bag before Howard married my mom. He couldn't hurt a flea."

166

"So Howard started hitting *her?*" Lauren asked.

"Not important right now," Harriet said quietly to her.

"Sarah, I heard from one of the Threads that your mom is the one who actually owns the senior center, that Howard just manages it. Is that true?"

"You want to hear something funny?" Sarah said, not waiting for an answer. "Technically, *I* own the place. It's been in a trust for me since my grandma died."

"Let me guess," Lauren said. "You take possession on your next birthday."

Sarah looked thoughtful for a moment.

"I guess that's right. I get it when I turn thirty-five. My grandma wanted me to get my degree and work before I had to worry about it."

"Oh, my gosh," Harriet said.

"What?" Sarah asked.

Harriet sat back in her chair.

"This certainly changes the picture." She could see that Lauren was about to speak. She shook her head slightly and glanced toward the door.

Lauren stood up.

"We should probably get going."

Harriet joined her, and Sarah looked up at them.

"Do you have any ideas about who killed Seth?" Sarah asked as she stood up.

"No," Harriet told her. "Not yet. But we're getting closer."

They followed Sarah upstairs to the large living room, where she pointed at a cardboard box that sat against the wall behind a worn upholstered rocking chair. Harriet slid it toward her then picked it up and set it on a coffee table that had been made from an old door. Sarah opened the box flaps with her good hand.

"Here are the blocks we've made so far," she said.

Lauren reached in and picked out a handful of the grandmother's flower garden blocks. She laid them out on the table. Harriet examined one of the blocks and then flipped it over to check the back side.

"These look really good."

"Don't sound so surprised," Sarah told her. "None of the group were quilters before they came here, but a couple of them do beading, and one woman knits."

Lauren rifled through the remaining blocks and pieces of blocks.

"I think you guys have more done than the people at the senior center."

Sarah put the blocks back in the box.

"Yeah, well, there's not much else going on here. We clean house, we go to therapy, and now we quilt. The people who have never worked have a job-training tutor, but the rest of us don't have much to do."

"Hopefully, you won't have to be here much longer," Harriet said.

Sarah looked around then lifted her wounded arm.

"I can't really do anything anyway, so I guess I might as well be here." Her shoulders drooped.

Lauren patted her awkwardly on her good shoulder.

"Well, hang in there."

Harriet looked at her.

"We better get going." She started for the door, and Lauren followed.

Chapter 23

"Hey," Harriet said when Aiden phoned two hours later.

"Want to come to my house for pizza tonight? Actually, in an hour?"

"That's a bit early. Is something going on?"

"Why would you ask that?" he asked in a voice that was so innocent, she knew he was hiding something.

"Come on, spill. What's really going on?"

Aiden sighed. "Okay, you got me. Michelle's kids are coming over. They're doing a school project on our family history—I have a bunch of Jalbert family records in the attic. Michelle dropped them off a couple of hours ago. She's staying with one of my mom's French friends from the old country. I told her I'd feed them before she comes to get them."

"Please tell me you don't expect me to be there when she is."

"It'll be okay. She's really trying to make amends. I think her therapy or meds or whatever they did for her at the hospital is working. And I told you she's been talking to Pastor Hafer."

Harriet studied the ceiling, hoping for advice from on high to descend on her. Finally, she sighed.

"Okay, fine."

"You won't regret it, I promise."

"That remains to be seen," Harriet said. "See you in an hour."

✂ - - ✂ - - ✂

"We go to a boarding school in Seattle," a dark-haired girl of about ten was explaining to Carla in a serious voice.

She was wearing an expensive-looking navy blue pleated skirt and matching cardigan. Harriet wasn't good with children's ages, but she could recognize a private school uniform at twenty paces.

"They have tutors so if we miss school when we visit Mother they can catch us up."

Harriet had another brief flash of déjà vu.

It was clear from the expression on Carla's face she didn't know what to say to that. Harriet stepped from the back porch into the kitchen.

"Knock-knock."

"Oh, hi, Harriet," Carla said with relief. "Have you met Aiden's niece Avelaine?"

Harriet extended her hand to the girl.

"We met at my house a few months ago. I'm Harriet."

The girl shook the hand and looked up at her.

"I'm Avelaine, but people call me Lanie."

"It's nice to meet you, Lanie," Harriet let go of the girl's small hand and slipped out of her jacket, setting it and her purse on a kitchen chair. "I hear you and your brother are working on a family genealogy project."

Lanie smiled. "We're tracing my mother's family. My grandmother came from France."

"Yes, I know," Harriet told her. "My aunt and your grandmother were very good friends. When I was just a little older than you are right now, I went to a boarding school in Bordeaux, which is where your grandmother lived before she moved here."

Lanie's smile faded.

"She died last year."

Harriet didn't think it was appropriate to tell a ten year-old what she knew about that.

"That's very sad, but it's terrific that she left you so many family albums and diaries."

"Have you seen them?" The girl asked.

"Yes, Aiden showed some of them to me. You're really lucky that your grandma was such a family historian."

"My brother Etienne is up in the attic now with Uncle Aiden. They're going to bring the one with the family tree in it down here. We're going to do DNA tests, too. My mother bought them for all of us. They'll tell us if we have Neanderthal in our background and what percent."

Harriet wasn't sure what to say about that. She hoped the family wasn't going to have any nasty surprises. With Michelle involved, anything was possible, but surely she wouldn't suggest it if there were a chance the kids weren't full siblings or, worse, if her husband wasn't the father of either.

Right on cue, a dark-haired boy in navy blue pants and a matching pullover came clattering down the kitchen stairs, followed by Aiden carrying two large bound books.

"Hi," Aiden said. "I see you've met Lanie."

"She was just telling Carla and I about the genealogy project you all are working on."

A squawk emanated from the baby monitor receiver on the counter and she turned and went up the stairs to retrieve her toddler Wendy. Aiden crossed the kitchen to the door that led to the dining room.

"Let's put the books with the rest and clear a space on the table."

Etienne followed him, and Harriet went to the oven where she found three pizza boxes. Carla had laid a stack of paper plates and napkins on the counter. Harriet stacked the paper goods on the pizza boxes and followed the men to the dining room.

✂- - -✂- - -✂

Harriet leaned over the table to get a good look at the family tree Lanie had drawn. They had finished their pizza, and the children had each taken a turn explaining what they'd learned about their French ancestors. Being eight years old and a boy, Etienne's report was heavy on the military connections. Lanie's emphasized how many generations back she could go. Apparently, her best friend didn't have nearly as many branches filled out on her tree.

"That's amazing," Harriet told them each in turn. "I'm sure you'll both get As."

"Of course they will," said Michelle from the entryway. Everyone was so intent on the presentations no one had heard her come in.

Carla grabbed Wendy and slipped back into the kitchen.

Michelle removed her fur coat and put it carefully over the back of a dining room chair."My children always get As." She turned to look at Harriet, her expression carefully blank. "Hello, Harriet, I'm glad you're here."

Harriet stared at her but said nothing.

"I suppose my brother told you I wanted to talk to you." Michelle pulled out another chair and sat down. "Avalaine, Etienne, go find something for dessert in the kitchen."

The children got up silently and left the room.

"I've discovered through my therapy that I may have been misguided in some of my conclusions and, therefore, my actions. I'd like to apologize. I'm sorry for all the problems I've caused you and your friends."

Harriet remained silent.

171

"Aren't you going to say something?" Michelle asked. "I worked very hard to be able to say those words."

"I appreciate how hard it was to say them," Harriet finally said. "I hope you've also learned in therapy that words are cheap and what really matters is actions. I'm willing to wait and see if your actions match your words."

Michelle smiled and held her two hands up in front of her.

"Fair enough, that's all I can ask. My counselor told me to expect skepticism."

Harriet started picking up crumpled napkins and pizza-stained paper plates.

"I *am* a good person, you know," Michelle said. "I sang in the church choir when I lived in Foggy Point."

Harriet carried the stack of garbage into the kitchen without looking back.

"Give her some time," she heard Aiden say before the door closed behind her.

Michelle's children were sitting at the kitchen table. Etienne's chin rested on his crossed arms on the table. Laine was leaning back, her chair rocking on two legs. She picked at her full lower lip.

"Did you guys find anything for dessert?" she asked them. They both shook their heads. "Want some ice cream? I happen to know your uncle never has less than three flavors of ice cream in his freezer."

Etienne straightened up.

"I love ice cream."

Laine pursed her lips.

"I guess I could have a little."

"Okay, then. Lanie, can you get three bowls, and, Etienne, could you get spoons?" She could hear the murmur of voices from the dining room, but she couldn't tell what they were talking about. "Let see." She opened the door to the side-by-side freezer. "We have mint chocolate chip, rocky road and lemon sherbet."

"Rocky road," Etienne said at the same time his sister said, "Mint chocolate chip."

Harriet pulled the two cartons out and began scooping ice cream, putting a little of each in her own bowl.

"Do you think my mother really is better?" Lanie asked in a quiet voice.

"I hope so," Harriet told her. "I guess we have to wait and see what happens."

Etienne took his bowl and carried it to the table.

"Do you think my dad will let her move back home?"

Harriet thought for minute while she let a bite of rocky road melt in her mouth.

"No one can figure that out but your parents. Whatever happens, your parents both love you, and nothing will ever change that."

Your mother just has a very strange way of showing it, she added to herself. Michelle probably loved her children as much as she was capable of, but her love affair with herself didn't leave much room for others — even her own kids.

"You know," she went on, "I took a photography class when I was in school in France, and I have a lot of pictures of Bordeaux. If you want, I can give them to Uncle Aiden, and you can look at them. Then, if you want, we can make copies for your report."

Lanie smiled. "That would be really cool."

"Hey, did you leave any ice cream for me?" Aiden asked as he came into the kitchen.

The kids laughed and that made Harriet smile.

✂- - -✂- - -✂

"Well, that was awkward," Harriet said when Aiden came back into the house after walking the kids to Michelle's car.

He pulled her into his arms.

"I'm with you—talk *is* cheap. I'm willing to give her a chance, but a cautious chance." He rested his chin on her head.

Harriet wrapped her arms around his waist.

"Are you really going to do the DNA test?"

"Yeah, why not? All I have to do is spit in a test tube. The kids are really into this school genealogy project. It will be fun for them. Besides, they already bought the kits."

Harriet pulled back reluctantly.

"I better get back home. Detective Morse dropped off a quilt she needs a quick turnaround on."

"Are you sure?"

She sighed. "I told her I'd get it done for her. It's a peace offering, of sorts. You know how upset she gets with us for poking around in her cases."

"Sounds more like a bribe."

"It's not like that. I'd have done it for her in any case."

"Okay. Whatever."

Carla came down the kitchen stairs, coughing to warn them before she appeared.

"Is she gone?" She slid Wendy to the floor when she reached the bottom step.

"Yeah," Harriet said. "She left a few minutes ago."

Carla got ice cream and two bowls and began scooping a snack for her daughter and herself.

"I thought I heard a car leave." She looked at her feet. "I'm not ready to talk to her yet."

"You don't have to," Harriet told her before Aiden could say anything. "Just because she's ready to talk doesn't mean you have to be."

Carla looked up at her as if to be sure she wasn't joking.

"Are you going to the Threads tomorrow at the quilt store?"

"I guess so. This last week has gone by fast. I really need to talk to the group, but I promised Detective Morse I'd work on her quilt." She slid her smartphone from her jeans pocket and glanced at the time. "Still, I can get a few more hours in tonight, so hopefully, I'll be able to go."

Aiden picked up Harriet's fleece jacket and held it out for her to slip her arms into.

"Thanks," she said with a smile. He bent his head and brushed his lips briefly across hers, and she felt her cheeks turn pink. She turned to Carla, who had busied herself with the ice cream. "See you tomorrow."

"I'll walk you to your car," Aiden said and grabbed his own jacket before opening the back door.

Harriet turned to him when they reached her car.

"Did you have a chance to talk to Hannah?"

"I tried, but she's all upset because now that Seth is dead, Howard wants her to go to pharmacy school. She has her heart set on becoming a vet tech."

"She doesn't want to be a vet like you?"

"I think that was her original idea, but Howard wasn't on board with that even before Seth died."

"Thanks for trying."

"I guess the office gals have talked to her about whether she was safe at home, given what happened to Sarah. She said she had a hard time believing Seth had done that, and that in any case, Sarah annoyed everyone in the family."

"That's terrible," Harriet interrupted. "Although, the people at the shelter told us that abused women are often blamed for their own abuse."

"Hannah also told them that, in her opinion, it was really Joshua who had been beating Sarah. She said Joshua spent time alone with Sarah at the cabin when Seth wasn't there."

"Wow, your friends are good. I'll have to bring them doughnuts. Sarah told us she let Joshua sleep there when Seth had overnight duty at the senior center. She didn't sound afraid of him, but then, she wasn't afraid of Seth, either."

Aiden pulled her into his arms again and this time kissed her thoroughly before he let her go.

"You're welcome," he said.

Harriet felt a familiar tingle all the way to her toes. She savored the feeling.

"I really do have to go," she said and smiled at him."I told Lanie I'd bring some pictures of Bordeaux to you for her to look at and potentially copy for her report."

"I'll talk to you tomorrow, then," he said and gave her the crooked grin that made the butterflies in her stomach take flight.

She opened her car door with a contented sigh and got in.

Chapter 24

avis got into Harriet's car and quickly buckled her seatbelt.

"If we hurry, we can swing by the Steaming Cup on our way to the hospital. Like I told you last night, Dr. O'Brian only has a few minutes before her first patient at nine. She has to drop her daughter at school at eight-thirty, so it won't do us any good to arrive early."

Harriet glanced at the car clock. The display read seven-forty-five.

"I think you got us started early enough," she said and laughed.

"Make sure you don't say she's the medical examiner. Pete says she's sensitive about it. You don't get to be a medical examiner unless your county's population is at least two hundred-fifty thousand. We're nowhere near that. There's a big difference in pay, too."

"Yeah, but we can't possibly have as much work as they do in the big counties."

"Very true. That's why we're meeting at the hospital. Dr. O'Brian fills in at the family practice clinic when things are slow for her. You know they don't autopsy everyone who dies. They only do it if the person wasn't under the care of a doctor or died from a weird cause or something like that."

Harriet pulled into the coffee shop lot and parked next to a familiar silver Beetle.

"I take it this isn't a coincidence."

"I figured Lauren would be here, since she always is in the morning, so I invited Beth and Connie along," Mavis said with a smile.

"I wonder how Sarah's mother could marry a man like that," Connie said when Mavis and Harriet sat down with their drinks at the table she, Beth, and Lauren already occupied. "I mean, he already had two wives dead under suspicious circumstances."

Harriet took a sip of her hot cocoa.

"Even if it turns out that both women legitimately committed suicide, you would think it would cause her to wonder."

Aunt Beth ripped open a yellow packet of sweetener, dumped the contents into her coffee cup and stirred.

"I think men like Howard Pratt target the sort of women who would believe whatever story he told them to justify his dead wives."

"Elaine was rather strange, if you ask me," Harriet said. "She may have her own agenda in marrying Howard."

Lauren sipped her coffee and gave Harriet a look.

"What?" Harriet said.

Lauren hit a key on her laptop, which was open on the table in front of her.

"Call me if you hear anything that can't wait until the Threads meeting this afternoon. I'll see if I can dig up anything else about Jill Pratt's death."

Harriet picked up her cup again.

"Will do."

"Thank you for agreeing to meet with us, Dr. O'Brian," Mavis said when the coroner came into the clinic waiting room.

"Please, call me Makenna. I'm sorry I don't have more time for you."

"We appreciate your seeing us this quickly," Harriet told her after Mavis had made the introductions.

Makenna led them to an office in the interior of the clinic and gestured toward two guest chairs as she sat behind the desk.

"What can I help you with?"

Harriet related the story Joshua had told her about being "arrested" when he tried to make an appointment to see the coroner and read her report on his mother's death.

"He's right to be suspicious," Makenna said. "I shouldn't be talking about this, but no one else seems to care about the case, so why not? I was new to this job when Jill Pratt died. There's no doubt that she died from a drug overdose. The question as to whether she took the drugs herself or they were administered is undetermined. Police found an empty prescription bottle beside her body and that was it."

"Didn't the police investigate it as a suspicious death?" Harriet asked.

"They did, but there just wasn't any hard evidence to be found. Remember, I was new. I honestly couldn't tell you if it was a homicide or a suicide. My understanding was, in a case like that, you open a coroner's inquest. I consulted my predecessor and was told that, since Howard Pratt was involved, an inquest wasn't necessary. If Howard said his wife committed suicide, than it was as good as fact. Inquests are held to establish facts, not fault, he told me. So that was the end of it. Her record says cause of death overdose, manner of death undetermined."

"What do you believe happened?" Harriet asked.

"To be honest, I don't know. As a matter of procedure, I x-rayed her body. She was either very accident-prone, or she was a victim of domestic violence. She had more healed fractures than I personally have ever seen. I'm guessing her life was miserable enough that she really could have committed suicide, just to escape her abuser."

"Do you think Howard did that to her?" Mavis asked.

"I didn't say that, and I will deny I even spoke to you if you try to tell anyone otherwise. As I understand it, Howard was her second husband, so the first one could be responsible for some of the damage I saw."

"Some but not all?" Harriet pressed.

"Don't quote me. I'm going out on a limb here just talking about this at all."

Harriet leaned forward in her chair.

"I don't mean to be rude, but if you're this nervous about it, why *are* you talking to us?"

Makenna leaned back. She was silent for a moment.

"Guilt, I suppose. I'm not sure what else I could have done. I talked to the police and the prosecuting attorney, and when I didn't get anywhere, I let it go." She stood up. "If that's all, I've really got to go see my first patient."

Mavis and Harriet stood up, too. Harriet extended her hand, and Dr. O'Brian shook it.

"Thank you for your candor."

"I'm not sure it helps. Let me know what happens, will you?"

Mavis shook hands with the coroner as well.

"If you weren't able to get anyone's attention, I'm not sure what we can do, but we'll be in touch if anything happens, and by the way, Pete says to tell you hi."

Mavis and Mackenna exchanged family news as the three women returned to the waiting room.

✂ - - - ✂ - - - ✂

Harriet turned to Mavis when they were both back in her car.

"I'm not sure how much that helped us. It confirms Howard as an abuser, but we still don't know if he killed Jill."

Mavis sagged in her seat.

"She stopped short of saying some of the injuries were too fresh to be from her first husband. And Howard still has an alibi."

"Let's go stitch with the rest of the Threads and run it past the group. Maybe they'll see something we don't."

"I was hoping we could stop by Sleepy Valley Quilt Company while we're this close," Mavis suggested.

Harriet started the car and drove out of the hospital lot.

"We've got plenty of time, and I've wanted to look at their wool. I heard they have a good selection."

"I'd like to check that out, too."

✂ - - - ✂ - - - ✂

With the exception of Jenny, all the Loose Threads were present and accounted for two hours later in the big classroom at the back of Pins and Needles quilt shop. In addition, Jo and Violet from the senior center were seated at the table between Connie and DeAnn. A platter of lemon bars sat in front of Violet.

"I hope it's okay that I brought food to your meeting."

Lauren slid the snack to the center of the table.

"Food is always welcome," she told Violet.

Harriet pulled out a ZipLok bag of precut squares of fabric and a plastic hexagon template then dug in her bag for a pencil. Beth reached into her own bag, pulled one out and handed it to her.

"I brought the flipchart. Should we go ahead and talk before we start stitching?"

Lauren got up and headed to the kitchen.

"Works for me, as long as we get to eat our snacks while we talk. Anyone need anything to drink?"

There were enough requests that Harriet got up to help her.

"Did you guys learn anything interesting from the coroner?" Lauren asked.

Harriet pulled cups from a hanging rack and set them in a line on the counter.

"Not really. She says it looks like Jill was a battered woman to the point that suicide could be a credible possibility. In any case, there wasn't enough evidence to determine whether she was killed or killed herself."

179

Lauren poured coffee into some of the cups while Harriet poured hot water into others.

"Howard has an alibi, in any case," Lauren said.

"Yeah, that's what Mavis was saying." She pulled a tray from the cupboard under the sink and set the cups on it. "Let's go see what the group has to say."

"Jo and Violet have something to report," Connie said as each one took the beverage of her choice from the tray.

Harriet reached back and set it on a table that sat against the wall behind the large main table.

"What have you got, Jo?"

"In my working life, I've had some experience in memory retrieval. Some people consider it to be hypnosis, but it's more just helping the person relax and guiding them to search their memories. Janice agreed to all this. In fact, it was her idea.

"She also did something risky. She's been combing the Internet for new research into memory recovery. The Chinese have done some promising research that involves a drug currently being used to treat Huntington's disease. You can imagine where this is going. She found a resident who was being given the drug and talked them into 'sharing' some of their medication. She took the medicine for a few days, and then I did my thing."

"Did it work?" DeAnn asked.

"I got her relaxed, and then we started talking about her life as a reporter. We got to her arrival in Foggy Point, and her memory still isn't perfect. She did remember having an affair with Howard, but she's pretty sure she was doing it to get information from him. That may be wishful thinking, but it's hard to tell. It seems like he's made a career out of charming vulnerable women.

"I don't think she remembers anything about the day of her accident. Memory is a funny thing. If you revisit a real memory or lack of memory enough times, it can change into whatever you want it to be."

"That could be huge, if she's right," Harriet said. "We know he was driving the car. If Howard was on to her, and he was driving the car…"

Aunt Beth took a sip of her coffee.

"Then she could be in danger living at Howard's center."

Robin cleared her throat.

"She's been living in Howard's 'house' for a long time. The only danger will be if he finds out she's trying to retrieve her memory."

"We made sure Howard wasn't in the building when we did our session," Jo assured them. "And believe you me, they sell us residents very short."

180

Harriet stood up, went to Beth's chair and pulled the flip chart from between hers and Mavis's chairs. She unfolded the stand and set it up on the table. Beth pulled a bag of markers from her quilting bag and handed them to her.

She flipped to the last page they'd written on. She added the new information under the heading "Janice's accident" then turned to the group.

"We're adding more and more information to support the idea that Howard is an awful husband who may have killed or attempted to kill more than one wife. He may or may not be doing something shady with the medications at the senior center. But, the fact remains, Howard has an airtight alibi for the night of the shooting and our car bombings."

Carla scooted her chair closer to the table then coughed into her hand.

"None of this gives us any reason to believe Howard would have to kill Seth."

"That's the more important point," Harriet acknowledged. "Aiden said Hannah is upset because Howard wants her to go to pharmacy school, now that Seth is gone."

"That makes it seem like Howard didn't want Seth dead," Mavis said.

Harriet set the marker back on the table and went to her seat, then picked up her pencil and started drawing hexagons on her fabric again.

"After talking to Sarah this last time, it sounds like Seth was marrying her to gain control of the senior center. Sarah inherits the place from her grandmother. Her mother has control until Sarah turns thirty-five, and then it's all up to Sarah whether she keeps it, sells it, or hires someone else to manage it."

"Diós mio," Connie said. "Sarah turns thirty-five this year."

"This changes everything," Robin said.

Harriet set her pencil down.

"What if Sarah was the real target?"

Robin looked thoughtful.

"That would only matter if Sarah's mom and/or Howard were set up to inherit. If they weren't, they were better off with her alive and under their control."

"Can we find that out?" Harriet asked.

Lauren set the cup of coffee she'd been holding down on the table.

"As far as I know, there's no requirement that a will be filed with any public entity before the person dies. She could just have it notarized or not and keep it with her personal papers."

"Her lawyer probably has it, but you're right, it could be handwritten," Robin said. "She'd want someone outside the family to know about it if she's not leaving everything to them. Otherwise, they could simply destroy the will and essentially do whatever they want."

"So, we have no way of knowing what she's done," DeAnn said.

Jo reached for a lemon bar.

"Can't you just ask her?"

The Loose Threads glanced around the table at each other.

"What?" Jo asked.

"You have met Sarah, right?" Lauren asked her.

Harriet started tracing hexagons again.

"What Lauren means is Sarah rarely gives us a straight answer to anything."

Robin got up and made a note on the flip chart about Sarah being the actual owner of the senior center. She turned back to the group seated around the table.

"So, where do we go from here?"

Mavis pulled two sandwich bags containing precut diamond shapes from her bag and set it on the table in front of her then dug in her bag for her needle and scissors.

"I can't think of anything," she said.

Harriet sat back in her chair and rubbed her hand over her chin.

"What are you thinking?" Lauren asked her.

"Jo's right. We need to talk to Sarah again and see who inherits if she dies. I'd like to have a chat with Joshua again, too. Sarah said she let him sleep at her place when Seth wasn't there. That implies they were close, or what passes for close in that family. His sociopathic tendencies notwithstanding, he's always seemed more normal than the rest of the crew."

She thought for a moment. "It seems like his goal is to survive Howard and get away from him. He has nothing to gain from Seth being dead or Sarah inheriting or not inheriting. I'd also like to know what, if anything, Howard gained when Joshua's mother died, and if he knows anything else that might shed light on who Seth's enemies might be."

"I don't know." Lauren paused while she reached for a lemon bar. "He hates Howard and thinks Howard killed his mother. If Howard stole his inheritance on top of that, maybe he killed Seth to punish him."

"That assumes Howard cared enough about Seth for it to hurt him," Harriet said. "Although I guess he did invest in making him his own personal drug expert."

Robin pulled a yellow legal tablet from her bag and made a note.

"If Sarah doesn't have a will or she hasn't filed it anywhere but her home office, I'm going to encourage her to write one, get it notarized, and also to hire an estate attorney to help her select an executor for her estate who isn't a relative. Once she's done that, she can let the family know, which should protect her from any thoughts her family may have about eliminating her."

Aunt Beth closed up the flip chart and put it back under the table.

"We're just going in circles. Everyone has a reason to hate Howard and wish him dead. Howard seems to be an abusive lout, but he has an airtight alibi. Have I missed anything?"

Everyone shook her head.

"I suggest we leave it be for a while and work on our quilting," Beth said. "Maybe if we stop thinking about it so hard for a while something will come to us."

Harriet looked at Jo and Violet.

"Do you two have anything else to add to the discussion?"

The two senior center residents shook their heads again.

"Do we have an inventory of blocks from the senior center and the shelter?" Connie asked. "We need to see how many we need to make to help finish the quilts in a timely fashion."

The rest of the meeting was spent quilting, but Harriet couldn't stop thinking about Sarah and Joshua and who had wanted Seth dead.

Chapter 25

A weak sun was trying to break through the clouds when Harriet took Scooter out for his morning walk.

"The detective is coming to look at her quilt this morning," she told the dog. "She's not here on police business, so be nice."

Detective Morse tapped on the studio door just as Harriet came in from the kitchen after showering and then eating a carton of yogurt. She wished her aunt could have seen her eating so healthy.

"Come in," she said. "I left your quilt on the machine so you can check it out and see if you like it. I can add more stitching if you want, but if you like what I've done, I'll take it to Carla's friend so she can start binding it."

"If you think it has enough quilting, I love it. My most important criteria is that it's finished. Besides, I've never seen you do a quilt that I didn't like."

Harriet stepped over to her machine.

"As you can see, I did an X in the center of each ring then used each leg of the X as the stem of a feather-like pattern."

Detective Morse rubbed her hand lightly over the surface of the quilt.

"This is fantastic. When you said it would be simple, I thought you would do something akin to stitch-in-the-ditch," she said, referring to the technique where the quilting outlines the seams in the quilt top. "This is much more detailed than I expected."

"If we'd had more time, I would have done something more intricate in the smaller spaces where the rings overlap. I would have done more in the border, too."

"If I'd had the time, I wouldn't have put a border on. I'd have carried the rings to the edge and bound off the resulting scallops."

"Oh, well, next time," Harriet said and laughed.

Morse turned away from the quilt to face her.

"I won't forget this. I know you put in a lot of hours in a short time. I expect your fee to reflect that extra effort."

"I'll trade my overtime for information. Do you have time for a cup of coffee or tea?"

Morse shrugged out of her coat and tossed it onto the wing-back chair.

"I thought you'd never ask. I really will toss you a few tidbits of info if you've got an old stale cookie or something to go with it."

"Follow me," Harriet said and headed for the kitchen. "You can choose your pod for the coffee machine while I go rummage in the freezer." She headed for the garage.

Ten minutes later, she set a plate of warm chocolate chip cookies on the table in front of Detective Morse. Morse bit into one of the warm cookies.

"Mmmm, these are delicious. Do you do a lot of cookie baking?"

Harriet laughed. "I wish. No, Mavis and Connie bring them by periodically. They decided that, since I have the studio space, which means we tend to meet here more often than anywhere else, it wasn't fair to expect me to always provide treats for the whole group. You can count your blessings, too. They're both much better bakers than I am. I just slice the dough and pop them in the oven."

"I suppose you want to know if there's anything new in the Seth Pratt investigation."

Harriet smiled and waited to see what the detective was willing to share.

"We really don't have anything new. As promised, I did ask my friend in Seattle to see what she could dig up on Howard. He still has an airtight alibi—that didn't change. I asked her to see what she could find about the deaths of his first two wives. His first wife's death is listed as an accident. She fell down a flight of stairs and landed on the cement basement floor. She died from head trauma."

"That's awful," Harriet said. "Did Howard benefit?"

Morse picked up a second cookie.

"As a matter of fact, he did. There was a life insurance policy to the tune of one hundred thousand dollars."

"That's a goodly amount. He could have gotten a good start in business with that."

"Only if he was conservative with his money, and that is not the Howard Pratt I know. Our Howard likes to throw his money around. He likes to buy favors from people in high places."

"How about wife two, Hannah and Joshua's mom?"

"I just visited the coroner about another case, so I know you've been to see her already about Jill's autopsy."

Harriet had the good grace to blush.

"So we found out that Jill's manner of death is undetermined. Did your friend find out if Howard benefited from her death, too?"

Detective Morse wrapped her hands around her coffee mug.

"Like most criminals, if he is a criminal—and that's a big if—he learned from his first crime. When Jill died, according to my friend's confidential sources, he not only collected two hundred and fifty thousand dollars in insurance he also gained control of a similar amount of money that was being held in trust for Joshua."

Harriet choked on the bite of cookie she was chewing.

"Whoa," she finally said. "That's huge. He adopted Joshua so he could control his inheritance and then makes the kid live like an indentured servant."

"Where did you hear that?" Morse asked her.

"Joshua told me. He lives in a garden shed on Howard's property and thinks he's on some sort of probation." Harriet stopped herself before she mentioned Lauren's background check on Joshua. She wasn't sure if Lauren and her geeks had hacked their way to that information or not.

"What do you mean, he thinks he's on some sort of probation?"

"Let's just say I have reason to believe the scared-straight diversion program Howard told him he's on is a program with only one client."

"Do I want to know how you came by that information?"

Harriet smiled. "Probably not."

"You're lucky I'm feeling so grateful about my quilt."

She tried to make a stern face, but the effect was ruined by a smear of chocolate on her mouth. Harriet pointed at it and handed her a napkin.

"To be serious for a moment, it's interesting to learn more about Howard and his possible past crimes. My friend and her partner in Seattle are going to look into the two deaths of Howard's wives, and if they think there's anything there, they'll pass on whatever they find to the proper authorities.

"What we keep coming back to, though, is that Howard has an alibi for the critical time and there is no conceivable motive for him to want Seth dead. By all accounts, Seth was involved in whatever Howard is doing at the senior center."

"Unless Seth began to suspect that Howard killed his mother," Harriet pointed out.

"But there's no evidence Seth suspected his father of anything. It could have equally been Joshua who suspected Howard of killing his mother. We know he hated Howard."

Harriet leaned back in her chair, her eyes unfocused.

"It's all a big circle. Everyone has a reason to kill Howard. Howard has reasons to kill any number of people if they've found out what he's done or is doing. But none of this has anything to do with Seth."

"Welcome to the world of police work. Everyone thinks police work is glamorous, but really, we spend all of our time interviewing and re-interviewing people, trying to figure out where their stories don't match."

"I'm going to take a page from your book and go talk to Joshua again. I think he knows more than he's telling. And I think he's the only one in the Pratt family that's likely to tell me the truth."

"I can't stop you from talking to anyone, but I strongly advise you not to. I have no real reason to believe Joshua is our killer, but you never know who's guilty and of what. He may have secrets that have nothing to do with Seth's murder, and who knows what lengths he might go to, to protect them. And there's always the chance he *is* the killer, in which case, it could be truly dangerous."

"His sister Hannah says he a sociopath."

"Seems like everyone's labeled a sociopath or psychopath these days," Morse said. "But, still, sociopath or not, stay away from him."

"Can you guarantee that Sarah is safe?" Harriet asked her. "If you can promise me that, I'll go back to my long-arm machine and not talk to anyone."

"You know I can't guarantee that, but leave the protection of Sarah to the police."

"I'll try," Harriet told her. "Want me to wrap up a couple of cookies to go for you?"

Morse smiled.

✂ - - - ✂ - - - ✂

Harriet was sorting pictures from her boarding school days several hours later when she heard someone tapping on her studio door. Reliving her school days through photographs was not the joyful experience it might have been if she'd had a more normal childhood.

Lauren stood on the porch. She held up two white paper coffee cups with the distinctive Steaming Cup logo stamped on the side. Harriet got up and opened the door, and Lauren handed her one of the cups as she entered.

"Mochas are us," she said and set her cup down while she slipped out of her jacket. She looked at the pictures spread out on the table. "Are you scrapbooking?"

"No, that would be depressing. 'Here's little Harriet having birthday cake with the headmistress and the dorm mother.' No, thanks. These are pictures of scenery from when I was in boarding school. Aiden's niece and nephew are doing a family genealogy project. They were talking about their grandmother being from Bordeaux, and I told them that I went boarding school there, and I took a photography class and would be happy to give them copies of the photos I have of the city if they wanted. They did, so here I am sorting."

Lauren slid a wheeled chair over to the table and sat down.

"How very generous of you."

"It seemed like the right thing to do. I mean, they have to live with Michelle as their mother."

Lauren sipped her mocha.

"Well, meanwhile, I've been tapping my fingers to the bone on my laptop, trying to come up with something we haven't considered yet."

"I'm going to drop the pictures off at the vet clinic this afternoon, and then I'll go try to reach Joshua and see if he is willing or able to tell me anything else about Seth. There has to be something we're missing."

"I get the same feeling," Lauren said. "But I've searched everyone involved. I can't find anything that helps."

"Morse came by today to get her quilt."

"That was quick."

"She was willing to keep it simple. Anyway, she dug up some information about Howard's first two wives. Whether he killed them or not, he certainly benefited from their deaths."

"Are you sure you should be going to see Joshua? I hate to sound like Morse, but maybe it's time to sit this one out."

"I take it you're not free this afternoon?"

"That would be correct. I have to meet with a client and try to figure out where the bug is in their new system. If I find it, I have to devise a workaround. They're a new client, so I need to try to impress them. Can you possibly wait until tomorrow?"

"I suppose I could. I don't think Joshua is dangerous. He seems more like a victim in this whole thing. He lost his mother, and if Morse's info is correct, Howard stole his inheritance. He also told me he's worried about Howard arranging an accident for him."

"Isn't that when a person is most dangerous?" Lauren asked her. "When they have nothing to lose."

"I suppose."

Harriet spent another thirty minutes sorting pictures then before loading the ones she thought Lanie and Etienne might be interested in into a photo box, took Scooter out. When she was finished, she picked up the receiver to her land line and dialed her aunt's number.

"Hey, Aunt Beth," she said. "Are you free this afternoon?"

"No, honey. Mavis and Connie and I are spending the rest of the afternoon sorting donations for the church rummage sale. What do you need? Maybe I can arrange a substitute."

"That's not necessary. I want to talk to Joshua, and Lauren isn't free. She said she's available tomorrow; I can wait until then."

"Are you sure? I don't want you going off by yourself. If what Hannah's telling you is true, he could be real dangerous."

"Don't worry. I'm going to go by the vet clinic to drop some pictures off for Aiden's niece and nephew while I pick up some more of Scooter's prescription dog food."

"If you change your mind, just give me a call."

"Okay, thanks. Talk to you later."

Harriet scooped up the pictures she wasn't taking with her and dropped them back into their original box.

"You behave while I'm gone," she told Scooter and Fred. She stroked Fred's head as he sat on the corner of the kitchen counter. "Don't think I don't know you're the one that's pushing paper products from the back of the toilet so Scooter can tear them apart. If you don't stop, you're going to have to be in time-out when I'm not here."

With her pets thoroughly admonished, she took her coat and purse from the kitchen closet and headed for the garage.

----- ----- -----

"Is Aiden available?" Harriet asked at the reception desk of the vet clinic. "Let me check." She disappeared into a hallway that led to the examination rooms. "He'll be out in a few minutes," she said when she returned a few minutes later.

Harriet sat down on a bench between a plump red-faced man with a bulldog sitting at his feet and a teenager with a stiff six-inch Mohawk holding a box with a lilac-point Siamese kitten in it. She was talking to the teen when Hannah came into the waiting room from the parking lot.

"Hi, Hannah."

"Hey, what are you doing here?"

"I have to pick up some of the prescription food Aiden wants my dog to eat. And…" She glanced at the photo box sitting on the bench between herself and the guy with the cat. "…I'm bringing some pictures for Aiden's niece and nephew for a school genealogy project."

"I hated it when we did family trees in school. It's embarrassing how many times my dad's been married."

"Three can't be that unusual."

"It's four, and get real. This is Foggy Point. Nobody gets divorced here."

Harriet wanted to grill her about the fourth wife—or more likely, a new contender for first wife—but the waiting room didn't seem like the place. She mentally added the question to her list for Joshua.

"Hannah, could you tell Joshua I'd like to talk to him again? I have a few more questions for him."

"What could he possibly tell you? He spends most of his time fooling around with plants in that horrible shed he lives in. Besides, I told you before, he's one sick puppy."

"I'll be careful, and I won't go alone," Harriet assured her.

"Harriet," Aiden called from the open door of exam room one.

Hannah turned when Harriet stood up.

"I better get to work," she said and opened the door next to the reception window.

"What about Joshua?"

"I'll give him the message. I can't promise anything. Like I've been trying to tell you—he's weird."

"I hope I'm not interrupting your schedule too much," Harriet said as she followed Aiden through the exam room and into the back hallway that linked all the exam rooms with the surgical suites, the kennel areas and the back of the reception space.

He put his arm over her shoulder and led her to the lunchroom.

"I've always got time for you." When the room proved to be empty, he pulled her into his arms and gave her a quick kiss. "Would you like anything to eat or drink?" He opened a white refrigerator and took a can of cola from the door.

"Do you have diet?"

He took a second can and set both of them on the table.

"Let me get a wipe before you drink that." He pulled a sanitizing wipe from a dispenser on the counter and wiped both cans before handing the diet to her. "I don't want you carrying any germs home to Scooter. He's still not strong enough to fight off an illness if he were to catch something. You

190

should wash your hands when you get home before you touch either of your animals, too."

"Thank you, Doctor Jalbert," Harriet said and smiled.

"You know, cobbler's kids go shoeless and all that. Our pets aren't going to suffer the same fate." He reached for the box of photos she had set on the table. "Are these the pictures for Lanie and Etienne? Are there any pictures of little Harriet?" he asked with that crooked grin of his.

"Are you kidding? Besides, I took the pictures, so I'm not in any of them."

He lifted several from the top.

"These are really good. How old were you when you took them?"

"I don't know. Eleven or twelve, I guess."

Harriet's phone rang. From the ringtone, she knew it wasn't one of her friends.

"Hello?"

Hannah came into the lunchroom carrying a white paper sack. Aiden held his finger to his lips as she crossed to the refrigerator and opened the door.

"Jo? Slow down and say that again…What do you mean, she remembered everything? The accident, too?…I'll be right over…Okay, you're right…Yeah, I'm free after dinner…Okay, see you then…Got it, patio door."

Hannah shut the door to the refrigerator, looked at Harriet and Aiden then ducked her head, pink spots on her cheeks.

"Sorry," she said and left the lunch room.

Harriet turned to Aiden.

"That was Jo from the senior center. Her friend Janice—the one in the wheelchair—she's the one who was an investigative reporter back when Howard's second wife died. She was in a car accident, and Howard was driving. She's never been able to remember what happened.

"She found a drug that's used for another disease but is showing promise in restoring lost memories. She got her hands on some and has been taking it. Until now, it was only making a minor difference, but Jo says today Janice remembered everything.

"She wouldn't tell me the details—she's afraid the place is bugged. She was out on her patio just now, but she said they have video cameras on the outside and someone would come to check up on her if she stayed outside long enough to be noticed. I'll go by after dinner and see what she has to say."

Aiden pulled her back into his arms.

"Are you sure she's playing with a full deck? If the place is bugged during the day, doesn't it stand to reason it's also bugged at night? Besides, could she possibly know anything that could help prove who killed Seth?"

"She said she and Mickey have some strategy for avoiding the cameras, but they have to wait until the evening staff come on. I guess there are fewer of them and they tend to be less vigilant. As for what Janice could possibly say—unfortunately, all she can do is add to the pile of evidence against Howard."

"Then don't go. I mean, if it can't help prove what happened to Seth, but it could be a threat to Howard, you could get caught in the crossfire."

"If I don't go, Jo might do something that puts that group of seniors in danger."

Aiden brushed back a lock of hair that had fallen into her eyes.

"If Jo was a CIA agent, she can take care of herself. And the one in the wheelchair has been living under Howard's control for years, if what you said is true. If he was going to harm her, he'd have done it years ago."

Harriet looked into his face and saw the worry lines etched into his forehead. She sighed.

"Tell you what. I'll call Detective Morse. If she wants to go talk to them, then I'm out of it. If she doesn't, I'll ask her if she cares if I go. If I do go, I'll talk to my aunt or Mavis and see if they want to go."

"I guess that's all I can ask. Do you think the whole memory-drug thing is for real?"

"Seems to be. Lauren looked it up on her computer when we had coffee earlier, and she found an article about it."

"Wow, that could be a game changer for plenty of folks if it's real."

Harriet glanced over his shoulder at the box of pictures.

"Those are all copies, so tell the kids they can use whatever they want."

"Thanks for helping them. You could probably tell, they don't get much attention from either of their parents."

"No problem," Harriet said. "I better get my dog food and get moving, I've got stitching to do."

"Want me to bring take-out Chinese by later?"

"Assuming it's not an attempt to keep me from going to the senior center, yes, I'd like that." She smiled at him then picked up her purse and left.

Chapter 26

Harriet went back home and put her next customer quilt on the long-arm machine, but she was too restless to start stitching on it. Her phone rang, and she hurried to answer it, but it was only Lauren.

"I can only talk a minute. My client is out on a smoke break," she said. "Did you talk to Joshua?"

"No, but I did hear something interesting from Jo." She gave Lauren an abbreviated version of her talk with the older woman. "I promised Aiden I'd tell Detective Morse about it. I left her a message but haven't heard back. I asked Hannah to have Joshua call me, but I haven't heard anything from him, either."

"You must be going nuts waiting for something to happen."

"Indeed, I am. I'm afraid to stitch on my client's quilt I'm so distracted. I guess I'll make a few more grandmother's flower garden blocks for the women's shelter quilt."

"Here comes my client. Let me know if anything happens."

Harriet's phone rang three more times before Joshua called. Aiden and Aunt Beth called to make sure she wasn't talking to Joshua or Jo by herself, and Lauren checked to see if she'd left on either mission.

"Fred, you keep an eye on Scooter while I'm in the bathroom," Harriet told the cat as she filled her upstairs bathtub with warm water infused with lavender-scented bubble bath. "If I can't get any stitching done, at least I can be relaxed when Aiden gets here."

She picked him up and set him down in the hallway, closing the door as she came back into the bathroom. She set a thick Ken Follett historical novel on her tub shelf beside her cup of herb tea. She'd just shrugged her jeans past her hips when the phone rang.

"Really?" she said to no one. She pulled her pants back up and made a run for the phone. It quit ringing just as she picked up the receiver. "Arghhh!"

She turned to go back to the bathroom, Fred on her heels, when the phone started ringing again.

"Hello," she said before the receiver was even up to her ear.

"Harriet," said a whispery voice.

"Joshua? Is that you? Your voice sounds odd. Are you okay?"

She heard a sharp intake of breath.

"Joshua?"

"I'm here. I'm a little under the weather, that's all. I must have picked up a bug somewhere."

"I was hoping to talk to you, but if you aren't well, it can wait."

"No, today would be...fine. I sound worse...than I am."

Harriet heard a muffled gurgling cough, as if he'd turned away from the phone.

"Now's good...can you come...now?"

"Are you sure? You really sound terrible. Can I call someone to help you?"

Joshua made a gasping noise. Harriet realized it was an attempt to laugh. "Who would that be?" he spat out finally. "I told you...there's no one."

"Can I bring you anything?" Harriet asked.

Joshua grunted. "Sure." He coughed again. "Bring something to drink."

"What would you like? Juice, soda, mineral water?"

"Harriet...please...come now...I'm at the garden shed."

"Sure. See you in a few minutes."

Harriet stroked Fred's head.

"That was weird." She picked up the phone again and dialed Lauren's cell number. She listened to it ring and then go to voicemail.

"Lauren. Joshua called and can see me today. In fact, he was pretty insistent that it be now."

She tried Detective Morse's cell phone with the same result. She didn't leave a message, since she'd left one earlier.

Fred jumped to the arm of the upholstered chair she was sitting on in her TV room. She thought for a moment then dialed Aunt Beth's cell phone. Her aunt had been planning a long day preparing for the rummage sale. Beth's phone went to voicemail immediately. Harriet repeated the same message she'd left Lauren, explaining that she was taking advantage of the opportunity to talk to Joshua.

"Besides, he sounds sick. I'm taking him some Seven-Up and crackers. It'll be my good deed for the day," she said and pressed the end-call button.

"Well, Fred, I tried—you're my witness. You watch your brother. Show him how to be a good pet." She rubbed his ears, went back to the bathroom and drained the tub.

From her house, it would have been quicker to go over Miller Hill and drop down to the residential neighborhood Sarah's parents lived in. Instead, she drove through downtown, stopping at Swan's market to get Joshua's soda and crackers before driving on past the dock area and the rocky beach then turning inland.

The Pratt property was one of the older homes in the development. It was located at the far side, where the homes backed up on a forested green space. Twenty minutes after Joshua called, Harriet was easing her car down the gravel driveway, past the main house to a wide parking area.

An older Honda sedan with at least three colors of peeling paint sat next to a late-model BMW. She got out and looked around. There were several outbuildings, but only one looked like it could be lived in. It had a cement porch, and the windows had curtains and screens. There was a pot of flowers sitting to the left of the door. This had to be Joshua's "shed."

She picked up the paper bag with Joshua's supplies and went to the door. She raised her hand to knock, but the door swung open before her knuckles reached the wood.

"Run, Harriet," came a strangled voice from inside.

She whirled, but before she could take a step, someone grabbed her arm roughly and pulled her inside, pushing her onto a sagging purple couch beside Joshua. She looked around wildly. The room was the size of a single-car garage. She was in the sitting/sleeping area. The couch, with a bookcase on one end and a table and lamp on the other, filled this end of the room. An oval kitchen table with mismatched chairs occupied the other end, and to the side of the table, an unpainted door led to what was probably the bathroom. Kitchen counters with a small sink and two burner stove lined the back wall.

"Hannah? What are you doing?"

"I'm putting an end to a nuisance. Two nuisances, really."

Joshua leaned into Harriet. His face was gray.

"I'm sorry," he whispered without looking at her. His eyes were fixed on the gun in Hannah's hand.

Harriet looked at the shiny revolver and then at Joshua. The appliqué quilt she had seen at Sarah's cabin was now draped across his lap. An irregular red stain blossomed in the white area between two blocks where it lay on his leg. Her eyes grew wide as she realized the stain was growing.

Hannah waved the gun back and forth between Harriet and Joshua.

"It's just a flesh wound," she said. "He wasn't going to call you, so I had to give him some incentive. Besides, it's nothing compared to what *you're* going to do to him."

Harriet stared at her.

"That's right," Hannah continued. "You and Joshua are going to have a shootout. He's going to go nuts on you, and you're going to shoot him."

"I don't have a gun," Harriet told her.

"Of course you don't. You're too nice to carry a gun. I have one for you. You found it lying on the table here." She bent and pulled a second gun from a backpack on the floor, keeping her weapon trained on Harriet the whole time. She backed up and set the second gun on the table.

Harriet glanced at Joshua. His breathing was uneven. She turned back to Hannah.

"Why are you doing this?"

"There you go with the questions. That's exactly why I'm doing this. You are too nosy for your own good. Seth wasn't *your* brother. How and why he was killed is none of your business. But you couldn't leave it alone. You wouldn't leave Sarah alone when she was at the senior center, and then you hid her. And my dad said you've been trying to damage his reputation, too. Now you have the residents of the senior center all riled up."

"You're not making any sense. I didn't hide Sarah, and the people at the senior center don't need my help."

"I heard them call you today at the clinic. You were going there tonight to hear what they think they know about my dad."

"Hannah, listen to you. If your dad killed your mother, don't you want to know that?"

"My dad didn't kill my mom. She killed herself and dragging it all up again isn't going to change that. All those old people can do is hurt my dad's reputation and cause people to not want to come to the senior center."

"Is that all that matters to you? How the business does? Don't you even care about your own mother?"

Hannah cocked the revolver she was holding.

"Don't you presume to tell me how to feel about my mother. You don't know anything about it."

Harriet felt Joshua stiffen where his good leg was touching her.

"How can you keep defending that monster?" he rasped at Hannah. "He beat our mother, he beat Sarah, and you know what he did to you. Even if our mother did kill herself, it was because of him. Her life was so miserable. Are you hearing me?"

196

Hannah sighed. "I'm way beyond caring about anyone but me. Everyone in this family is screwed up. I'm a survivor. You never learned that lesson, big brother—or I should say big stepbrother.

"If he were your real dad, you'd understand. We Pratts are practical. You do what you need to do to stay on top. Right now, what I need to do is clean up my mess. Dad said if I clean up my mess, I can go to veterinary school, and he'll hire a pharmacist.

"Don't you see, Josh? If you had been a little more respectful, he probably would have let you be his drug guy."

Harriet looked at Joshua.

"What's she talking about? What mess is she cleaning up?"

He shuddered.

"Haven't you figured it out? It took me a while, but I finally got there." He took a deep breath. "I couldn't understand why anyone would kill Seth. Howard needed him to keep his drug-cutting scam going, and he needed Seth to date Sarah to keep her in line until he could make his move to take the center from her, though I admit I didn't realize the lengths to which he would go.

"When Hannah told me Howard was making her go to pharmacy school, it became clear. He didn't kill Seth or have anyone else do it. Why would he? So, who *would* kill Seth? Sarah had motive, but she was too in love with him so, no one." He stopped talking and took a series of shallow breaths.

"We've all been looking at the wrong victim," Harriet said. "Seth wasn't the intended victim. It was Sarah. With Sarah gone, her mom would inherit the senior center, and we all know what happens to Howard's wives. It all makes sense.

"Howard wanted Sarah dead, and whoever was trying to kill her hit Seth instead. Maybe the bullet deflected when it went through the window, or maybe Seth moved into the way at the last second. In any case, he took the bullet intended for Sarah.

"I'm still confused, though," she said and looked back to Hannah and the gun. All of a sudden it became clear. "You're the shooter? Why?"

"It took you long enough. Dad doesn't like to involve outsiders in family business. I've been training with a rifle since I was twelve. I'm a medalist at that distance. I could have done it in my sleep."

She shook her head. "I'm still not sure exactly what went wrong." She held the revolver up and sighted down its short barrel, reenacting her shot. "I had it all lined up, and then, just as I squeezed the trigger, Seth hit her with a roundhouse right and put himself right into the path of my bullet." She sighed. "I'll admit, I didn't see that one coming.

"I must have practiced that shot a hundred times. I've even practiced shooting in the dark." She shook her head. "It should have been easy."

"You can't possibly think you're going to get away with this," Harriet said.

"You know, if you and your busybody friends had left Sarah alone, this would not be happening. Sarah's pain pills were laced with poison while she was in the senior center after she broke her arm. If she'd cracked and taken even one, we wouldn't be here.

"We could have administered the poison another way, but you people were always there, bringing her food from the outside, taking bites from her tray and asking questions about everything that was happening in her room. Dad couldn't risk having one of you die at the center along with her."

Harriet looked around the room to see what possibilities it held. Before she could formulate a plan, someone knocked on the door.

"Hello?" Lauren called. "I know you're in there. I can see your car, Harriet."

Hannah started for the door, but Lauren opened it and came in.

"Well, well, well, what have we here?" she said as she sized up the situation.

"What we have is a complication," Hannah said, pointing the gun at her and motioning her to the couch with it. Lauren sat down on the near end of the couch, with Joshua between her and Harriet. She picked up the edge of the bloodstained quilt.

"Isn't this the quilt from Sarah's cabin?"

"Sarah made it for me," Joshua said with a small gasp.

Lauren turned to look at him, taking the opportunity to assess his condition.

"Wait a minute, here. We've all seen Sarah's handiwork, and it doesn't look this good."

Joshua took a shallow wheezing breath.

"No one is allowed to be better than Howard's blood children. Hannah doesn't even care about quilting, but when Sarah made me this quilt, Howard made her pay, and then he threw it in the garbage. I fished it out and took it up to the cabin. Seth didn't say anything, because he had his own battles to fight." Joshua sank back into the cushions on the couch. "It's all so sick."

"Sarah didn't really make it," Hannah said. "He just wanted her to have made it for him. She bought it at a quilt show."

Joshua looked like he was going to argue, but he didn't have the energy. Harriet looked at the bloodstain on the quilt. It was growing at an alarming rate. If something didn't happen, and soon, he was going to bleed to death.

"Hannah," she said, "give it up. Your plan isn't going to work now that Lauren is here."

"I'd like to hear the plan," Lauren said and looked at her.

Harriet lifted the edge of the quilt and looked at Joshua's leg.

"If you want to have any hope of staging this as a shootout, we need to put a pressure bandage on his leg. Otherwise, he's going to be dead before you even get started."

Lauren scooted a little closer to Joshua and took a look.

"You should look at this," she told Hannah. "It's a mess. You're going to have to clean up some of this blood on the sofa and floor, or it's going to be very obvious what really happened here."

Hannah paced across the room to the kitchen. Harriet looked at Lauren and held the edge of the quilt up, raising her eyebrow as she did. Lauren gave her a nearly imperceptible nod.

Hannah whirled and came back to the sofa.

"Why did you have to come here, anyway?"

Lauren smiled and shrugged.

"Just curious, I guess."

"Yeah, well, I guess you know what curiosity did for the cat." Hannah smirked. "Now, what am I going to do with you three?"

She paced to the kitchen and back again, passing the revolver from one hand to the other and back again. Her face became redder as she paced.

"If you let us get help for Joshua, we won't call the police until we have him at the hospital. You can head for Canada and disappear," Harriet suggested.

Hannah bent to stare at her.

"What kind of idiot do you think I am?" she screamed, drops of spit spraying Harriet's face.

Harriet and Lauren sprang up, each holding an edge of the quilt. They threw it over her head and torso and pulled it toward them, pulling her off her feet. Both brought their weight to bear against the thrashing woman.

While they struggled to subdue Hannah, Joshua lurched to his feet and staggered to the kitchen table, picking up the second revolver as he slumped into a chair. He quickly popped the cylinder to the side, confirmed it was loaded and snapped it back into place.

"Hannah, I'm holding a gun pointed at you," he said. "Slide your gun out from under the quilt, or I swear I'll shoot you."

The quilt-wrapped bundle struggled more at his words. Lauren balled her right fist and slugged the quilt.

"Ouch, stop that," said Hannah's muffled voice.

Lauren hit her again, hard. They heard a grunt.

"You want more?"

"Okay, okay, stop. And get off me, I can't breathe." The gun appeared from under the bundle. Harriet kicked it away.

Harriet dialed 911 while Lauren picked up Hannah's gun. Harriet looked at Joshua; his head was down on his arms.

"Do you have something we can tie her up with?"

He pointed to a drawer next to the small kitchen sink.

"Duct tape," he wheezed.

Harriet noticed a second wound near his armpit. It didn't appear to be bleeding as profusely as his leg, but it couldn't have felt good.

"Give me your hands," she commanded Hannah when she'd pulled a strip of tape free from the roll. When the hands appeared, she made quick work of pulling them behind the girl and taping them together. She moved to Hannah's feet and bound them tightly, too.

"Give me your belt," she told Lauren and, for once, her friend complied without argument.

Joshua groaned when Harriet lifted his leg so she could slip the belt around his thigh.

Lauren fished around in the kitchen and came up with a clean looking dish towel and a tray of ice. She handed Harriet the towel and found a baggie for the ice and then handed that to her friend, too.

"I'm afraid that's as good as we can do for now," Harriet told Joshua when she had a tourniquet on his elevated leg and the towel and ice covering the second wound. She patted him on the shoulder. They all heard the sound of sirens in the distance.

Lauren walked over to where Hannah lay on the floor. She poked the woman with her foot. "I take it we found our murderer?"

"Ow," Hannah complained.

Harriet pressed her lips together and tried to smile.

"We have, indeed."

"On the up side, I think Sarah's better off without Seth, and she's definitely not going to miss this viper," Lauren said.

Harriet did laugh at that.

"Let's not share that thought with anyone else, okay? Besides, Sarah's still got to deal with Howard."

Lauren came to look at Joshua. She held his wrist and felt for his pulse.

"Your pulse feels strong enough," she told him. "Too bad we couldn't have gotten something on Howard. Then Joshua and Sarah could truly be free."

Harriet was quiet. Lauren looked at her.

"I know that look. You have an idea, don't you?"

"According to Jo, Janice has had some sort of memory breakthrough. She remembers what she had learned about Howard. Maybe about the accident, too."

"And?" Lauren prompted.

"If Detective Morse is willing to go along with this, we could make sure Howard doesn't find out about Hannah immediately, and that he does find out about the sudden retrieval of Janice's lost memories. Maybe he'll incriminate himself."

"That'll never happen," Lauren said. "Not the Howard part. Morse will never agree to it."

"Agree to what?" Morse asked as she came through the shed door just ahead of the paramedics. She stepped aside so they could pass. "What's going on here?"

Harriet went back to the couch and sat with a sigh. Lauren plopped down beside her. The adrenaline rush from subduing Hannah was beginning to catch up with Harriet, and she assumed the same thing was happening to Lauren.

She took a slow deep breath.

"Hannah is the one who killed Seth. She was actually trying to shoot Sarah. She says her father put her up to it."

Detective Morse started to speak, but Harriet held her hand up. She could see a uniformed officer getting Hannah to her feet and removing the duct tape, replacing it with metal handcuffs.

"I got a call this afternoon from the senior center. Janice, the woman who was in the car accident with Howard years ago, was investigating him at the time. She's just recovered her memories, and they want me to meet them at the senior center to hear what they have to say. You might be able to catch Howard in the act of trying to shut her up if he doesn't know about Hannah by then."

"That's assuming Howard did something wrong in the first place and also that he'll come after the woman," Morse said, but it was her turn to hold her hand up. She signaled the patrol officer to stop. He was moving Hannah toward the door but paused. "I need to think about this, but for the time being, let's put the prisoner in an isolation cell as a Jane Doe. Call her a material witness and keep it off the radio. Don't take the cuffs off, but put them in front and cover them with a coat.

"Don't turn your back on her. She's to be considered extremely dangerous." She made eye contact with Hannah. "Make no mistake, these officers have my permission to taze you, shoot you or whatever else they feel is necessary to keep you in custody."

"I want my attorney," Hannah spat.

"Until further notice, I'm going to assume you were the one who planted bombs on US soil. I'm going to consider that to be the act of a domestic terrorist until I have evidence to the contrary. That being the case, you have no rights. You can consider yourself lucky I'm not turning you over to the Feds until we sort this out." She turned back to Joshua, who was now on a gurney, being attended to by three jumpsuited paramedics. "That silence order applies to you folks, too, patient included."

Joshua managed a weak smile as he was wheeled out.

Morse punched numbers into her phone then spoke to someone in hushed tones before turning back to Harriet and Lauren.

"He'll have a police guard at the hospital, and the staff will keep his name off the records for now. Now, tell me everything you know about this woman and her memories."

Harriet filled Morse in on what Jo and Violet had told them as well as what Aunt Beth had dug up at the library. She ended by relating the memories her aunt, Mavis and Connie had from when the accident had happened.

"We don't have any evidence whether Howard killed any of his wives. By the way, there's one more than we knew about, according to Hannah. It's suspicious that at least two of them have died," Harriet told her.

"And we saw evidence in Howard's office to back up the talk about him running some sort of drug-cutting scam," Lauren added.

Harriet stood up, wobbled a bit, steadied herself and went to the kitchen cabinet. She found glasses and filled them with water from the tap, giving one to Lauren then offering another to Morse before sitting and taking a long drink of her own.

"I don't know if you can believe anything Hannah says, but apparently, Howard or Elaine tried to poison Sarah while she was in the nursing wing of the senior center, before the shooting. They tampered with her medication."

"That makes more sense, actually," Morse said. "I mean, shooting someone is messy. Poisoning someone who is already sick or injured gives you a lot better chance of getting away with it."

Harriet set her glass down on the end table.

"I guess it's a good thing Sarah's paranoid. For once, it paid off."

"Okay, let's go to the station and let me talk to my boss. If he's good with it, we'll set it up."

"I'm going to have to tell my aunt and Mavis something. I'm surprised they haven't come here. I left Aunt Beth a message telling her I was meeting with Joshua."

"Call her and let her know you're helping me with some research and that everything's okay." Morse looked at Lauren. "Do *you* have anyone who's likely to pop out of the woodwork at an inopportune moment?"

Lauren shook her head.

"I'm good."

Chapter 27

"Let's go over the plan one more time," Morse said.

Harriet and Lauren sat on one side of a table, flanked by two undercover cops and across from Morse and a young male Hispanic detective.

"This is going to be complicated, Martinez," she told the detective beside her. "Your mother already lives there, so you're going to be our inside guy. You'll walk Officer Welke in. She'll be wearing your wife's coat and a rain hat, so at a glance, you and your wife are coming to visit just like normal.

"Welke will be made up to look like Janice. Maria, you're a new temp. The service sends new people on a daily and nightly basis. We've already contacted them. Andy and Nate are also coming in as temps. They'll work in the laundry.

"Martinez is going to get Janice out of her chair and into a laundry cart, and Welke will replace her. Andy and Nate will move Janice to the laundry room. When and if Howard goes to Janice's room, they will wheel the cart to the back door and out.

"Mickey and Violet will tell everyone they're going out to dinner. Maria will be in a storeroom with a laptop monitoring the security system using the codes Lauren provided us. She'll keep eyes on Howard. When he's away from both the independent living wing and the security monitors, we'll move Jo, Micky and Violet out through Jo's patio door.

"At the critical moment, the monitors are going to go black for thirty seconds, long enough to be sure no one accidentally sees the exodus out the patio. When the residents are safe, Andy will put on his wig and Jo's bathrobe and join Welke for an evening cup of tea.

"Everyone clear so far?"

The police officers nodded. Harriet and Lauren looked at each other.

"What about us?" Harriet asked.

Morse looked at her.

"You're going to bait the trap. You're going to call Elaine on the front desk and tell her that Jo says Janice wants to tell you something important tonight. She told you it's urgent, that Janice has remembered something important. Tell her you can't be there until eight o'clock. You're worried about whether the front door will be locked and if there's an alternate entry for night visitors."

"Okay," Harriet said.

"Just for good measure, tell her Jo told you to keep it secret."

Lauren took a sip from the paper cup of coffee sitting in front of her. She grimaced and set it back on the table.

"Isn't that laying it on sort of thick?"

"If you've ever spoken to Elaine, you know she's not the brightest bulb in the box. That doesn't mean she isn't dangerous, but she is definitely not the brains of the operation."

"What are we supposed to do in the meantime?" Harriet asked. "I need to take my dog out."

Morse looked at Lauren.

"What about you?"

"I can call my neighbor girl to take my guy out. Thanks for asking."

"I'll have an officer take you both back to Harriet's in an unmarked car then bring you back here to make the call. There shouldn't be any issues, but I want you here, with us listening, just in case Elaine has any surprises for us."

Chapter 28

*W*hen the operation was over, the Foggy Point Police Department had made it seem simple.

Elaine played her part admirably. She'd clearly reported to Howard after Harriet's call, and as expected, he'd gone back to his office then on to Janice's room. In a twist Detective Morse hadn't revealed during their meeting, Janice's role was to be played by a blow-up doll duct-taped to the wheelchair while Andy hid in the bathroom, the door cracked enough to allow him to sight his gun on the entry door. They'd turned the lights off. It looked like Jo and Janice were watching TV.

"Imagine his disappointment when he plunged his syringe full of poison into a plastic doll," Morse told Harriet, Lauren and the rest of the personnel gathered in the conference room, where the two quilters had been told to stay until the operation was over.

"Is attacking a doll enough to charge him with attempted murder?" Harriet asked.

Morse poured a cup of coffee from a carafe that sat on the middle of the table.

"It will be when you combine it with Hannah's testimony. As soon as we told her things would go easier for her if she told us the truth right from the beginning, she started singing like a bird. She may have been willing to kill for her dad, but now that we've assured her he won't be able to get to her ever again, she's decided to go the victim route."

Harriet twirled the red plastic stir-stick from her coffee between her fingers then tossed it into her empty cup.

"The sad part is, she probably *is* a victim. Howard abused all the other women in his life. Why would she be different? Joshua alluded to as much when we were at his shed."

"She can tell it to the jury," Morse said. "She still killed a man, and so far she hasn't shown a bit of remorse. That won't play well in court."

Harriet stood up and gathered Lauren's empty cup along with her own and threw them in the wastebasket.

"Are we free to go? I'm sure my aunt and Mavis and probably the rest of the Loose Threads are beside themselves wondering what's going on."

Morse stood up, too.

"I know I've warned you ladies not to get involved in police matters, and I still stand by that, but thank you for your help tonight. Your persistence led to the arrest of two people who needed to be off the streets. Thank you, but let's not do this again, okay?"

Lauren finally got to her feet.

"I've learned my lesson. I don't want to be held at gunpoint by a crazy person ever again."

Morse looked at Harriet.

"Is she making fun of me?"

"She would never do that," Harriet said with a smile. She turned to Lauren. "Let's get out of here before you get us arrested for sassing an officer."

END

About The Author

ARLENE SACHITANO was born at Camp Pendleton while her father was serving in the US Navy. Her family lived in Newport, Rhode Island, before settling in Oregon, where she still resides.

Arlene worked in the electronics industry for almost thirty years, including stints in solid state research as well as production supervision. She is handy, being both a knitter and a quilter. She puts her quilting knowledge to work writing the Harriet Truman/Loose Threads mystery series, which features a long-arm quilter as the amateur sleuth.

Arlene divides her time between homes in Portland and Tillamook she shares with her husband and their dog Navarre.

About The Artist

APRIL MARTINEZ was born in the Philippines and raised in San Diego, California, daughter to a US Navy chef and a US postal worker, sibling to one younger sister. For years, she went from job to job, dissatisfied that she couldn't make use of her creative tendencies, until she started working as an imaging specialist for a big book and magazine publishing house in Irvine and began learning the trade of graphic design.

From that point on, she worked as a graphic designer and webmaster at subsequent day jobs while doing freelance art and illustration at night. April lives with her cat in Orange County, California, as a full-time freelance artist/illustrator and graphic designer.